D1799377

A LETHAL FIXATION

Four weeks after his body was found, the death of medical student Keith Mayhew is still puzzling detectives. Was he murdered or did he kill himself? The inquiries of Detective Inspector Richard Montgomery and his sergeant, William Bird, are complicated by a parcel bomb in the office of a senior lecturer in physiology. Then the gruesome killing of a second student shatters the whole community. With its intricate plot and vigorous characters, *A Lethal Fixation*, Stella Shepherd's fourth crime novel, is a real delight.

A LETHAL FIXATION

A LETHAL FIXATION

by

Stella Shepherd

Dales Large Print Books
Long Preston, North Yorkshire,
England.

British Library Cataloguing in Publication Data.

Shepherd, Stella
    A lethal fixation.

A catalogue record for this book is
available from the British Library

ISBN 1-85389-681-0 pbk

First published in Great Britain by Constable and Company,
1993

Published in Large Print July, 1996 by arrangement with
Constable Publishers Ltd., and Jacintha Alexander Associates.

Dales Large Print is an imprint of
Library Magna Books Ltd.
Printed and bound in Great Britain by
T.J. Press (Padstow) Ltd., Cornwall, PL28 8RW.

For Diana and Terry

1

'Well, Mr Mayhew?'

Hubert Pomeroy's soft but penetrating voice arrowed across the hushed lecture theatre as if to further impale the cringing figure before him. The peculiar bleached eyes stared unremittingly, accentuating the sarcastic sneer beneath.

'I—I—what was the question?'

Dr Pomeroy gave an exaggerated sigh. 'We were discussing digestion, Mr Mayhew. Stomachs and their secretions. Schoolboy biology—except that you purport to be a second-year medical student.' He flicked his fingers in a peremptory gesture. 'Stand up! Now, I'll put my question again. It's a simple one, something I expected even your limited cerebral capacity to cope with: what is the composition of gastric juice?'

'I...' Keith Mayhew swayed and had to grasp the long desk to support himself. He cleared his throat. 'Electrolytes,' he croaked. 'Hydrochloric acid...er...intrinsic factor.'

'And?'

'There's an enzyme to break down proteins—um, gastrin.'

From his eyrie in the back row, Christopher Shallet suppressed a groan at the gaffe. Now Hubert would really tear poor Keith to pieces. Anyone else would recognize the futility of proceeding once the testee had been reduced to gibbering confusion, but not Hubert; he seemed to reserve an especial venom for Keith, lashing him again and again with that chilling whispery voice as if in punishment for some dark misdemeanour.

'You don't appear to know the difference between your hormones and your enzymes,' observed Hubert Pomeroy with affected weariness. 'I presume you meant pepsin.'

'Yes.'

'The hormone gastrin is secreted into the *bloodstream*, not the gastric juice. It circulates, then acts on the gastric glands, which release proteolytic enzymes and hydrochloric acid into the stomach lumen. Does your imagination find this basic concept difficult to grasp?'

'Yes—I mean, no.'

'Good...good,' he said silkily. 'If it's all so clear, then you'll have no trouble in listing some trigger factors for gastrin production.'

Keith Mayhew stood mute.

'*Any* trigger.'

Silence. Chris was mesmerized, but hurriedly looked elsewhere as Hubert lifted his vindictive face to scan the upper echelons of the lecture theatre.

'Mr Brunt?'

In the seat next to Chris, Morgan Brunt stirred and uncrossed his lanky legs. 'Vagal stimulation,' he offered in bored tones. 'Distension of the antrum. The presence of proteins and polypeptides—or ethanol.'

There was a brief, uneasy titter at this last point.

'Thank you. Now, Mr Mayhew...' Hubert focused his attention once more on the wilting boy, who had remained standing either by instinct or by sheer paralysis. 'We have discussed the stomach at some length this morning. No doubt you're ready for your lunch. Tell me, do you *need* a stomach?'

Keith blinked, startled out of his fugue. 'I—yes.'

'It's vital for digestion and absorption?'

'Yes.'

'Hm. Gastrectomy patients will be most upset to hear that. You may sit down.' He paused. 'You will all be aware that next week's practical was to have concerned the collection of gastric secretions from human volunteers. It has been brought to my attention, however, that the latest batch of Ryles tubes is faulty. I have therefore rescheduled the experiment for the beginning of next term, and you will

11

have an extra histology session instead.' The gaze from the pale eyes swept in an arc around the class. 'This will, of course, have no effect on your examinations in a fortnight. Professor Byrne is expecting good results; I have to say I am not so sanguine. Rarely have I met a group of Sherwood University's so called *crème de la crème* more over represented by lazy yobbos and congenital cretins.'

'Typical verbosity,' murmured Morgan. 'True cretinism *is* congenital.'

'...so I suggest you all apply yourselves to your books and ignore the Christmas festivities going on around you—that is, if you wish to avoid emulating Mr Mayhew here and resitting the papers. That is all.'

'Hubert's a real bastard,' said Chris to Morgan as they walked briskly up the hill towards their hall of residence, shivering in the December dankness. In summer, Sherwood's rolling campus was green and attractive; it was situated three miles to the west of Nottingham city centre, and its open aspect had appealed to Chris during his first look-round prior to interview. There was even a lake at the bottom of the hill, to which the general public had access during daylight hours. A further plus was the ready availability of residential accommodation; Chris felt he was lucky to

12

live in venerable, ivy-clad Calverton, the second largest of the men's halls.

Now the campus was dulled by winter, and the lake was as grey as the smudge of Nottingham's industries on the far horizon.

'True,' came Morgan's reply, 'but Keith's such a wet Nellie, he does rather ask for it.'

Chris smiled at the northernism. Morgan, a rugby-playing Yorkshireman whose mother had grown up in the Rhondda Valley, had little sympathy for failures like Keith.

'It was cruel,' stated Eleanor Ransome, drawing level with them. 'He was shaking. It was obvious he was in such a panic that he couldn't think straight. Why does Dr Pomeroy persist when it's counter-productive? He seems to single out Keith for special humiliations.'

'I can't imagine,' said Chris. 'Do you know, Morgan?'

'Oh, I can think of a reason, but I don't know for sure.' Morgan carried on walking with long, athletic strides.

'Don't just leave it there! Tell us your theory!' exhorted Chris.

'I think Hubert propositioned him,' answered Morgan breezily. 'Some time last year. And Keith turned him down.'

'Honestly!' Chris peeked nervously over his shoulder, but no one else was within earshot. 'What a dirty mind you've got. Have you any evidence?'

'The evidence of my own eyes—and something Fay said once.'

Chris was unimpressed; Morgan's girl-friend imbibed her opinions from whoever she had last spoken to. 'Hearsay,' he muttered.

Unexpectedly, Eleanor was nodding at Morgan. 'Yes,' she said. 'Fay mentioned that to me, as well.' She turned to Chris. 'It was just some odd behaviour at Medics' Ball.'

Chris thought back. He could scarcely remember...or could he? Oh, yes; it was Keith who had turned up for the annual shindig with a petite, pert-nosed geography student, shortly before she became Morgan's girlfriend. So perhaps Fay *was* in a position to comment... Nevertheless, he felt he didn't want to hear the details. 'So you think Keith's gay?' he asked Morgan.

'Keith: I'm not sure. But *Hubert?*' He gave a grotesque leer. *'He's* as bent as a nine-bob note.'

In the Physiology Department of the Medical School, senior lecturer Laszlo Kovacs sat anxiously in his office, re-hearsing various turns of phrases for the forthcoming confrontation. Delicate

14

personnel matters always confounded him; he was much more at ease with hard scientific facts, apparatus, formulae... Unfortunately there was no convenient formula with which someone could accuse a colleague of homosexuality.

A tap on the glass door disturbed a promising line of euphemistic obfuscation. He looked up to see the smiling face of Michael Chan, his PhD student. The expression meant nothing; Michael, a Hong Kong Chinese, always looked as if he was smiling.

'I thought you should see this, Dr Kovacs,' he explained on entering. 'It's the latest student magazine, and the Animal Concern people are more strident than ever. Here on page five...this article only just stops short of inciting students to take matters into their own hands! They haven't mentioned us by name, but "the abhorrent practice of animal experimentation on our own campus" leaves little to the imagination.'

Laszlo skip-read the article, taking in its gist with practised ease. 'You are right,' he said, handing it back, 'but there is nothing we can do. They are simply exercising their right to express an opinion.'

'Taking their democracy for granted,' said Michael darkly. Laszlo gave him a sympathetic smile; he knew Michael had worries for his family's future when the colony entered into reluctant wedlock with its vast communist neighbour. He understood such fears only too well, having left his own native Hungary as a young man in the wake of the 1956 uprising and constructed a new life in England.

'Shouldn't we reply?' went on Michael. 'Write a piece ourselves, explaining that we only use dead or anaesthetized animals here, with the aim of furthering medical knowledge, and would they rather we experimented on babies?'

'I think,' said Laszlo after a pause, 'that we would find ourselves in an undignified contest, a tussle waged through the medium of columns of print. Our seeing fit to offer justification would be regarded by them as a capitulation of sorts. Our energies are better spent on the work in hand.'

'But they should *know* about this work!' exploded Michael. 'Your success in the field of diabetes...I could tell them. I could set up a debate and air all the issues. That would stop this one-sided sniping!'

Laszlo slowly shook his head. 'No, Michael. It would take more than that. But I am not worried. This group, Animal Concern, are not like their cousins in Bristol. Animal Militancy start fires. Here, the students simply talk and write. No one is hurt.'

Badly satisfied, Michael made as if to leave, then turned again as he reached the door. 'Did Fred tell you about the animal house?' he asked.

'Yes. I believe he found some scratches on the padlock last week. But the door hadn't been forced, and nothing has happened since. It is an inconclusive incident.'

'Well, I know what I think,' said Michael Chan, and left exuding umbrage. Laszlo wondered fleetingly whether Michael would try to enlist support from other seniors in the department, but dismissed his prospects as poor. Professor Byrne would take a brusque, Blimpish view, Magda Hepworth, the taciturn new lecturer, was unlikely to involve herself in any public relations scheme, and as for Hubert...

A qualm of nervousness assailed him as he thought again of Hubert. Where was he? After morning lectures he usually returned to the department to deposit his notes and slides prior to walking to his campus flat for lunch. Perhaps today he had gone directly...

Having steeled himself as far as he was able to the prospect of tackling Hubert, Laszlo wanted to get it over with as soon as possible. He left the office, nodded at a passing technician, and proceeded down the Physiology corridor, glancing into each laboratory he passed. There was no sign of Hubert, although he spotted the broad back of Magda as she bent over a spectrophotometer. Yes, Magda would work through lunch and utter no syllable which was not deemed strictly necessary.

The Human Morphology corridor below had a coffee machine set in a small offshoot from the main thoroughfare, a niche which also contained informal padded chairs and a noticeboard. In mid-morning this area hummed with activity, but just now it was silent: all the students had dispersed to the campus eating facilities. Only Hubert stood there, pinning a memo to the board.

Laszlo approached him. 'I would like a quiet word with you, if you have a few minutes,' he began tentatively.

Hubert frowned. 'What's it about?'

'It would be easier to discuss it upstairs. Would you like to come to my office?'

'I was just going for lunch. Is it departmental business?'

'Er—indirectly.'

'Can't it wait till this afternoon?'

Laszlo's diary for the rest of the day was full. 'I am afraid not,' he said.

'In that case, tell me now.' Hubert folded his arms, making little effort to conceal his impatience.

'It's about—your private life,' said Laszlo, his voice pitched discreetly low. 'Are you sure you will not come upstairs?'

'Absolutely certain. What about my "private life"? And what is it to do with you?'

Laszlo swallowed. How was he to put his point across without provoking a storm of resentment? He cast his mind back to the previous weekend when he had taken his wife Anna for dinner in town. The air had held an atmospheric wintry tang, and the words of a French carol had floated out to them from a small side street church, sung with the innocent tonelessness of young children: *'Eel ay nay, lur diveen onfont...'* The mood of peace and elevation had lasted throughout the excellent meal at the Rhinegold, only to be sullied on their way back to the car...

'I saw you on Saturday night,' he said slowly. 'You were coming out of a club with a—companion...' He spread his hands and waited for Hubert to speak. Nothing happened. 'It was a male companion,' he went on.

Anger flared in Hubert's pink-rimmed eyes. 'So?' he hissed.

Laszlo flinched. He heard again the coarse laughter thrusting from that upper window, despoiling the image of the children, and saw, as he clutched Anna's arm tightly, the smooth predatory face of his colleague's chosen analogue.

19

Hubert was staring at him. 'I'll thank you to keep your nose out of my business,' he said softly, but very precisely. 'What I do outside the department is no one's concern but mine.'

'Hubert.' Laszlo found his voice again. 'My opinion is not important here. It is more the fact that if I saw you, anyone else might have done, and some of the people in positions of power at this university have very strong views on—such matters.'

'Professor Byrne, you mean. Yes, I've heard his declamations. I suppose you've been blabbing to him?'

'No, I have said nothing.'

Hubert curled his lip. 'Impressive, isn't it? Here we are at the end of the twentieth century, and my career has to tremble before the prejudices of others. Good old Prof Byrne knows what he likes. A department full of foreigners is fine by him, but let the token Englishman deviate even slightly from the norm as defined by our worthy professor, and suddenly his prospects aren't worth a pin!'

'Hubert, you are wrong. No one has complained about your work. Even if he discovers your personal secrets, Professor Byrne cannot remove you on those grounds.'

Hubert gave a hollow laugh. 'No, but he would find some other excuse. At best I'd be passed over for the next twenty years. So what now? Are you going to tell him?'

'I did not come to make threats, Hubert, simply to warn you. But there is an area where I am uneasy. You live on campus. You have a flat in Calverton Hall where, I believe, you are what they call a "morals tutor" for some of the resident boys, advising them when they are vulnerable. I feel this should not continue. You would be better to leave hall and make your home away from the campus. I know your warden well, and his views reflect Professor Byrne's. He would be horrified if he found out the subject of our discussion; I have no doubt that he would remove you from your post the moment he knew, and that could indeed affect your position at the Medical School.'

'I see. I am to be blackmailed out of my flat. If I don't go voluntarily the whispers will start and I'll be thrown out. I didn't expect to hear this sort of thing from you, Laszlo.'

'You have misunderstood. I only want what is best for everyone.'

With a snort, Hubert Pomeroy turned away and walked towards the glass-doored entrance foyer with his peculiarly undulant gait. Laszlo watched him thoughtfully. One might have imagined his orientation was obvious to all, but it hadn't been quite so

21

simple. Before the earthy evidence of the Lynx Club, he had pigeonholed Hubert as one of those effete, asexual types of academic, and was fairly confident that Professor Byrne shared this view. Saturday night had been a shock. It hadn't even been a case of 'the Love that dare not speak its name', that stalwart of Oxbridge literature from a certain era. No, this had been the casual pick-up, physically degrading, emotionally impoverishing, and Laszlo had abruptly been forced to confront his own attitudes.

He retraced his steps to the first floor, and found himself wondering what Hubert would choose to do.

Inside room D9 of Calverton Hall that evening, students were crowded on Morgan's chairs and bed, drinking after-dinner coffee from an eclectic collection of mugs. The three other medical students—Chris, Bradley Pike and Steven Listerfield—tended to migrate there on a regular basis, while neighbours from the corridor joined them more sporadically.

'These blasted exams!' grumbled Steve, above a background pounding of heavy rock music from deep inside the building. 'We're never free of them. I'd rather have a summer all-or-nothing than tests every term.'

'The Medical School gives you both,' said Bradley. 'It's supposed to be for our benefit: a kind of continuous assessment.'

'Continuous harassment, more like.' Steve turned to the boy from D6, who sat quietly in the corner. 'Do the Chemistry lot subject you to similar tortures, Jason?' he asked.

'No—sounds a bind. We get the usual summer blow-out.'

'What are you revising tonight, Chris?' asked Bradley.

'Oh...endocrinology, I think. And you?'

Bradley was about to reply when they heard the distant thud of D block's main door, followed by a light pattering of feet on the stairs.

'That'll be Fay,' said Morgan, his tone not wholly enthusiastic.

Chris opened the door in anticipation, causing Oswald, Morgan's articulated skeleton, to jangle from the hook where he hung. Fay entered with a giggle, her cheeks flushed with cold, and stopped to push the generous sheaf of corn-coloured hair away from her face before rushing to embrace Morgan.

Behind her came Eleanor. 'Thanks for the loan of your Samson Wright,' she said to Morgan, holding out the volume. 'Now I know where Dr Pomeroy gets most of his lecture notes.'

'Coffee?' he offered.

'I'll make it,' said Fay, and flitted round the room collecting mugs for topping-up, happily proprietorial.

'Those dog experiments are all explained,' went on Eleanor. 'It's really interesting. Before Pavlov's gastric pouch, people didn't know that the vagus is the secretory nerve to the stomach, so the logical basis for selective vagotomy to alleviate gastric ulcers wasn't appreciated.'

'Dogs shouldn't have to be sacrificed just for human comfort,' scowled Jason. 'No animal should. We don't have the right.'

'I think it's reasonable if they're treated humanely and there's no other viable option,' said Morgan. Fay looked uncertain. 'And more than mere comfort is involved: some medicines tested on animals have meant the difference between life or death for patients. Where would diabetes be today if Banting and Best hadn't spent that awful sticky Ontario summer 1921 isolating pancreatic extract from dogs? We've now moved on to genetically engineered insulin, but Dr Kovacs in the Physiology Department here is trying to go one better. He wants to obviate the use of exogenous insulins altogether.'

'Using animals for the tests?'

'At this stage, yes.'

'I thought so,' said Jason stiffly. 'In my book, moral arguments can't bow to pragmatism. If the human race wants to improve its quality and length of life then let its members find ways of using their own tissues to achieve these ends.'

'We already do, with transplantation,' commented Bradley.

Jason swung round, his deep-set eyes aflame. To Chris, watching, it seemed that he had found an opening he had been waiting for.

'Yes,' sneered Jason, 'and why is that? Because animal hearts, and lungs, and livers, and what-not would be *rejected*. Or would be the *wrong size*. No other reason. Certainly not moral principle. If animal spare parts fitted the bill, could you seriously imagine us *not* clamping creatures into cages of misery, making them drag through the days until the next recipient had need of their organs? Huh!'

Bradley looked surprised at the outburst he had provoked from Jason. The chemistry student rarely volunteered opinions, and could sit with them for hours without contributing to the general conversation. Sometimes they wondered why he came at all: it could hardly be for the quality of Morgan's instant coffee. Jason's appearance gave no particular clue to his cryptic temperament: he was smallish, dark and very ordinary-looking; only the occasional fanatic flash below his jutting forehead had previously signalled any depth of feeling.

Chris felt embarrassed. 'You'll be pleased to hear that we'll be the guinea pigs in a few weeks' time,' he said lightly, hoping to dispel the sudden tension. 'We'll have to swallow rubber tubes and have our stomach secretions measured.'

Fay shuddered. 'I'd be sick,' she said in a little-girl voice, snuggling up to Morgan.

Morgan gave a lazy smile. 'Hubert told us of an alternative way of obtaining gastric juice for study. Apparently a fellow called Alexis St Martin blasted himself in the stomach with a load of duck-shot in the 1820s. He was left with a fistula, a permanent opening between the stomach and the outside air. Another chap called Beaumont used him to study human digestion; no need for fancy tubes.'

'Stop it! You medics always find something revolting to talk about.'

'But you still love us.'

She raised her face, with its neatly upturned nose, towards him. 'One of you, anyway.'

'Speaking of Hubert,' said Bradley, 'I really think he's going too far with Keith.

He victimizes him. Keith looks terrible these days—all shaky and attenuated. I think he's heading for a nervous breakdown.'

Eleanor's eyebrows drew together in concern, but Morgan simply shrugged. 'He's always been a bit of a jelly,' he pronounced. 'I don't think he's cut out for medicine. You need a good memory for facts, and he's hopeless.'

'His nervous state's probably affecting his memory,' said Eleanor. 'That gives him more to worry about. It's a vicious circle.'

'Well, let him go to the Health Centre and get some pills.'

'You don't sound very sympathetic.'

'I don't hold with the idea of depressive states and nervous breakdowns. These people should get a grip on themselves.'

'And you studying to be a doctor! Shame on you, Morgan. I predict you'll feel differently when you've done your clinical training.'

'I suppose it's possible.'

'Course you will,' said Chris heartily. He had been watching Fay during this small exchange, because her expression had caught his eye. Her face, lustrous with love for Morgan which she never attempted to conceal, had grown taut and pale. Her gaze was unfocused, and she held her body tensely against his side. Morgan appeared to have noticed nothing amiss; the arm draped across her shoulder remained casual, and he regarded Chris with untroubled eyes.

'Mental illness is no problem,' murmured Steve from across the room. 'Everyone knows it's all in the mind.'

'Time we got on with some work,' announced Morgan half an hour later, and proceeded to shoo people from the room.

Fay lingered at the door. 'Are you sure you won't come carol-singing with me on Saturday night?' she asked him.

'Fay, after a rugby match, there's only one place to spend the evening—in the pub with the lads.'

'He can't sing anyway, despite his Welsh mother,' grinned Bradley. 'You should hear him in the shower.'

'I *have* heard him in the shower, thank you. And he *can* sing.'

'We'll go out on Sunday,' Morgan promised. 'I'll give you a call.' He accompanied her along the corridor, whistling, then waved as she went down the stairs with Eleanor.

Chris sighed, unlocked his own door, D8, and prepared for another evening's slog.

2

Laszlo Kovacs peered out of the window at his still, bleak garden, where a sparrow pecked fruitlessly against the rigid ground. 'It is so cold,' he said, 'that I believe we shall have snow before the weekend is over.'

'I hope so,' smiled Anna. 'It will remind me of home.' She walked across the room to join him, her carriage erect, her blonde hair still prevailing against the encroaching grey. To Laszlo, she had changed little from the vibrant girl he had first met in Hungary nearly forty years earlier.

'Isn't this now our home?' he asked softly.

'Yes—of course. I am sorry. I should have said it will remind me of youth.'

Youth... For a moment Laszlo savoured his own nostalgia. He envisaged snow, gentle flakes falling on the fine buildings of Buda Hill, covering the squares with a carpet of white, clean as the fleece on a lamb. He inhaled the steamy warmth of the *eszpressós* where the coffee was always piping hot and the student gossip cogent. Happy days, or not? Not for Hungary. He hadn't wanted to care, but politics had been all around him, a pressure for change voiced ever more urgently in the streets and the cafés, and even the laboratories at his university. So his youth had abruptly died...

'Something is worrying you?' asked Anna.

'Oh...just things at work.'

'Is it the animal rights people? I read in the paper that they demonstrated in Nottingham last weekend. There was some violence...do you think there is danger at the university?'

He hastened to reassure her; Anna was both formidable and tenacious when aroused by matters of principle; she would hector him for new details every day. 'The people in Nottingham were picketing a department store which sells furs,' he said. 'They were a visiting group from Bristol who had enlisted some local support—just for the day. There has been no violence at Sherwood.'

'Good.' She glanced at him shrewdly, but decided to let the matter drop. 'Look at this Christmas card,' she said, holding out a cherubic depiction of the infant Jesus. 'It is from Tibor and Agota. Would you believe that Ferenc is now twenty-two? He has passed all his accountancy exams. We must congratulate him when we write.' She sorted through the rest of the cards, offering them for his inspection then slotting them into a cheerful display holder topped by a robin; at the finish, she stepped back with a nod of satisfaction.

'Will you be receiving fan mail again this Christmas?' she teased. 'Will there be a card from that funny little girl who studies geography?'

'No,' he said firmly. 'Not this year.'

In the reverential hush of the Science Library Keith Mayhew crouched numbly over his books. Few other people were there on this Saturday afternoon, but those few who were wore faces of intelligent application. How oblivious they were to their great good fortune! None could know his grim struggle against panic and dismay, the paralysis of thought which left him staring at the same anatomical diagram for minutes at a time without any benefit.

They would know at the Medical School, though... After last summer's exam fiasco they would be watching him, noting everything: his difficulty with the practical experiments, his sparse contributions to seminars, his lack of rapport with the other students... Only the Christmas exams could save him; if he failed again, he would be taken on one side and politely asked to leave.

Keith's eyes stung; he almost sobbed aloud. His parents would be utterly crushed—and his sisters! How could they understand? His father owned a modest jeweller's shop in Lincoln; there were no doctors in the family. At school, Keith had done well through sheer hard work and self-discipline. Only now did he realize that he had been a big fish in a small pool. Here at Sherwood the intellectual baseline was so much higher that his meagre self-assurance was sapped from the start, and his faculties frozen by the fear of comparison.

He grasped convulsively at the notes on the table, bunching them up in his hand. A thin pink sheet slid out from between two of the pages, and he picked it up with trembling fingers; it was a perky letter from his sister Marjorie, received three weeks before. Against his will Keith found himself unfolding and re-reading it, lingering over the colourful vignettes of home and school (so ordered, so *safe*), yet knowing that the closing paragraphs would be turgid with hero-worship as Marjorie's estimation of his academic powers ran riot:

'We can't wait to consult you when you're in Harley Street,' she had written. 'Claire is already designing a plate to put beside your door, with lots of room for all the letters you'll get. Guess what? Pattie Soames's brother has gone to Sheffield to study medicine. He's nowhere near as clever as you. We always imagined he'd be a bank teller, or something. At least you'll be qualified *long* before he is.

'Spare a thought for your poor, house-bound sisters as you while away the evenings exchanging lively intellectual conversation. Dad's really strict about our homework at the moment; he's even stopped us watching *Suburb*—says it rots the brain. He also accuses me of thinking about boys too much. He's right...'

Keith's eyes smarted anew as he skipped to the affectionate valedictory words, words full of trust and unquestioning confidence in his future accomplishments. They were all relying on him to justify their pride—no ifs, buts or maybes. And he was equally certain that he was about to let them down.

With a shudder he buried the pink sheet once more among his notes and staggered to his feet. He could scarcely breathe...the foreknowledge of failure, that poisonous dark sludge, was swamping him. He had to get out of this library now; he had to find somewhere else to think.

Chris Shallet pulled up the collar of his jacket with numbed fingers and bowed his shoulders, retracting the head between like a penguin. Brr! What an icy wind! If it wasn't for the fact that the reference book he wanted was in the Science Library, he wouldn't have stirred from Calverton Hall. Morgan must be mad, playing rugby in weather like this! All those exposed knees...

As he reached the lee of the building, a familiar figure pushed feebly at the glass doors and emerged with a zombie-like tread. Keith Mayhew's face was set in a tortured mask, and his raw eyes stared straight ahead. It would have been convenient to let him walk past, locked in with his demons, but Chris's conscience was too well developed for that.

'Hi, Keith,' he said. 'How's it going?'

Keith started. 'Oh—Chris. Badly. I can't think—I can't learn anything. My head's full of cotton wool.'

'Oh dear,' he said, infusing a kind of jolly sympathy into his voice. 'There is a lot to remember, isn't there? But I've managed to boil much of it down to basics, and as for the rest—acronyms can help, the sillier the better!'

'There's no time...I'm going to fail, Chris. They'll kick me out this time—and how can I face everyone at home?'

'You won't fail,' said Chris, grappling for some concrete suggestion to offer, and wishing he was in the warm library.

'I will. Dr Pomeroy will make sure of it. He hates me.'

'No...no. He just uses you as an example to stir up the rest of us. He could have picked on anyone. Look, if it's physiology you're worried about, I could lend you my notes. Or even better, why not go and ask one of the lecturers for some extra help. Then the responsibility for your performance becomes *theirs*. Yes—tell them you're anxious and request some personal tuition.'

'Who would I ask? I can't approach Prof, Dr Kovacs teaches the other seminar group and Dr Hepworth only takes us occasionally. It would have to be Dr Pomeroy, and—I can't!'

'Well, think about it. It would put the onus on him.' Out of the corner of his eye Chris saw Steve Listerfield scuttling up the slope towards them. 'Do come round if you want the notes,' he said hurriedly to Keith. 'I'm in D8, the room before Morgan's.'

Steve drew level and together they watched as Keith trudged away, every lineament downcast.

'You playing agony uncle?' asked Steve. 'Sort of.'

'Morgan's right, you know. Keith *is* a bit of a jelly.'

'I feel sorry for him.'

'So do I, but only up to a point. These exams are facing us all. Are *you* ready for them?'

'Heavens, no. My revision's about a week behind. You wouldn't catch me on a rugby pitch at this stage in the term.'

The great glass door swung towards them.

'What it is to have brains,' Steve said.

Chris chewed his pen absently and glanced at his watch. Apart from half an hour for dinner—the typical chips-and-beans-type fare still fighting a feisty rearguard action in most of the men's halls—he had worked right through the evening and now felt jaded and stiff. Ten past nine. Morgan would be in some pub, quaffing his grant money and playing 'bunnies' or singing rude limericks... Chris gave an involuntary smile as he remembered the one about the Woman from Nod. He stood up, stretched and walked over to the small hand-basin in the corner, intending to splash cold water on his face.

A double knock sounded at the door.

'Come in!' he called, and to his surprise Morgan ambled into the room. 'I thought you were out with the lads,' said Chris.

'That's what I told Fay,' twinkled Morgan.

'How was the game?'

'We trounced 'em. Twenty-two nine. *And* I got my own back on their hooker—that ape who split my lip last year.'

'Good. I presume you're here for some quiet revision, then, uninterrupted by admirers. Want a coffee?'

'No, thanks.' Morgan pushed the door shut. 'No on both counts, in fact. I've got a plan, and I wondered if you wanted to be part of it.'

'A plan? Take a seat; what's it about?'

The bed creaked as Morgan sat down heavily. 'Hubert goes out on Saturdays. Take that as fact—I know. Tonight he's left his window open.'

'In this weather?'

'He smokes, remember. And his rooms are on the second floor, so security's not an issue...or should I say *oughtn't* to have been an issue...'

'Morgan, what are you getting at?'

'You're going all pink, Chris. Stay cool. Do you recall last summer's physiology exam, Hubert's little gem? We knew the stuff, but the questions ranged from the idiosyncratic to the totally irrelevant. He claimed to be testing our "adaptability", if I remember rightly. Steve complained to Prof but got nowhere.'

'Ye-es.'

'Well, I happen to know that Hubert's

37

already prepared this term's paper, and is keeping it in that black briefcase of his. One of the lab techs told me.'

'Really.'

'Chris...' Morgan leaned forward and subjected Chris to his considerable personal magnetism. 'If we get a look at the paper tonight, copy down the questions, we could give Hubert such a shock!'

Chris was outraged. 'I've never heard anything so mad in my life! I think the only person who'll get a "shock" is your father when you're sent down. You don't need to cheat, Morgan. You've got a fine brain.'

Morgan shook his head impatiently. 'You're missing the entire crux,' he said. 'We'll distribute the questions to every member of our year—even Keith, or perhaps especially Keith. We could devise some model answers, as well, with variations. Hubert won't know what's hit him.'

'Yes, he will,' said Chris grimly. 'He'll know someone nicked the papers.' Despite his reservations, he felt a germ of fascination beginning to unfold in his brain. It would be nice to repay Hubert in his own coin for once. He would be baffled; let him dare to give poor marks! And, more important, Keith's greatest source of fear would be removed...

Chris's next objection was purely practical. 'How do you know Hubert is out?' he demanded.

'His car has gone, and—I know there's a place where he goes on Saturdays.'

'And how do we get to the second floor? I mean, how do *you* get to the second floor?'

Morgan grinned at the slip. 'There's a handy chestnut tree just outside the bedroom sash window: that's the one which is open a crack. Along with the Boston ivy on the wall, I reckon that should prove a feasible route.'

Gamely Chris argued against the scheme, but all the while he felt his resolve disintegrating. Not for nothing was Morgan a founder member of the 'Forfeits Club', a select group of students who played poker for imaginative penalties. Morgan's own brand of rugged charisma ensured that others were willing to follow his lead.

Within ten minutes Chris found himself sliding between the bushes of Calverton's outer garden. 'One of us is certifiable,' he muttered, 'and I've a nasty suspicion which one.'

'Consider this an act of philanthropy.'

'You're *sure* he's out?'

'Ninety-nine per cent.'

They crept across the lawn, avoiding the rhomboids of light cast from random windows. Hubert's flat was situated in a partly disused wing of the hall, by his own request; to one side were students' rooms, to the other a deserted corridor. Chris was thankful that the wind had dropped, although the chill seemed to be deepening with the night. He wore a padded zipper jacket, dark trousers and black non-slip trainers, and leather gloves encased his fingers. He had half expected Morgan to produce a balaclava with holes cut out.

'That's the window,' hissed Morgan, pointing. Chris grunted an acknowledgement; he could just make out the dark silhouette of the tree rearing above them, and confirm that its trunk rose slightly to the left of the last illuminated ground-floor window. Some of the curtains were drawn. As long as no one took it into his head to peer into the winter night, Chris judged that the chances of detection would be slight. Anyone passing between the various blocks and common rooms of the hall would use the quandrangle, the inner garden, to minimize time spent in the cold.

'What now?' he whispered when they reached the shelter of the creeper-clad wall.

Morgan leaned close and explained with the aid of gestures. 'We climb the tree until we reach that branch hanging above and to the left of Hubert's window. Then one of

40

us helps the other to step across to the sill and get a safe purchase—there's plenty of ivy round the window to grab. That person opens the window, then lends a hand in his turn.'

Chris stared upwards doubtfully. From that angle he couldn't assess the true distance between branch and sill. How reliable was the ivy? He knew it grew from thick, gnarled roots and attached itself to the wall by means of tendrils. He tugged at a nearby piece; yes, it seemed secure enough.

'I'll give you a leg-up,' said Morgan. 'That first branch is rather high.'

'Oh, *I* see. I'm first up the tree, and first on to the sill...'

'Shut up and put your foot there. You're lighter than I am, that's all.'

Chris made a laborious progress up the tree until he came to the branch which overhung the window. He noted that the curtains were open. Now for the tricky bit, he thought, then abruptly froze as he realized that the quality of darkness inside the bedroom was not absolute.

'What's the matter?' whispered Morgan behind him.

'I can see the bedroom wall, and it's not as black as it should be. There must be a light on somewhere—which means he's home after all.'

'More likely he's just left a lamp switched on. Go carefully.'

That was an admonishment Chris didn't need. He was already tensing his muscles as he edged along the chosen bough, flexing a little at the knees, steadying himself with the aid of a higher, more delicate branch. Dead twigs scratched across his trousers, sending a flurry of pieces into the black void below. Another few inches and he would be able to see inside...

He crept forwards, stopped again and risked a quick peek. For a moment he saw nothing significant, then his innards gave a great jolt. A figure was lying on the bed, thinly illuminated by a bar of light from the partially open door opposite. Chris could only see the head and shoulders, and the face was turned away, but he knew with sickened certainty who that person was: Keith Mayhew.

'Have you got a good grip? Shall I come and give you a hand?' Morgan was still in his fool's paradise.

'No.' Chris's voice sounded muffled to his own ears. He felt a hundred years old. 'There's someone in there. I'm coming back.'

'Who?'

'For God's sake! If Hubert returns to the room he'll see us. Move, Morgan—or let me come past.'

'I want to look for myself.'

'You do. I'm going down.' As Morgan stepped on to a creaking side branch, Chris skirted cautiously round him and grasped the main trunk with relief. He cringed as he heard the nearby scrape of a sash window opening, and shrank into the shadows, expecting to hear a shout of fury. Instead, there was a hollow ring followed by a repeat of the rasping.

'Someone just put their milk out on the sill,' murmured Morgan.

'Oh.' Chris levered himself downwards, his arms feeling shaky and weak. 'See you back at base,' he said uncompromisingly.

In the safety of D8 Chris opened the cupboard above his wardrobe, drew out a hidden bottle of whisky and splashed it into two glasses. 'Whisky Mac?' he offered, unscrewing the cap of a ginger wine bottle.

'No, thanks. I'll have it neat.' Morgan tossed his head back and drank the spirit in one gulp, then slammed the glass down on the desk. 'What a turn-up!' he said with an unconvincing laugh.

'Yes,' agreed Chris, feeling the specious warmth of the ginger dissolve the icy lump that was his stomach. His hands still trembled; he thrust the left one into his trouser pocket and gripped the glass more firmly with the right. 'I wish we hadn't done it,' he said. 'I wish we hadn't seen...I feel— Unclean.'

Morgan nodded. 'Who would have thought Hubert would have resurrected his efforts with Keith?' he mused. 'I thought that was a damp squib; he finds his partners in town.'

Chris wasn't entirely concentrating, and so a few seconds elapsed before the purport of Morgan's words filtered through. When they did, a ghastly thought slammed into him, robbing his legs of muscle power and making him grope for a chair.

'It's my fault,' he said in a faint, appalled voice. 'Morgan—I'm responsible.'

'Don't be daft. How can it be your fault?'

'It *is!* I met Keith outside the library this afternoon; he looked exhausted and depressed, as usual. He said he was frightened of failing the exam, especially the physiology. I suggested he speak to one of the lecturers, ask if he could have some personal tuition, make them share the problem.'

'I think he's had personal tuition, all right. Sorry, Chris—go on.'

'Well, that's just it. I never meant...but it must have put the idea in Keith's head. He must have felt that the only way out was to—sell himself.'

'If that's true, then he'd have done it

anyway, without any help from you.'

Chris wasn't prepared to let himself off so easily. 'I didn't believe you,' he said through clenched teeth. 'The other day, when you commented on Hubert and Keith. I thought it was just salacious talk. But you were right. How did you know?'

'About Hubert?' Morgan grinned. 'I landed an interesting penalty once in the Forfeits Club—this is last year, before you joined. I was required to spend two hours dancing in the Lynx Club; Brad went along to check that I didn't default, and nearly got picked up himself! It was a hairy evening, I can tell you, and half-way through it became even hairier when I suddenly saw Hubert at the bar. He was canoodling with a real weirdo. I had to lurk in dark corners until my time was up.'

Chris felt his mouth gaping open. 'I can't imagine you in that place,' he said. 'What an awful experience... Did you just guess about Hubert and Keith?'

'Not exactly. Keith behaved very oddly when he took Fay to Medics' Ball. He kept parading her in front of the high table where the medical staff were sitting at dinner, as if he was determined to show her off. When she made a joke about it, Keith muttered, "I want him to see you, I want him to see you," and later she

45

noticed he became very tense every time one particular person came near him. That person was Hubert.'

'God, if only I'd known,' seethed Chris through his knuckles. 'What do we do now?'

'It's easy.' Morgan shrugged and turned to leave. 'We keep our own counsel and get back to our revision.'

3

'Yes, Sally. Walkies!'

Dorothy Holt affectionately patted the flank of her golden retriever, reached the lead down from its hook and clipped it on to the dog's collar. Sally wagged her plumy tail in eager anticipation, and strained towards the kitchen door.

'We'll go to Sherwood Forest.'

Mrs Holt drove the old estate car at her own pace, noting how empty the streets were so early this Sunday morning. The wan light revealed that there had been a thin snow-fall during the night—just enough to relieve the grey drabness of winter. More would be needed before children could hurl themselves down the slopes on their toboggans.

She parked in a rutted lay-by and held on to the lead while Sally sprang joyfully from the vehicle. Together they set off down a broad footpath which today was firm with a light powdery coating where snowflakes had swirled through gaps between the ancient trees. This wasn't the 'tourist track' to the Major Oak; it was a more personal pathway, much beloved by her husband Charlie when he had been alive.

'All right, girl. Off you go!' Mrs Holt knelt to release the lead, and Sally shot away into the depths of the woodlands. Once she had gone, everything seemed very still. Silent, too: the birds were saving their energy. Dorothy Holt briskly swung her arms and strode away under the canopy of trees; there was a good hour to enjoy the exercise before she would have to return and change her clothes for church.

Ten minutes later she was still alone. Sally usually came bounding back at five-minute intervals, but if something caught her attention it could be longer. It was amazing how dogs could be excited by scents even on the bleakest day.

'Sally!' she called.

Shaking her head in rueful amusement, Mrs Holt ploughed on. She knew the path opened out into a clearing less than a quarter of a mile ahead; Sally would probably be sniffing around the felled trees which had not been removed since the last gale.

'Sally!'

She heard a distant answering bark, but the dog didn't come. Overhead, the pearly sky widened as the trees thinned out, and soon she had reached the edge of the clearing. A tawny shape was scrabbling and worrying at something in the centre. Mrs Holt frowned; it looked like a bundle of old clothes. People really shouldn't dump such things in a beauty spot; it was very selfish. They must have driven along the track to reach this place.

'What have you got there, Sally?' she asked, approaching the heap.

Sally broke off her investigations and raised her head, panting, open-jawed. She had scraped snow away from one portion of the amorphous mass, and Mrs Holt could see a patch of dun-grey gaberdine, like a raincoat or a jacket. She put a hand on Sally's collar and leaned forward for a closer look.

Breath hissed in her throat: it was the body of a young man.

At his home in Carlton, Detective Inspector Richard Montgomery was spreading a knife-ful of marmalade on to his slice of Malted Grain. Across the table sat his dark-haired wife Carole, but the other two places were unoccupied.

'Where are those two adolescents of ours?' he asked.

'Still in bed, I'm afraid,' she said. 'I thought I'd give them another few minutes: they were very tired last night.'

'So they might be, going to a pop concert!'

Carole smiled. 'You have to enjoy being young. We went to pop concerts—don't you remember? Anyway, let's make the most of the peace and quiet this morning. I need to go through the Christmas card list with you.'

'Oh—I thought I'd better look at the car. The suspension needs checking.'

'It's been making that creaky sound for six months. Don't think you can wriggle out of communal obligations so easily! As it is, most of the outstanding cards are for your relatives...'

She broke off as the telephone bell rang in the hall. Montgomery displayed his sticky fingers, so Carole slid from her chair and went to answer the call. Within seconds she was back.

'It's Will,' she said.

Hastily Montgomery rinsed his hands, dried them and picked up the receiver; William Bird, his sergeant, was on call that weekend, covering for a constable with 'flu, and his own threshold for seeking help was not low.

'Will? Richard here.'

'I'm sorry to disturb you, sir,' came Sergeant Bird's mellow tones, 'but we've just received information that a young man's body has been found on the outskirts of Sherwood Forest. The local bobby says the cause of death isn't certain, but it looks suspicious. I'm going up there now, and Frobisher knows.'

'Where exactly?' Montgomery took down the directions with speedy precision. 'I'll meet you there,' he said.

Carole's face wore a familiar expression of resignation when he returned to the kitchen. 'You're going out, I suppose,' she said. 'Well, wrap up warmly and take care.'

'I shall.'

'What has Will found for you this time?'

'I won't know till I've seen for myself. But it might be murder.'

Montgomery parked his Sierra a sensible distance from the scene and walked along the edge of the forest track until he reached the cordoned-off clearing. Frobisher, Nottingham's Home Office pathologist, was already crouched over the body, and the bulky figure of William Bird stood sentinel on the other side.

50

Montgomery gave each a brief greeting and stared down at the corpse. It lay curled on one side, one arm flung out as if craving a benison from the frozen earth with its numbed fingers. His colleagues had excavated the upper part of the body from its thin covering of snow, but the lower part still remained shapelessly shrouded. From what he could see, Montgomery estimated this victim to be a boy of about twenty years.

'He was found at eight-thirty by Mrs Holt, a local widow,' supplied Sergeant Bird. 'This lady was exercising her dog in the forest, and the dog started scrabbling at the snow here. PC Goole is driving her home just now; he hoped to be back before you arrived.'

'No matter.' Montgomery knelt down and made his own examination while Frobisher delved in his case for a thermometer. Rigor had set in. The visible left side of the face was a faint dusky blue while the right cheek, gently raised from its hostile resting-place, showed the expected post-mortem lividity. A crooked pair of spectacles clung to the nose.

The gaberdine jacket seemed inadequate protection against the bleak weather of the previous hours; its pockets yielded only a handkerchief and a few coins. Before Frobisher had a chance to descend,

Montgomery checked the pockets of the grey woollen trousers, and this time had more luck: he extracted a printed card with a photograph of a bespectacled boy in the corner.

' "University of Sherwood Students' Union",' he read. ' "Keith B Mayhew, Faculty of Medicine".'

'Poor lad,' said Sergeant Bird. 'I wonder what happened? Was he strangled?'

'There's no evidence of a ligature,' answered Montgomery, 'and no bruising on the neck. But here's the expert...'

Frobisher crouched down, made his own assessment, then peered at them over his half-moon spectacles. 'I can't tell you at this stage,' he said. 'It *looks* like asphyxia—see these petechial haemorrhages on the eyelids?—but the method is uncertain. You're right about the neck—there are no marks at all.'

'When did he die?'

The pathologist pursed his lips. 'Difficult to say. Core temperature is useless as a guide in these conditions, even though one feels obliged to record it. Rigor is fairly well developed, as is the hypostasis. I'd say between nine and fourteen hours ago. I'll be able to be more precise when we've ascertained whether the blood has coagulated in the vessels, or not.'

Montgomery nodded, and moved aside

with Sergeant Bird while Frobisher dictated notes into a small machine.

'Apparently the snow-fall was between six and seven,' said William Bird.

'So the body's been in this clearing at least three hours... I wonder if this is where he died? If it isn't, then someone must have driven out here last night, and dumped him. We'll be lucky to spot any tyre marks; the ground's been rock-hard for days.' Montgomery glanced up as the sound of an approaching car engine reverberated through the forest.

'That'll be PC Goole, or maybe the SOCO boys,' said Sergeant Bird.

'I hope they have the wit not to drive too close.' He turned back towards the body, brows drawn together in contemplation. 'Doesn't this strike you as odd, Will?'

'What, sir—the position of the body?'

'Yes. If the boy's been murdered, which is probable, then why is he lying in the most wide open space this part of the wood has to offer? I know burial would be nigh impossible with the ground being so solid, but why didn't the killer put him in a ditch, or behind a tree, and pull a few branches over him? Why didn't he drag him even just a few yards away from a track that people use?'

'It's almost as if he *wanted* the body to be found.'

Sergeant Bird returned to headquarters from Lincoln just before lunch the following day, and made his way to Montgomery's office.

'I had a good chat with the Mayhews,' he said, accepting the invitation of a chair. 'An uncle and aunt were there as well as the parents—the same couple who came to help them with the identification yesterday. They were still shocked, of course, but they were ready to talk about Keith.'

'He was the eldest of four, wasn't he?'

'That's right. His three sisters are still at school. Everyone sounded very proud of his achievements; they even had his A-level certificate framed on the sitting-room wall! Basically, he was a bit of an introvert, worked hard at his studies and didn't go in for sports, except for enjoying an occasional country ramble. In the vacations he was perfectly satisfied with low-key family life?'

'What feedback had they received regarding his attitude to university? Did he write letters home?'

'Yes, but they were stilted affairs. I looked at five or six of them, spanning last spring, summer and the whole of this term. He only wrote about his course work, and made polite queries about how things were at home. There was no mention of friends, or parties, or fun, with one exception: a single line to say he'd been to the Medics' Ball.'

'What did his last letter say?'

'Very little; there was certainly no hint of potential suicide.'

'Did he join any university clubs?'

'The Craft Club in his first year—he brought home a pewter bowl he'd made. Then he changed to the Chess Club.'

'Hm. So what impression did the family have of Keith's state of mind while he was away?'

'They thought he was coping; he'd said nothing to suggest he was unhappy. I asked them in a vague way about his exams, and they reckoned he was doing fine. It was clear that they were unaware of the resits; he's been protecting them. There was something else, as well. The aunt managed to confide to me that Keith's parents got a lot of reflected glory from his status as a medical student. They would embarrass him in restaurants by loudly proclaiming the fact, or introduce him to perfect strangers as Keith, "who's about to be a doctor". It's understandable, because his father's a shopkeeper and there are no professionals in the family, but it must have added to the strain on Keith... Have you heard from Frobisher, sir?'

'Yes. He confirms that the boy died of

asphyxia, but can't tell us the cause beyond saying the appearances are consistent with suffocation or smothering. It's very odd. The time of death is as vague as ever, too: Keith hadn't eaten for some hours, so stomach contents were unhelpful.' Montgomery stood up from the desk and walked round to Sergeant Bird's side. 'Haslam and Grange are making enquiries at the Sherwood Forest end of this mystery,' he said, 'but the information we want is almost certainly at the university. Jackson and Smythe are down there right now, to catch the students in their lunch break. I propose we join them without delay.'

4

'Chris! Something dreadful has happened...'

Chris had been assaulting the Medical School's recalcitrant coffee machine, determined to receive either a drinkable beverage or his money back; one look at Eleanor's white, strained face, however, prompted him to leave the monster to the next thirsty student.

'What is it, Eleanor? Have you had bad

news from home?'

She shook her head, and they walked up the corridor for privacy. Just outside the Human Morphology Department she whirled round and stared at Chris with shocked brown eyes.

'It's Keith,' she said in a low voice. 'He's dead; Jenny from Faculty Office just told me.'

'Dead?' he repeated stupidly. 'How?'

'They don't know. The police rang the registrar at home yesterday, and he had to come in. They wanted Keith's family address, and asked lots of other questions. They said he'd been found dead in Sherwood Forest... Isn't it awful! He's been so anxious all this term... He must have killed himself.'

Chris could hardly take in the news. 'I noticed he wasn't in the first lecture this morning,' he said slowly, 'but then I didn't give him any further thought.'

'Neither did I,' said Eleanor, 'and that's been the trouble. I did try to help him once: I mentioned Hubert's bullying to two of the other lecturers, but neither was prepared to interfere; they said it was a matter of teaching style. I didn't bother after that...Keith never seemed to want to help himself, and we all had our own problems. Oh Chris, how miserable he must have been!'

Someone called 'Lecture!' from the other end of the corridor, and the crowd milling around the coffee machine hastily dispersed. Chris touched Eleanor's arm and they followed automatically, parting company just inside the door. He watched as she went down to her usual seat near the front, then plodded numbly towards his own place next to Morgan...Morgan! The sight of his friend slouched there, genial and unaware, jolted Chris from his torpor. They had to speak, and the sooner the better.

Someone entered the room and droned for an hour about the analysis of epidemiological studies, but Chris heard none of it, and the pen idled in his hand. As soon as the lecture was over, he dragged Morgan out of the Medical School and down the slope towards the campus lake.

'What's up?' protested Morgan. 'Can't we have lunch?'

'No.' Chris waited until they had reached the edge of the still grey water, then quietly imparted the news.

'Oh, God,' said Morgan in disgust. 'I suppose he must have topped himself. What a mess... I thought the campus helpline was meant to stop people doing things like that.'

Chris shivered. 'You know why he did it, don't you?'

'I should imagine he was ashamed. He thought selling out to Hubert was the lesser evil, then discovered that it wasn't.' Morgan had immediately grasped the situation, with minimal time to think—he was like that. Nevertheless, he lacked the sensitivity to appreciate Chris's agony of personal guilt.

'Eleanor told me the police are asking questions,' said Chris. 'What do we do? What do we say? I think we should volunteer all we know about Saturday night.'

'Don't be ser daft!' A broad band of Yorkshire cut through Morgan's speech whenever he was aroused. 'What will you say to them: we were just about to break in to copy Dr Pomeroy's exam papers when we saw Keith lying on his bed? That'll go down well, won't it? Not only will *our* reputations be shot, but so will Keith's. If we keep quiet, everyone will put this death down to exam-worries. Let's face it, there's a sizeable historic precedent for exam-related suicides at Sherwood.'

'I still think...'

'Look, if we hadn't been there on Saturday night, we wouldn't have seen anything.'

'But we were, and we did.'

'All right...but you'll agree our presence didn't *alter* the course of events.'

59

'I suppose not.'

Morgan clapped him on the shoulder. 'Attaboy. I'd be as willing to pipe up as you if I thought it would achieve anything, but I don't. At best it's a futile exercise in self-sacrifice. Don't worry, Chris. I doubt the police will even want to speak to us; Keith's room is in A block, and we weren't known as especial friends of his.'

Chris stared blankly out at the lake. 'He didn't have any friends,' he said.

In the event, Morgan was wrong. The two students had just finished their pasty and chips when Steve Listerfield peered into the dining-room and darted across to their table.

'Ah—there you are,' he announced in a conspiratorial undertone. 'A police inspector has been looking for you.'

'Me?' asked Chris faintly.

'Yes. It's about Keith—you've heard the news, haven't you? That's a relief. Well, this inspector says he's trying to piece together Keith's movements over the weekend—who he spoke to, what mood he was in, etc. I last saw Keith outside the library with you on Saturday afternoon, so obviously I had to mention the fact.'

'Obviously,' echoed Chris sarcastically. 'Thanks a bundle, Steve. Where's this policeman now?'

'Lurking somewhere near your room.'

With Morgan, Chris traversed the quadrangle to D block, and opened the sturdy outer door; his heart missed a beat as he saw a solid, rosy-cheeked man of about forty-five standing there with an air of officialdom.

'Remember!' whispered Morgan, disengaging himself from his friend with a nod at the officer. Chris swallowed and approached the stalwart figure directly. 'I'm Christopher Shallet,' he announced. 'I believe you were looking for me.'

'My inspector is,' smiled the man. 'He's just talking to one of your colleagues. Perhaps we could have a little chat in your room afterwards? I'm Detective Sergeant Bird.'

Any relief Chris felt at the approachability of this representative of the law was soon dissipated on the arrival of Detective Inspector Montgomery. This man had none of the sergeant's air of openness, of acceptable familiarity. Above a narrow mouth and pale, chiselled facial planes his eyes were a cold steely blue which seemed to say, 'I know your innermost thoughts; don't even try to hide them.' When he spoke a few conventional words in a quiet, well-modulated voice with the barest hint of a Nottinghamshire accent, Chris felt no reassurance. He was sure his own face was already scarlet, and surreptitiously brushed the back of his fingers against the cheek to check. Perhaps it wasn't *so* bad...

'We're sorry to detain you, Mr Shallet,' said Montgomery. 'I hope this won't take long.'

'Oh—it's all right. We're only doing dissection this afternoon and it's six to a cadaver anyway, so the people on the left-hand side will be glad to get a bit more room...' Chris broke off. What was he *saying*? 'That is,' he blundered, 'I can catch up later.'

'Good. Did your friend Steven tell you why we wanted a word?'

'He said it was about Keith. I'd already heard he was—dead, from another friend.'

'When was that?'

'Today; earlier on this morning.'

'What were your thoughts when you heard the news?'

'I...' Chris struggled to identify the implications of the question. 'I felt very sorry. But I didn't know him well.'

'Steven seemed to think that Keith was coping badly with the medical course. Was that your impression?'

'Yes. He resat several of the exams last summer, and was struggling again this term. I noticed he found seminars a particular ordeal, because everyone is expected to contribute something, and he had trouble speaking up.

'When did you last see him?'

Chris affected a thoughtful mode, but almost faltered under the cool scrutiny of the inspector. 'It was Saturday. I think. That's right—outside the Science Library. Keith had just been doing some revision, and we met by the door.'

'Did you speak?'

'Briefly. He said he was worried about the forthcoming exams. In this Medical School there are tests every term; the course is compressed into five years, so there's a lot to learn.'

'Can you remember exactly what he said?'

This time the pondering was real. 'Er—he said he was going to fail and they would kick him out. He said his brain was full of cotton wool.'

'How did he appear?'

'Ill—anguished, pinched...but he's looked like that for as long as I can remember.'

'What did you say to him?'

Chris wriggled in discomfort, transferring his weight from one foot to another. He wished he had thought to offer them chairs, then he could have sat down himself. Too late now... 'First, I tried to jolly him along,' he said. 'Then, I offered him my notes.'

'Did he accept?'

'No.'

'And you never saw him after that?'

'Er, no.'

'Tell me, Christopher, have you ever seen Keith on a bicycle or at the wheel of a car?'

The switch took Chris by surprise. 'No.'

'Did Keith have any friends with a bike or a car?'

'I—I don't know. I don't think so.'

'Who were his friends?'

'I can't really say. Sorry.' Chris found he couldn't meet the inspector's eye. 'He lived in A block,' he added lamely.

Montgomery gave a brief nod. 'What time was your conversation outside the library?' he asked.

'Oh...four, half-past...it was already getting dark.'

'And did Keith give any intimation of how he proposed to spend the evening?'

A vision of Hubert's window swam in front of Chris; he stared at the floor but it was there, too, showing him the dim room beyond, a bar of light, Keith's head and shoulder...

'No,' he croaked.

There was a long pause, then Montgomery's voice came with surprising gentleness. 'I'd like you to think for another minute, Christopher,' he said, 'then tell me if Keith said anything else to you, anything you haven't so far mentioned.

Or you to him. Anything at all.'

As they waited for him, the vision transmuted into Hubert's face, his sardonic sneer, the creepy-distorted stance, and from the closeness of the room came the bullying lash of his whispery voice. How could they let him get away with it? He had crucified poor Keith in public and in private, and only respect for Keith's posthumous reputation hung against the sudden lust for justice which surged into Chris's bones and lent them strength. He found he no longer cared about his own situation.

He raised his head. 'Keith was particularly anxious about the physiology paper,' he said clearly. 'I suggested he ask one of the lecturers for help. He may have followed my advice.'

In the Medical School, Montgomery paused outside the Faculty Office and consulted the list he had just been given. Jackson's enquiries among the students of A block had so far thrown no light on Keith's movements on Saturday night; Christopher Shallet's idea that Keith might have informally approached a physiology lecturer, while it sounded unlikely, might just provide a clue.

'You wouldn't bother a tutor at the weekend, surely,' said Sergeant Bird.

'Normally, no. But Keith was running

65

out of time: the exams were less than a fortnight away. Perhaps he contacted one of them to make an appointment.'

'What's the hierarchy? We'll have to see the top man first.'

'Professor Byrne runs the department. He's not here today; he's giving a guest lecture in London. The senior lecturer, Dr Kovacs, lives in Bramcote, but these other two lecturers, Drs Pomeroy and Hepworth, have flats in campus halls of residence.'

'Pomeroy lives in Calverton!' exclaimed Sergeant Bird, leaning over the list.

'Yes, but as you pointed out, we'll have to observe the usual courtesies. Dr Kovacs is waiting for us upstairs.'

Laszlo Kovacs proved to be a tall, spare man in his late fifties, with thinning grey hair and a mild expression. Despite having spent the bulk of his life in England, he dispensed his civilities in a voice which was both soft in tone and strongly accented.

'I am sorry this office is so small,' he apologized, offering them two tightly-wedged seats between his desk and the wall. Through the glass partition Montgomery could see the purposeful activities in the laboratory itself. At one bench, a young man of oriental appearance flashed them an evanescent glance while pretending to concentrate

66

on the liquid he was pouring into a beaker; across the room a large plain-faced woman spoke earnestly with a white-coated technician.

'Our registrar told me that you wanted to discuss the student Keith Mayhew,' said Laszlo. 'It is a terrible tragedy.'

'Yes,' agreed Montgomery. 'His family were very shocked; from their point of view there had been no warning signs. We are trying to establish whether he seemed depressed here on the campus...?'

Laszlo exhaled and gave an infinitesimal shake of the head. 'It is difficult to give you an answer,' he said. 'Our second-year students are sixty in number, and the physiology contribution to their medical course comprises lectures to the entire class, small group seminars and practical work. I did not personally encounter him in seminars—I believe Dr Pomeroy had more contact—but Keith was notable in a more general way because he was the only student to fail in three subjects last summer. He did particularly badly in the physiology paper.'

Something evasive in the scientist's otherwise frank expression when he mentioned 'Dr Pomeroy' caught Montgomery's eye: he decided to let his instinct take command.

'Did Keith get on with all the lecturers,

or were there any personality clashes?' he asked.

'I—er, heard that he, er, sometimes irritated Dr Pomeroy.' Laszlo Kovacs was clearly grappling with the ambivalence of whether or not to close ranks with a colleague.

'In class? In public?'

'I—er, believe so. That is, er, I was told this in confidence by another second-year student.'

'Just Keith?'

'Not exclusively, but mainly.'

'I see. Were these occurrences recent?'

'I—I really don't have first-hand information, but I thought perhaps you needed to know...'

With a little prompting, reflected Montgomery. Briskly he continued his catechism. 'We know that Keith spent Saturday afternoon revising in the library, and told one of his classmates that he was anxious about the forthcoming Christmas exams, especially the physiology. This boy suggested that he ask one of the lecturers for extra coaching, and felt that Keith may have taken the advice. We're trying to trace Keith's movments that Saturday evening...did he contact you at all?'

'No. I was at home with Anna, my wife.'

'Have you heard anything from any

68

colleague which might throw light on Keith's whereabouts that evening?'

'Nothing. I am sorry I cannot help.'

'Never mind. Thank you for your time.' Montgomery stood up and manoeuvred his way to the door in order to give Sergeant Bird maximal room to lever himself out of the narrow corner seat. 'We're hoping to speak to any staff who have actively taught Keith over the last fifteen months. Would that be Dr Pomeroy in the laboratory?' He indicated the oriental who, recognizing their interest, gave an ironic little bow.

'No,' said Laszlo. 'That is Michael Chan, our PhD student. But Magda is with us—Dr Hepworth. I shall introduce you, and you must use my office to talk to her.'

The office seemed even smaller to Montgomery once Magda Hepworth's solid figure had been substituted for the thin frame of Laszlo Kovacs. Her plain, serious face betrayed a hint of impatience, perhaps because of the interruption to her work; the detectives responded by remaining standing.

'I only came here this term,' she said. 'I can't pretend that I know all the students personally. I don't encourage discussion in my lectures. The purpose of lectures is to teach facts. Seminars are the fora for discussion. Keith must have been one of the quiet students.'

'We heard that Keith didn't always get on with Dr Pomeroy.'

'That doesn't surprise me.'

'Why not?'

She gave a heavy shrug. 'Dr Pomeroy is full of paranoia because of the way he is. He sees prejudice all around him, but dare not speak out openly, so he channels his frustrations into aggression towards the students. He is not a likeable man. But his *own* prejudices...they are valid in his eyes. He finds it almost intolerable to share the department with foreigners like Michael Chan and myself.'

'Ah...' Montgomery had detected some unusual nuances in her speech, but the name 'Hepworth' had told him nothing.

'Are you Polish?' he asked lightly.

'Czechoslovakian.'

He nodded, as if one eastern European accent didn't sound very much like another to him.

'Prague?'

'Ostrava—but later Prague.'

Montgomery nodded again. 'You said that Dr Pomeroy encounters prejudice *against* him, "because of the way he is". Can you explain what you mean?'

For the first time a slight curl appeared in Magda's upper lip.

'You will see for yourselves,' she said.

They ran Hubert Pomeroy to ground on the lower floor, between 'Multidisciplinary Laboratory Number One' and the Human Morphology Department. Once again Laszlo, having effected the introductions, discreetly removed himself from the scene.

They saw a slim man with a loosely rotated stance, thinning sandy hair and pink-rimmed eyes which were almost colourless. Homosexual, thought Montgomery immediately. Rightly or wrongly, that still went against the grain with many establishments. They had their ways of showing displeasure...the dead-end career path, the careful exclusion of the tainted entity from the real fruits of the academic tree—the venerable committees and titles, the influence and responsibility. But that was only people's response to *him*... What type of person was Hubert Pomeroy: a pleasant, sincere individual who formed stable, fulfilling relationships, or a thwarted, aggressive social inadequate scratching in the midden of casual pick-ups and sex-for-sale? Those attributes were quite independent of sexual orientation. One thing both detectives were sure about: Hubert Pomeroy looked defensive.

'I can't help you,' he said in a whispery, singsong voice when they had broached their subject. 'Keith was making

71

poor progress, but I have encountered worse students, and they haven't killed themselves.'

'I believe there was pressure from home for him to do well,' said Montgomery. 'He was anxious about the coming exams. Did he make any request for extra tuition?'

'Not to me. All the facts are in the textbooks, anyway.'

'You live in Calverton Hall, I think.'

'Yes. I have a tutor's flat.'

'Did you see Keith at all last weekend?'

'No. I don't eat in the dining-room at weekends: the food is so stodgy. I was off campus anyway, much of Saturday.'

'You're sure you never saw Keith? Not even a glimpse?'

A muscle twitched in Hubert Pomeroy's left cheek; his hissing answer came a second late.

'Absolutely not,' he said.

Montgomery and his sergeant climbed the hill from the Medical School to rendezvous with Jackson and Smythe at Calverton Hall.

'Nice building, this,' commented Sergeant Bird as they approached the creeper-clad walls. 'Much more character than those modern halls on the northern perimeter. The wistaria must look a treat in autumn. Or is it Boston ivy?' He

72

continued to muse over this conundrum as they passed into the inner quadrangle, where the garden hid its secrets behind a bleak winter façade.

A door opened just ahead, and Detective Sergeant Brian Jackson scurried out of A block with his partner Graham Smythe, a detective constable with a singularly poetic face, having waited some minutes in the warmth.

'We've interviewed all the students we can find on Keith's corridor,' said Jackson hastily, 'and their consensus is pretty uniform. They say he was peevish and antisocial. Those who did attempt friendly overtures got rebuffed. The only times he deigned to speak were when he was asking them to turn down the volume of their tapes and CDs.'

'What about weekend sightings?' asked Montgomery.

'There's one of relevance. He was seen entering his room about twenty to five on the Saturday by the lad from two doors down.'

That would fit with Christopher Shallet's library encounter at half-past four.

'Our witness can't say when Keith came out, though,' continued Jackson. 'He went off boozing himself just after seven, and says he could hear Keith using his washbasin as he went past.'

73

'Well, we haven't had much joy with the physiologists. They merely confirm that Keith was struggling with his work. Have you seen any of the hall staff—the bursar, the catering people?'

'We were just about to, sir.'

'Hm. Let's go and talk to the warden again, see what he can arrange.'

From the centre of the quadrangle they tramped back into earshot from the surrounding windows, feeling chilled now as the December afternoon darkened. They passed through a door into Calverton's foyer, where a line of wooden pigeon-holes stretched behind the porter's desk. William Bird paused to speak to the porter, a heavy-jowled but loquacious individual, and much nodding punctuated their earnest discussion.

'Well?' asked Montgomery when his sergeant returned. 'What have you found out?'

'It is Boston ivy, sir—*Parthenocissus tricuspidata*. I should have known: it has three leaflets per leaf, not five like Virginia creeper or eleven like wistaria. But you still get a blaze of autumn colour—Taff there says it looks like a russet tapestry...'

'*William!*'

'Oh, I've got the night porter's details, as well. He may have seen Keith on Saturday.'

Shaking his head with minimally amused exasperation, Montgomery led the way into the depths of Calverton Hall.

5

Montgomery removed the Christmas cards from his office three days before Twelfth Night. Their aura of jaded festivity irritated him, like a drunken party guest still asleep on the kitchen floor the following day. They were also a reminder that the 'party' itself had been less than successful: the unresolved death of Keith Mayhew had cast its blight on Montgomery's enjoyment of Christmas, and through him that of his family. Only the good humour of their companions, Sergeant Bird and Carole's daredevil young cousin Mark, had saved the occasion.

It was impossible, he thought, to conduct meaningful enquiries on a university campus once the students had gone home for their vacations and many of the staff were away visiting family. If only he could have wrapped up the case in the first week all would have been well. Keith himself could have been laid to rest, his parents could have begun the long haul towards acceptance of their loss, and Montgomery's small CID team could have felt the satisfaction of a job completed. Unfortunately, it hadn't worked out like that...

Montgomery grimaced as he reviewed the threadbare profile of Keith they had so painstakingly assembled. He had been quiet, studious and polite, a seamless family member in Lincoln, but an unpopular recluse on Sherwood's campus. His academic prowess had been adequate for school, good even, but sadly unequal to the demands of the medical course... All this Montgomery had known on the second day. What new facts had they uncovered in the weary round of subsequent interviews? Keith had auditioned for a minor part in the Drama Group's production of *Caesar and Cleopatra,* but had been turned down; he had never reappeared. He had joined the Craft Club and made a pewter bowl for his mother, but after two terms his attendance there had ceased, too. He had made, then cancelled an appointment with his campus GP the previous summer.

Young Keith had been colourless and unremarkable by anyone's standards—yet his death was puzzling a whole cohort of supposedly intelligent detectives. Asphyxia was undisputed as the cause. He had died because air had been unable to reach his lungs. But how? And why? He had ruffled the feathers of his neighbours in Calverton Hall by his peremptory demands for silence, but that was hardly a provocation for murder. No one else appeared to have even a whisper of a motive. What about suicide, then? Reasons for despair were not hard to find, but if that was the answer, it raised more questions than it solved.

Almost more difficult to contend with were the physical aspects of the case. Keith Mayhew, a student with no personal means of transport beyond his own two feet, had been found dead in the middle of a wood several miles from the campus. If he had been dumped there by a killer, why hadn't more effort been made to hide the body? If he had killed himself after somehow reaching the clearing, then *how* had he done it? The nose and mouth had been clear, and analysis had failed to reveal exotic drugs in his bloodstream. There had been no suicide note.

There was one other possibility: some sort of accidental death. Meeting the epicene Dr Pomeroy had reminded Montgomery of the diversity of humankind; he had fleetingly wondered if Keith had perhaps died during some bungled sexual experiment. Autoerotic asphyxia, they called it. Physical evidence, however, was completely lacking; the body and clothes had been examined with great care by Frobisher and others. No weird contraptions had been found at the scene... (*The scene?* Who would play such games in Sherwood Forest on the coldest night of the year? Keith would have been found in his room, surely.) And if someone else had been involved, then who? Keith had had no known girl- or boyfriend. He had taken a geography student to the Medics' Ball the previous spring, but had had no dealings with her since, according to his colleagues and neighbours. On the whole, misanthropy seemed to have been his favoured creed.

Montgomery had felt an instinctive mistrust towards Hubert Pomeroy himself, but the physiologist had had no known connection with Keith outside the Medical School. As more tales of savage public grillings had emerged, it seemed less and less likely that Keith would have sought help from that quarter on the Saturday night. A few discreet enquiries revealed that Dr Pomeroy had driven away from Calverton car-park alone just before seven, a time when Keith was known to be still in his room. No, thought Montgomery, Pomeroy's defensive manner stemmed from guilt and shame: he probably imagined he had harried Keith to his death.

So that was their situation, a death still

designated 'suspicious' nearly four weeks later. The inquest had been adjourned, of course, but evidence for firm conclusions would be required soon. An open verdict would not only represent failure, it would mean ongoing mental torment for Keith's family.

Montgomery fingered the glitter frosting on one of the Christmas cards before throwing it into the bin. Jackson had earlier asked him something idiotic about New Year resolutions, and received a dusty answer. They didn't need resolutions, they needed to shake off their festive hangovers, restore a businesslike atmosphere to the department, and do some serious detecting. He would see to it that they did.

'Eleanor! I haven't seen you since we got back. How was your Christmas?'

Eleanor paused in the corridor of Wellington Hall as Fay rushed towards her in a flurry of words and corn-coloured hair. Even in winter she managed to look like a refugee from the hippy era, with a long skirt, ethnic jewellery and homespun shawl.

'Fine, thank you,' Eleanor answered politely. 'Too much food and alcohol, not enough exercise...a fairly normal Christmas. How was yours?'

'Much the same. Will you have a cup of tea with me?'

Fay hadn't always been so welcoming, recalled Eleanor as she made a courteous acceptance. When she had first become involved with Morgan she had regarded Eleanor as some kind of rival, and resented the fact that she spent every day in his company at the Medical School. It took some time for her to grasp that Eleanor was simply a friend to both Morgan and Chris. Now that all was clear, her overtures were friendly, but Eleanor was wryly aware that her own revised role was that of sounding-board or, occasionally, trusted messenger.

Fay's study-bedroom was in the old part of Wellington Ladies' Hall, the core of the building which stood for decades before two long extensions were added in the early 'seventies to help provide accommodation for the increasing numbers of female students at Sherwood. The room was large and dark with a squeaky floor, but Fay had done her best to disguise its more forbidding features. Tapestries, macramé and silk-screen prints hung from every wall, and plump quilted cushions covered the chairs and bed. No surface was allowed to be free from embellishments; even the narrow window ledge was jammed with figurines.

Eleanor found that the confusion of styles gave a cloying effect: the crocheted bedspread was at odds with the chintzy valance beneath, and home-made terracotta pots made uneasy companions for porcelain ballet-dancers. Fay's choice of clothing was often a similar hotch-potch: Laura Ashley goes Creole. It seemed to reflect a certain naïvity in her nature—wanting to do the right thing, but immature in her approach, easily swayed by conflicting enthusiasms.

'Here,' said Fay, holding out a pottery mug with an odd-smelling liquid inside.

'Er, camomile tea?' asked Eleanor, taking a sip and disciplining her facial muscles.

'That's right. It's best without milk. I drink gallons of the stuff—it's supposed to be good for you.'

'You like it?' murmured Eleanor.

'Not really. Oh! Let me show you something!'

Fay had sat down on the bed, her remarkable curtain of hair pouring over her shoulders like molten silk, but now she sprang up and reached a small cosmetic jar from the top of a chest of drawers.

'Guess where I went last night?' she said, unscrewing the lid.

'Where?' asked Eleanor obligingly.

'I went to a meeting of Animal Concern, down at the Lakeside Bar.' She giggled. 'I didn't tell Morgan. He wouldn't have approved at all! I bought this cream there—they had a stall of cruelty-free

81

products. All the ingredients are natural, and really cooling—try some.'

Eleanor smoothed a little of the white substance along the back of her hand. 'Yes,' she said. 'It's not at all sticky.'

'It's barbarous to experiment on animals!' Fay exclaimed abruptly. 'They have no say in the matter. Why should *they* suffer for our vanity? No cosmetics company should be testing its paints and pastes on God's creatures! If this cream can be formulated without cruelty, then they all should be.'

Eleanor hesitated while Fay sat back, flushed with indignation. An animal-lover herself, she heartily agreed with the gut sentiment. But there was a vein of speciousness in the declamation, and she debated with herself the value of trying to point this out. Usually, when Fay had decided on a stance, such efforts were futile.

'I agree,' she said slowly, 'and if it was just cosmetics I'd say ban the lot. But it's not quite so straightforward; we need protective products like sunscreens, and lotions to prevent nappy rash. European law requires that every new chemical be tested on animals before any contact with human skin, in case it causes inflammation, or something worse like cancer. That means companies who claim to avoid animal testing are simply using ingredients already known to be safe...but these will have been tested on animals by someone else, perhaps many years ago, in order to reach that conclusion.'

Fay's lower lip protruded mutinously. 'That's silly,' she said. 'You don't need tests if you use natural ingredients. Everything in this jar is natural—and pure. There are no additives at all.'

She glowered at Eleanor with a closed, stubborn look, and Eleanor knew instinctively that it would be unwise to pursue the topic. Fay had a poorly developed sense of logic; already she had blurred and broadened the issue, probably without realizing it. 'Natural' components such as lanolin were actually more likely to cause allergic reactions than synthetic ones, and without preservatives they were prone to bacterial contamination and general decay. As for the virtues of 'pure'...! Arsenic could be 'pure'... No, best not to tease Fay.

'It might be wise to keep it in the fridge,' she said mildly.

Fay nodded and relaxed, similarly shying away from conflict; Eleanor was more use to her as a captive confidante. 'Guess who else was at the meeting?' she asked.

'Tell me.'

'Jason Gower. You know, the boy who

lives down the corridor from Morgan and Chris. We got talking; he's really sincere in his views. He told me what a widespread problem animal cruelty is—and how much is going on on this very campus!' She leaned forward, and the hair slid off her shoulder. 'I've got to stop Morgan doing physiology for his Medical Sciences degree next year. He's bound to need animals for his project. I want to persuade him to choose a subject like Community Medicine. Will you help me?'

It was almost risible. Fay, who had survived as Morgan's girlfriend for eight months mainly by saying 'yes' to his every demand and having no mind of her own, was actually going to take a stand with him on an issue. But did she really believe he would change his career plans just to protect her sensibilities? Eleanor suspected the submission would go down like the proverbial lead balloon. Morgan wanted to specialize in anaesthetics eventually, so a preclinical physiology degree would be useful to him. The Department of Community Medicine, by contrast, was staffed by woolly academics who spent all their time talking. What had Morgan once called them? Ah, yes: 'prattling twits, who don't know one end of a syringe from the other.' He would find no kindred spirits there. As for her own situation, Eleanor planned to do her first degree in biochemistry, where again animal tissue would be needed for study. In the context of improving medical knowledge, she was able to find this acceptable.

'Well?' asked Fay eagerly, her eyes sparkling as they always did whenever Morgan's name cropped up.

It was time for the truth. 'I'm sorry, I can't help you there,' said Eleanor. 'But best of luck with your endeavours.'

Laszlo Kovacs picked up the parcel which had appeared on his desk and tugged ineffectually at one end of the wrappings. It was a stout padded envelope, swathed in masking tape, and there seemed to be no easy 'open sesame' mechanism. He paused as Professor Byrne tapped on the door.

'Ah, Laszlo. My lecture at the Sheffield symposium next week has been rescheduled: I shan't be back in time to teach the second-years here. Can you cover that? Friday at ten. Thank you.'

He sailed out again before Laszlo could do more than nod. Friday... Laszlo quickly consulted his diary and found a cast-iron prior engagement. Oh dear. Hubert Pomeroy was the logical choice as a fill-in, but their relationship had been very strained since their delicate discussion a month earlier. It would have to be Magda.

Michael Chan appeared in the open doorway. 'Dr Kovacs, I have some results here which don't make sense. Look, the insulin uptake should have been...'

'Wait a moment, Michael, and we shall discuss them in detail. But first I must have a word with Magda.'

'She's in the secretary's office. I'll fetch her.'

Michael was back in less than a minute. 'She's coming.' He jogged impatiently on the spot.

Laszlo, meanwhile, attacked the parcel again. Under the tape was a row of staples; he took a small pair of scissors and prised them open one by one. Then he began to slide the contents of the envelope on to the desk.

He looked up as Magda's brisk footsteps crossed the lab. She was wearing her usual uncompromising expression, but as her gaze fell from Laszlo's face to the package in his hand her demeanour underwent a startling change. He saw fleeting puzzlement, then a shock of understanding and horror.

'Dr Kovacs!' she gasped hoarsely. 'Stop! Look at the package!'

Beneath fingers gone suddenly icy, he saw a loop of wire protruding.

6

'Laszlo Kovacs!' exclaimed Sergeant Bird when Montgomery told him the news. 'We know him. Who's the investigating officer?'

'Jack Bayliss. There's nothing to link this incident with *our* case: it's got all the hallmarks of an animal rights attack. Nevertheless, I've pumped him for as much information as I can get.'

'What happened?'

'It seems that someone left a parcel addressed to Dr Kovacs on the porter's desk in the foyer at lunchtime, and the porter nipped up to the Physiology Department himself to deliver it. There was a stamp, but no sign of franking. Dr Kovacs didn't find the package until early afternoon; he was just in the process of opening it up when Magda Hepworth yelled at him to stop. She'd seen some wires emerging. They wondered what to do for a minute; Michael Chan, the PhD student who was also present, suggested lowering it into a bucket of water, but in the end they did the wisest thing. They evacuated that whole portion of the building and rang for

Security, who contacted the police.'

'Was it live?'

'Oh yes. Quite a nasty little device—enough to maim and possibly kill at close range. Luckily the bomb disposal people deactivated it intact, so we've got the wrapping to analyse. There's a bit of a label on one of the batteries used which might give a clue to where it was bought. Jack's team are working through ARNI, the National Index, to ascertain which known animal rights sympathizers should be investigated.'

Sergeant Bird frowned. 'It's wrong, you know, when you can't do a vital job without laying yourself open to this kind of thing. I thought only Animal Concern was active locally, and they've always confined themselves to written propaganda, or the odd demo. It bodes ill if they've decided to take the militant road.'

'Perhaps they haven't. This could be the work of an isolated maverick. Or maybe they've been infiltrated by another group. Jack will find out.' He gave a gloomy sigh. 'What's the betting he'll have solved this long before we've cracked our own case?'

'Magda must come to dinner! Ask her, Laszlo; she has saved your life.'

Laszlo gave Anna a rueful smile, and carefully placed his tumbler of *barack* on

88

the table beside him. He hardly ever drank, but here, in the privacy of his own home, he had been able to acknowledge how shaken he felt.

'You don't know Magda,' he said. 'She is so antisocial. Only the work matters, and time spent fraternizing with colleagues is time wasted.'

'Ask her anyway. I want her to know how grateful we are. She must go out sometimes? Surely you introduced me to her at the Dean's dinner in October?'

'That is right. But she had only just started her post here...and you do not turn down an invitation from the Dean!' He paused, reminiscing. 'I think that is the only time I saw her smile. Yes! Hubert had said something funny. He had drunk too much sherry, and told us he was in a gun club and possessed a firearm.' He laughed. 'The very idea! We were all amused...Professor Byrne said we would have another Alexis St Martin for experiments. That is a man who filled himself with duckshot and became a very useful human guinea pig for studies of physiology!'

He laughed again, but more shakily this time. Violence and all its associations made him feel ill. Unbidden, his mind scampered back to visions of that package and he shivered. Diabolical though the contents had been, with their potential for indiscriminate injury, the most chilling part was outside the envelope. Handwritten capitals...his own name.

'Stop him! Stop him!'
The roar of the crowd surged around him in a great suffocating wave. He felt anger, but more than that, blind fear, threatening to release the floor of his belly like a hangman's trap. He limped a few steps, but despite the strong new boots his cursed left foot let him down. Still they yelled and pointed.
Suddenly—pain in his shoulder as though he'd been kicked. Long moments of silence which were only in his head. Then he stumbled on...
So little blood. So little blood.

Laszlo awoke, shuddering violently, his pyjamas soaked with sweat. He felt confused, disorientated. Beside him Anna stirred. 'Laszlo?'
'They want to get me,' he muttered feverishly. 'My name is on the list. We must cross the border.'
'Shh.' Her hand was on his shoulder, warm and comforting. 'You've had a nightmare, that's all. Shall I put on the light?'
'No...I'm sorry. I didn't mean to wake

you. It was that parcel...it seems to have triggered memories.'

'I know. I understand.'

'I felt that they were still after me, that they would never give up.' He found that his fists were clenched, and made a conscious effort to relax. 'I'm sorry,' he said again. 'Please go back to sleep.'

'Would you like a drink of cocoa?'

'No. I shall be all right, thank you, Anna. Good night.'

'Good night, my dear.'

He stared into the darkness as her breathing slowly became deep and regular. Peace...all he wanted was peace. He had crossed a continent to find it, and now he had to live with being afraid again.

'Why Dr Kovacs?' asked Steven Listerfield bemusedly. 'Why not Prof? He's head of the department, after all.'

Bradley Pike gave an ironic smile. 'Prof Byrne's never here.'

'Dr Kovacs's work is better known,' said Morgan. 'Those diabetes papers he published last year represented a real breakthrough—keep still, Chris; I'm trying to put drops in your eye.'

'Poke it out, more like,' grumbled Chris, shrinking away from the small bottle in Morgan's large hand. He backed into the bench, and submitted with minimal grace. 'What was that, homatropine or the placebo?'

'Best if you don't know,' soothed Morgan, recording the time of instillation on his notepad.

'Huh!'

'It gives you the creeps,' went on Steve. 'If a sickie's on the loose, any one of us could be his next target. We already made use of animal organs for pathology and some physiology, and next year when we do our Medical Science degrees we'll be using a lot more. Ergo, we condone it.'

'First Keith, now this. I'm ready for something cheerful,' said Brad. 'I'm really looking forward to Forfeits Club tonight.'

'What's this?' Eleanor had wandered over from her group and now stood regarding them with quizzical amusement. 'Is your gambling coterie still going strong?'

'You're not meant to know about that, Eleanor,' he chided. 'The proceedings are secret.'

She chuckled. 'Like Freemasons? I suppose you make strange signs at each other across the dining-room. Gosh—perhaps Dr Pomeroy is a member. And there was I, thinking his spasms were just a nervous tic! Can I join, please?'

'Absolutely not. It's for men only.'

'I know how to play poker.'

'The game is *stud* poker,' leered Morgan.

'Pity,' she said. 'I think brag would be more appropriate.'

Morgan grinned and consulted his watch. 'Five minutes exactly,' he said. 'Come here, Chris. I want to measure your pupil.'

Chris had been watching Eleanor through a fog. 'I can't see,' he complained. 'Everything's blurred on the right.'

'That's just your ciliary muscle getting paralysed,' said Morgan approvingly. 'The pupil's enlarged, too—you look quite odd.'

'Thanks.' Chris staggered to the bench and sat on a stool. 'I suppose this is what they mean by a single blind trial.'

The room was steamy-hot and Chris felt very stiff. It was twenty-past one in the morning, but rather than drooping with fatigue his three companions were straining forward, anticipating the culmination of the night's play and—most important—who would have to carry out the 'forfeit'.

The club had been founded a year earlier with medical students who had since moved out to the hospitals for their clinical apprenticeships. At first, it had embraced 'dangerous sport' elements, and Chris had declined his invitation to join, but more recently the nature of the forfeits had softened, and he had succumbed to friendly pressure from Morgan. Now he enjoyed the evenings, and tonight's tournament provided welcome relief from the more disquieting events on the campus.

He glanced across the table at Morgan, Brad and Steve, then back to his cards. In some ways, he thought, Eleanor was right to compare this club with the Freemasons. Besides being exclusively male and supposedly secret (one of the former members must have talked), they undertook a series of rituals which were scrupulously observed. First, the forfeits were written on identical pieces of paper, folded, then placed in a hat guarded by Oswald's bony fingers. The spirit of the club demanded a certain spice, and the individuals vied with each other to produce something daring and original; each was piquantly aware, however, that there was a four in one chance of having to carry out the instructions himself. The second ritual concerned the purchase of neat little piles of twenty-pence coins from Morgan; although the use of real money lent a greater feeling of danger to the proceedings, they all knew that the true prize was avoiding the forfeit. Additional rituals punctuated the evening, standard procedures for any serious card game, but the zenith for three people was to occur at one thirty precisely, when the overall loser stood before Oswald's throne, selected a piece of paper from the hat, and read his fate out loud.

Tonight, Chris was struggling to avoid being that person. Brad had played in his usual boisterous way, lacking subtlety but finding inordinate luck with the cards. Morgan had matched his badinage, played well and reached a respectable position. Steve, who possessed cunning, self-discipline and a perfect poker face, had received poor cards for much of the evening, as had Chris, but had managed by means of an uncharacteristic bluff to keep ahead of Chris. Chris himself, prudently folding hand after dismal hand, had seen his shiny pile of coins inexorably leak away in antes. This was his last chance to avoid paying the forfeit.

He looked at his cards, and consciously kept his face neutral: Morgan was watching him. They weren't scintillating—a queen and five, unsuited. Morgan had insisted on playing 'Hold 'Em', a trendy variant of stud poker as played in Las Vegas; it enabled him and Brad to spout more jargon at each other. Unlike the more standard draw poker Chris had dabbled with as a schoolboy, this game involved fashioning a hand from one's own cards and three communal face-up cards, 'the flop'. If betting continued, two further single face-up cards came into play. Assessment of an opponent's hand was thus quite different to draw poker: instead of making deductions from the number of cards drawn, one based much of the calculation on the values of the face-up cards.

'Are you in, Brad?' asked Morgan when the flop had been revealed.

'Not me.' Brad threw down his cards and took a swig of lager.

'Steve?'

Steven shook his head.

'Chris? Want to call it a night?'

Chris stared at the three cards in the centre of the table. Queen of hearts, ten of spades, five of clubs. That gave him two pairs, queens high. But what did Morgan have? He had raised before the flop, indicating that the hand was a strong one. Two aces, perhaps? Ace-king? If the latter, Chris would be sunk if a jack came up. He should play vigorously now...but supposing Morgan had two queens, or two tens? That would mean he was now sitting there with three—

Chris made a modest bet. His fear of the forfeit was greater than that of losing good money after bad. He had only landed the forfeit once before, and the experience had not been pleasant. For a full week after he had removed the ornate crest from the gates of a neighbouring university he had cringed in his room, waiting for the men in blue to come to his door. Returning it had doubled the terror, but brought profound relief. Incitement to commit a felony had subsequently been frowned on by the club.

Morgan raised. Did he have the three? Chris wasn't at all sure. He swallowed, and called.

'Fourth Street,' announced Brad, glorying in his Las Vegas jargon as Morgan flipped another card on to the table. It was the two of spades; their status quo was unaltered. Both players checked, and Chris took a drink of his lager. Morgan, the host of the evening, had handed out powerful Special Brew before surreptitiously switching to low-alcohol Swan Light for himself. Brad had fallen for this piece of gamesmanship and was now moderately drunk; Steve had kept his head by sipping daintily at his can for hours, while Chris had made it clear to Morgan that he wanted Swan Light, too.

Morgan prepared to deal again, and Chris's heart began to thud in his chest with genuine nervousness. This last round could give him the money he needed to beat Steve—or it could plunge him into disaster. If the card should be an ace, a king, a jack or a ten, Morgan might find what he was looking for.

Across the table Brad craned forward, hot-eyed, waiting for the kill. Steve sat like a statue...Morgan dealt.

The card was the queen of clubs. Full house! Chris hastily used his lager-can to suppress the radiant beam he was sure was about to burst forth from his features. Morgan couldn't have queens. Even if he had two aces, that would still only give him two pairs. And the straight no longer mattered...

'You betting, Chris?' asked Brad.

Chris was contemplating his strategy. The pot wasn't big enough for him to overtake Steve and avoid the forfeit. He needed to draw Morgan in, make him stake heavily... He waited, sucking his lip, glanced doubtfully at the sprawl of coins and made a largish bet.

'You're bluffing, Chris,' grinned Morgan.

Chris smiled twitchily back. 'Am I? Do you want to find out the expensive way?'

'No.' Morgan raised, his face now smooth, and everyone turned expectantly back to Chris. He hesitated, eyes flickering between his own coins and the 'pot' in the centre of the table, then with an air of wild decision thrust his entire residuum forwards.

'Chris,' chided Morgan mockingly, 'I don't want to take *all* your money.'

'Drop out, then,' said Chris, fervently hoping he wouldn't.

'Come on, Morgan,' growled Brad. 'Play the game.'

Morgan shrugged. 'Okay,' he said, and matched the bet. The cards were rolled; his pair of aces failed to match up to Chris's queen. 'Yer jammy bastard!' he burst out.

Chris pulled the coins lovingly towards him. 'I think Steven has an appointment with Oswald,' he said.

'No, I haven't,' came Steve's quiet voice. 'It's Morgan.'

They looked again at the piles of winnings and discovered that this was true.

Morgan laughed, and shook his head philosophically. 'We haven't caught you yet, Steve,' he said, 'but just you wait.'

'I'm good at that.'

Chris, pink with success, joined Brad and Steve as Morgan solemnly approached the judicial figure of Oswald. The skeleton sat upright in a corner chair, its thin fingers cupping an inverted top hat they had bought at some second-hand shop. Inside the hat lay the four papers.

'Incompetent wretch, read out the challenge,' boomed Bradley, who as overall winner of the evening had become master of ceremonies.

Morgan, face averted, dipped his hand into the depths, drew out a paper and slowly unfolded it. 'Spend the night with Magda Hepworth,' he read, 'and bring back a token of your success.' He swore as they roared with laughter. 'What did you have in mind—a battered Durex?'

'A pair of knickers would do,' said Steve.

Chris was wondering who was the author of this forfeit. Open speculation was forbidden—the remaining papers were to be destroyed unread. Nevertheless, he had a shrewd idea. The challenge was typical of Bradley.

Morgan was shaking his head, his mouth twisted unreadably. 'Real paper bag job, that,' he said. 'I'd rather abseil from the Post Office Tower.'

'Do you *decline?*' enquired Bradley portentously.

'No; I'll do it.' Refusal meant unthinkable loss of face.

'You might be in luck,' speculated Steve. 'She could be frustrated. Mike Chan says she spends nearly all her free time in the lab, working on research. Perhaps she has nothing else to do.'

'Or isn't interested in anything else,' countered Chris.

'How will you go about it?' asked Brad with prurient eagerness, swaying slightly on his feet.

'Dunno yet. I'll need a plan of campaign.

Perhaps I'll take Ogden Nash's advice.'

'What's that?'

' "Candy is dandy, but liquor is quicker." '

They guffawed again, and Bradley staggered against a bookshelf. 'Wassup, Chris?' he asked when all Chris could summon up was a tight, forty-per-cent smile. 'Haven't you any suggestions for Morgan?'

'I was just wondering...' Chris swung round to address the remark to Morgan himself. 'This is all very well—but what about Fay?'

It was true, thought Morgan as he stared through the doors of the physiology lab Magda Hepworth did work late: solitary and dedicated, she put in the kind of hours one normally associated with postgraduate degree students. Much of the work was manual, repetitive procedures which others would delegate to technicians, but like a Marie Curie she persisted, jealously presiding over her own kingdom as if no one else could be trusted.

Her square profile was all he could see, but he knew the rest well enough. She was big, but not fat: muscular, like an eastern European athlete. Her voice, when lecturing at least, came over in a clipped contralto, but no trace of personality was ever allowed to leak out with it.

He paused, his hand against the door. Could he really go through with this? He could pretend—they'd never check. No...without honesty the Forfeits Club was a sham. He'd show Brad, and sly little Steve.

He entered the lab; she looked up from her print-out but said nothing.

'Hello,' he said. 'I'm Morgan Brunt from the second year.'

'Yes?'

'You gave us a lecture on the liver at the end of last term.'

'I know.'

'I, er, was just packing up downstairs in the MDL, and I saw someone else was working late. I wondered if you'd like to come and have a drink with me.'

'Why should I want to do that?'

'It was just an idea.'

'There is a kettle here.'

'I meant wine. I'm going to the Lakeside Bar.'

'Enjoy yourself, then,' She turned back to her print-out of wiggly lines.

Morgan stood in the middle of the lab, thwarted, but giving up was not in his Yorkshire nature. Girls constantly told him he was attractive. They liked his blunt talk and sense of humour, conquests were easy. This woman, though, was of different fibre. Each disdainful accented monosyllable represented a challenge, and he realized that he would have to modify his approach, formalize it in some way, if he was to succeed.

'Dr Hepworth,' he said, 'I would be greatly honoured if you would accompany me.'

She lifted her head slowly, her expression registering surprise at his persistence, and under the harsh artificial lighting he saw that her skin was as fresh as that of a young girl, and her eyes were the colour of peat. 'That place is noisy,' she said, 'and anyway, I haven't finished my work.'

He held his breath; she hadn't actually said no. 'I have wine in my room,' he answered, locking her gaze into his and taking a step closer. 'As for work—there's always tomorrow.'

After the cold walk up to Calverton, during which few words had been exchanged, the central heating of D block felt positively decadent. Morgan unlocked D9, ushered his guest into the sanctum and hung her coat behind the door. Oswald lounged in a chair, a scarf wound around his neck and a cigar clamped between the grinning jaws.

'Who is your anorexic friend?' asked Magda drily.

'That's Oswald. I can put him in the wardrobe if he bothers you.'

'The living tend to be more dangerous than the dead.'

Morgan felt curiously gauche; usually, the battle was more than half won once you had enticed a girl into your room, but with Magda, he wasn't sure how the revelation of his true intentions would be received? Would she hit him? Cry rape? Make trouble at the Medical School? He switched on a shaded lamp in the corner and turned off the overhead light.

'That's killed the spotlight,' he smiled. 'Now, can I get you something? I can offer wine, or tea, or coffee...'

Her face was in shadow, but the quirk of amusement at the side of her mouth was just detectable.

'I'd like coffee, please,' she said. 'Afterwards.'

Morgan woke up once in the middle of the night and stared into the blackness, feeling joy and disbelief in equal measure. Magda's willingness, her lack of inhibition, had astonished him. In contrast to the pale acquiescence of Fay there had been participation from a real woman, which had stirred him to feats he had only read about before. All cats might be grey in the dark, but this one yowled. She made him feel...yes, she made him feel very much a man.

7

Thin January light stole under the curtains as Morgan climbed out of bed and began his exercise routine. Today there was to be an important rugby game against a visiting Scottish team, but already he was wondering how soon he could decently abandon the evening celebrations and repeat the exhilarating manoeuvres he had just experienced. Fay wouldn't be expecting his company...

Magda was just beginning to stir and, belatedly remembering the point of the night's industry, Morgan seized the sensible pair of white cotton knickers which lay by the foot of the bed, and jammed them behind the radiator. He then stretched to the ceiling, touched his toes, executed several lunges to left and right, and finished with a series of press-ups. By the time he rose, panting, she was watching him.

'Quite the man of action,' she said.

'I've got to keep in trim; we're playing Stirling's First Fifteen this afternoon—rugby. As the home team we should beat them.'

'I thought professional players avoided—

over-exertion—the night before a match. Doesn't it weaken the legs?'

'Received wisdom is for receiving, but not necessarily for acting on,' he answered, pulling back the curtains. 'I find it spurs me on to greater things... Would you like a shower, or some breakfast? If the bread hasn't gone mouldy I can give you toast, or there's Weetabix, or fruit...'

'No, thank you,' she said, swinging her legs to the floor. 'I should go right now. It's nearly nine o'clock, and your neighbours will be out and about at any moment.'

'No, they won't. They're lazy sods at weekends. Stay a bit longer.' He couldn't resist touching her again as she sat there, skimming his fingers along the smooth, supple skin of her shoulder, tracing the collar-bone to its junction with the breastbone, and sliding downwards...

He was halted by her expression.

'Morgan,' she said, taking his hand, nipping it gently between her teeth and relinquishing it, 'this was a mistake. It mustn't happen again.'

He felt thunderstruck. 'What do you mean?'

'What I said. We'll both put last night behind us. Whatever your motives were—some kind of dare, I should imagine —they don't matter. Neither does my reason for co-operating. Call it weakness, if you like. But as an episode it's past.'

'No! I want to see you again. I *must* see you again.'

'Not like this. It's over. Where are my underclothes, please?'

He gaped at her, feeling inexplicably faint as frustrated rage washed through him. 'Damn your underclothes!' he choked. 'You can't just leave as if nothing happened. It was good—admit it! More than good. The best one you ever had...the best *three* you ever had!'

'Yes,' she agreed calmly.

'Then come here again—tonight.' He crouched down to her level and seized her arms. 'We've got something special going; don't let's...'

A sharp triple knock sounded on the door.

'Go away, Chris,' called Morgan.

'It's not Chris. It's me!'

He stiffened: Fay! He hadn't expected her until Sunday; her shopping and his rugby should have taken care of today. Hastily he pulled on his trousers.

'Hang on a minute, Fay!' He glanced out of the window, but his room was fourteen feet up and Magda shook her head ironically as she slipped into her own skirt and blouse.

'Morgan?'

'Just a tic...' He clumsily straightened the bed before a peremptory tattoo made the door shake.

'Morgan! I feel silly out here! Let me *in!*'

With a sigh of resignation he walked to the door and opened it, interposing his large frame between Fay and the room. 'Sorry, Fay, I can't ask you in,' he said. 'It's not very convenient at the moment. I'm just sorting a few things out.'

Her expression of happy anticipation rolled away, leaving the small face pinched with hurt. 'I—I can't I—?' she began, before realization sprang into her eyes. 'Sorting things out...' she repeated slowly. 'You've got someone in there, haven't you? *Haven't you!*'

Importunately she pushed past him and stopped, chest heaving, at the sight of Magda standing petrous by the window. 'I knew it. You *bastard*, Morgan! You swine!' Her eyes were glazed and rolling wildly; her tortuous head movements made the long hair writhe, Medusa-like.

Magda picked up her jacket. 'I was just leaving,' she said.

'You and me both,' spat Fay. As she wheeled round, her gaze seemed to focus and she frowned at Magda, puzzled. 'Don't I know you?' she whispered. 'Haven't we met before?'

'I live on campus.'

'No... Years ago... Oh!' She clapped a hand to her mouth and stood there, rigid, her pale face suffusing with pain and humiliation. 'I must go,' she muttered, and stumbled past a silent Morgan into the corridor. Magda crisply followed.

In the bathroom by the angle of the landing, Chris had been unable to avoid hearing the commotion. He pulled his dressing-gown round him, reluctant to run the gauntlet back to his own room just at this moment, and waited by the half-open door. People were probably poised, ear-to-keyhole, all over the block. Certainly Jason was interested—he had just opened his own door a would-be-nonchalant crack.

Fay staggered up the corridor, then stopped mere feet away, waiting for Magda to catch up.

'You remember, don't you,' she stated flatly.

'Yes.'

'I know. I have to ask you something... I don't want to, but I must. Please don't tell him. Please.'

'I had no intention of doing so. I regard it as a professional confidence.'

'You—you mean that? You promise?'

'If I were you, I would leave it there.'

'Yes...' She clattered down the stairs,

and Chris heard no more.

Morgan, when Chris deemed it safe to seek him out, was sitting on his bed looking strangely blank, kneading a pair of white knickers between his hands.

'You got the trophy, then,' said Chris in an attempt at cheerful banter.

'What?... Oh, yes. The trophy.'

'Marks and Sparks, are they? I think Steve was hoping for Janet Reger.' This wasn't working; Morgan seemed totally dazed. 'Are you worried about Fay?' Chris went on more quietly. 'Give her time, and she'll come round. It was just the shock. She's really fond of you; she won't let this spoil it.'

Nothing.

'Morgan?'

Morgan swivelled his eyes towards Chris's face, but still he was dumb.

'Tell her it was a one off. Assure her it won't happen again.'

Morgan flushed and appeared to grit his teeth. 'You don't understand, Chris,' he rasped. 'You don't get it at all. It's *going* to happen again. Fay and I are finished—and I've found that I don't care.'

'What have you got, Jack?'

Montgomery usually avoided the smoking area of the station canteen, but DI

Bayliss was alone in the corner, slumped in the centre of a cogitative blue cloud.

Bayliss greeted him with a lazy smile. 'You mean the Sherwood case? Not a lot. The device was a crude, amateur effort. In some respects it's not unlike two recent devices found in a Bristol laboratory and disarmed, but frankly anyone with an ounce of nous can put one of these things together once they'd acquired the main explosive component—or made it—and a detonator. I've been on to SO13, but they can't throw light on this particular attack. Neither can Special Branch. It doesn't seem to be part of a concerted campaign.'

'Were there fingerprints, excluding the porter and Dr Kovacs?'

'Yes, but they don't tally with any of our known troublemakers; they could well belong to the shop assistant who sold the padded envelope.'

'What about your enquiries at the scene?'

'The parcel was definitely left on the desk in the Medical School foyer at lunchtime, between twelve forty-five and one o'clock. The porter had gone to the washroom for a few minutes; he saw the packet immediately he returned, and decided to take it up to the Physiology floor himself, as it had missed the usual postal run.

He went through Dr Kovacs's lab to his office, and deposited the packet on the desk. Only a woman and "someone of oriental appearance" were in the lab at the time—we've confirmed that these were the lecturer Magda Hepworth and Michael Chan, the postgraduate student.

'Obviously, the Medical School foyer can be reached from both inside and outside the building. Lectures finish at twelve, and after an initial flurry as staff and students go off for lunch, the area is quiet. Someone could have waited behind, or alternatively an outsider could have come in. In addition to the foyer entrance itself, there are two rear doors, one opening into a car-park from the administrative corridor, the other leading from Human Morphology out past the animal house to a path which links with both the School of Physics and the School of Chemistry.

'Now, this animal house is interesting because apparently its main lock was tampered with early in December. Unexplained scratches were found on the padlock, although the door was never forced.' Bayliss dragged deeply on his cigarette. 'We've focused our enquiries on Animal Concern,' he went on. 'They used to be a purely campus-orientated bunch, but the founder members left the university three years ago and the group now has a broad local base. The ongoing campus "chapter", as it were, is headed by Andrew Tait, a minerology student. He hotly denies any connection with the parcel bomb; in his words, they're trying to win hearts and minds, so violence, or any action which will lose them sympathy, is counterproductive. I think he's sincere.

'He told me that an inflammatory article appeared in the student magazine *Campus Connection* last term which hadn't been vetted by any of his people, and pointed out that individuals might share many of Animal Concern's views but not be actual members. After a bit of a hassle he let me have the names of his members; I'm going to chat to them individually and see if they have any personal suspicions.'

'What about the article?' asked Montgomery.

'It was anonymous. The editor tried to give me some baloney about "protecting his sources"—jumped-up little toe-rag—but when I grilled him some more it turned out that he'd accepted and printed the contribution without querying its provenance. It came perilously close to incitement to violence, yet he stood there squeaking about freedom of individual expression. I pointed out that he was a puppet: it seemed anyone could use his precious magazine as a propaganda tool.

He didn't like that.'

Bayliss stubbed out his cigarette in the ashtray. 'That's it to date,' he said.

'Thanks.' Montgomery was considering what he had heard. 'I wonder if this could be remotely linked with Keith Mayhew's death?' he mused.

'Why should it be?'

'Well...there's a common factor, albeit a tenuous one.'

'What's that?'

'Physiology—the lab, the staff...Keith had the most difficulty with this subject, and possibly tried to contact one of the staff the night he died, with a view to extra coaching. No one admits to having seen him—but it's just occurred to me that he might have stumbled on the bomber trying to plant something near one of their homes, or the lab, and been silenced.'

Bayliss shrugged. 'I s'pose there could be mileage in that,' he conceded. 'Or maybe Keith was a member himself—I didn't think to check for him on the list. Perhaps he inadvertently unmasked a militant.'

Now it was Montgomery's turn to sound unconvinced. 'I'd be surprised if that was the case. I think Keith was too fixated by his own concerns to have energy to spare for anything else. No...that's an unlikely scenario. There's a further angle I'd like to see explored, though—Laszlo Kovacs himself. Could the bomb have been a *personal* attack on him, rather than an attack on his working methods?'

'Nah.' Bayliss lit up another cigarette. 'Parcel bombs bear all the hallmarks of militant groups. And remember the padlock.'

'I know it's unlikely, but it should be excluded. Someone might be using the animal protesters as a cover.' Montgomery stood up. 'Do you mind if I have a few words with Laszlo Kovacs? I've met him before.'

'Be my guest.'

The Kovacses' house stood in Bramcote, an exclusive district to the west of the university, where many of the hospital consultants lived. Their own home was relatively modest, but beautifully maintained and welcoming; lamps and potted plants dispelled the cheerlessness of a winter evening.

'You must have a hot drink,' insisted Anna as soon as Montgomery had crossed the threshold. 'We do not follow the rule here that coffee is only for mornings or after dinner: we like our *presszókávé* any time of day. It is an old student habit from Hungary.'

'Thank you,' said Montgomery politely,

and followed Laszlo through into the sitting-room where they made small-talk until she reappeared. Anna was statuesque, he noticed, a handsome woman just beginning to succumb to the weight problems of middle age. Her hair was a greying blonde, but plenteous, and her accent remained markedly eastern European despite decades of life in England. Behind her pleasant, open features he sensed a forceful character.

She placed something on the table in front of him and he looked down; next to the cup of strong black coffee was a huge piece of home-made torte. William Bird would have given much for such an offering, but Montgomery knew that Carole was preparing his meal at home.

'Cream in your coffee, Inspector?'

'No, thank you.'

'Good; we also drink it black. A dash of *barack*?'

'Thank you, but no. I'm driving.'

'Ah, yes.' She sat down next to Laszlo, and they regarded him expectantly.

'I was talking with Inspector Bayliss today,' said Montgomery. 'He is interviewing the various campus animal rights sympathizers on the very reasonable assumption that that was the motivation for the attack on you, Dr Kovacs. Most of them will no doubt be appalled by the incident; we know that Animal Concern's leader is deeply dismayed. They may have suspicions of a new member—or perhaps someone from among their ranks has been voicing radical ideas. We hope his enquiries will bear fruit.'

Anna nodded vigorously; Laszlo looked wary. 'Your perspective is different, Inspector?' he asked.

'Not necessarily. A maverick animal rights protester, or group, is the most likely perpetrator. Letter bombs and incendiary devices are the trademarks of these people; explosions are dramatic and newsworthy. But they have also been used in more personal crimes... That is why I'm here.'

'Personal crimes...' repeated Laszlo. The hands on his lap had clenched into fists.

'Is there anyone,' asked Montgomery carefully, 'who could wish you ill for a reason *other* than the nature of your work?'

Laszlo's discomfort visibly increased. 'No—I don't think so,' he said.

'Could someone be jealous of your position in the Physiology Department, or your recent acclaim?'

'No...I am only a senior lecturer; I am not the professor.'

'Tell me about your colleagues. Do you get on with them?'

'Well enough for the purposes of work.

But we are all self-contained in our own way. I confess that my personal friends come from other departments—that is not unusual.'

'Mm. Where were your colleagues at lunchtime on the day of the parcel bomb?'

'Professor Byrne always goes to the restaurant in the Trencher Building each lunchtime—that is next to the Clock Tower Building at the centre of the campus. Magda brings sandwiches to the lab and works on her research, and Hubert returns to Calverton Hall. As far as I am aware, they followed their normal routine on the day of the bomb. For myself, I was in the cafeteria near the chemical engineering laboratories, just behind the Medical School. It is cheap and convenient.'

'I see. Had you received any threats, or any warning of danger? Perhaps something you discounted at the time?'

'No... No.'

Anna leaned forward to interject. 'There was a highly irresponsible article in the student magazine a few weeks ago,' she said. 'It gave an emotive account of animal sufferings, and incited students to take matters into their own hands. Someone of weak mind might have acted on this advice.'

'I've read the article,' said Mongomery.

'Inspector Bayliss is trying to trace the author...but you're sure that neither of you can think of a more specific enemy?'

Laszlo repeated his denial, but somehow Montgomery did not feel convinced.

'Have you ever been in serious personal danger before?' he asked. As soon as the words were out of his mouth, he feared that they were inappropriate. The Kovacses had left their mother country in times when genuine oppression was more likely to be the reason than economic hardship. That it had not been done lightly was evident from the Hungarian memorabilia all round the room: wooden carvings, a fireside rug woven in red, white and green, paintings and photographs, one of which he identified as a view of famous Chain Bridge in central Budapest.

Anna confirmed his reasoning. 'We came here in 1956,' she said with a wry smile. 'As students in Budapest we were involved in the uprising against the Stalinist regime and yes, there was danger! Along with thousands of others, we had to flee for our lives. But that was long ago...'

'Are you happy here?'

'England has been good to us,' she answered. 'We can speak and walk freely. Laszlo has a respectable job and our children are leading responsible, productive lives in Cambridge.' She pointed to a

119

photograph of two young people resting on the mantelpiece. 'That is Noel, our son; he is a medical student at the Addenbrooke Hospital. And that is Elizabeth, our daughter; she is a teacher.' The daughter, a laughing blonde with her mother's good looks, appeared several years older than the thin youth by her side, but Anna's pride in her son clearly transcended primogeniture.

'What about yourself?' asked Montgomery.

'Oh, I teach a little German at evening classes.' She smiled as his eyebrows flickered upwards. 'We are all trilingual in the family: it is a throwback from the Austro-Hungarian Empire, and we have also lived in Germany for a short while. Apart from that—I am just a housewife.'

'There is no such thing,' said Laszlo. 'I must tell you, Inspector Montgomery, that Anna is the hub of the household. Without her organization I would be nothing, and when relatives come to visit us from Paris and from Canada, she is totally unruffled. I do what I am told—'

'As little as possible,' chuckled his wife.

'—and I retreat to my study when the jollity becomes too much.'

'More torte, Inspector?' invited Anna, lifting a piece with a silver serving slice and hovering over his plate.

'No, thank you. It was delicious, though.

I should be going...' Once more he eyed the Hungarian artefacts around the room. 'Have you been back to Budapest?' he asked. 'Has it changed much?'

He was addressing them both, but seeing Laszlo's cheeks suddenly blanch he turned to Anna to spare the physiologist embarrassment.

'I have longed to,' she said after a pause. 'We did not go through all that hell in 1956 to leave our country behind. But it had to be, and since then, democracy has taken a long time to establish a fragile root. There has been much tension. Only recently was Imre Nagy finally disinterred from his shameful grave in Romania, brought back to Hungary and given the honour which is his due. So we have not been able to return.'

Montgomery was faintly puzzled, and let it show.

'We were on the AVH blacklist: the secret police. We call them by their old name, the Ávó. All were bullies and cowards. They kept their death lists for years in vaults, like the Stasi.'

'Surely they aren't a threat now,' said Montgomery, trying not to stare at Laszlo, whose face was like parchment.

'That is what I say,' agreed Anna. 'They were disbanded long ago. Myself, I would go back tomorrow, but Laszlo is more cautious.'

Laszlo at last seemed to realize that his lack of contribution was odd. 'We live in England now,' he said in a strained voice. 'It is always best for a break to be clean.'

8

Chris scanned the shelves in the Union shop and paused by the toiletries section. 'Endeavour' was in stock, the fresh, lemony aftershave Morgan had been wearing ever since its promotion the previous spring. Chris was tempted to buy a bottle for himself—it really had a knock-out scent—but he didn't want to be a copy-cat. Life, with its little choices, could be difficult sometimes...

He turned a corner and there was Fay, examining wooden ear-rings. Before he could back away she had caught sight of him and plunged forward wrathfully.

'He's still seeing her, isn't he?' she shouted. 'He's still screwing that—that old woman!' Heads nearby turned in fascination.

'I, er, can't say,' he answered. (How old

was Magda? Less than forty, surely.)

'No—you only live next door. I suppose you're stone deaf!' She shuddered, and abruptly her tone lost its sarcastic crust. 'I hate him,' she croaked. 'I could have forgiven him a one-off slip if he'd been drunk, or if she'd caught him while he was vulnerable...' (Morgan vulnerable?) 'I would have done it, for him. But he doesn't care! He—he's just *wallowing* in it!'

Chris felt his cheeks flame, and heard muffled titters from the other side of the toiletries shelf. Crabwise he began to sidle towards the exit, hoping to steer Fay out of the shop.

'*You* don't care either, do you? You don't want to help me.'

'I think this is something you must sort out with Morgan.'

Her face crumpled into a small child's mask of single-minded anguish. 'I hate him,' she repeated. They were almost at the door. Chris abandoned his purchasing intentions and led the way outside, crossing a corridor to the main exit and open air.

'I'm sorry, Fay,' he said, 'but I'm not going to interfere. Morgan's his own man. Why not send him a letter to tell him how you feel?'

'I—I don't know. It's probably too late now.' They walked down the stone steps at the front of the building and Chris waited to see which way she would turn; he would go the opposite way, however inconvenient.

'Chris...?'

'Yes?'

She blinked up at him uncertainly. 'Has—has that woman said anything to Morgan about me?'

Chris was fairly sure they didn't do much talking, but such a response would hardly please Fay. 'Not that I'm aware of,' he said.

'Oh.'

She halted where the steps changed direction and stared down the hill towards the Medical School, shivering in an inappropriately thin dress.

'This always happens,' she whispered. 'They leave me every time.'

'We don't talk much, do we?' observed Morgan as he lay on the bed, hands clasped behind his head.

Magda was slouched in a nearby chair, wearing his dressing-gown. 'I thought that was what young men wanted,' she countered with an ironic smile, '—a competent partner who keeps her mouth shut and doesn't babble endless pseudo-psychological claptrap about the state of their relationship.'

'Do you think we have a relationship?' he asked curiously.

'Within mutually acceptable limitations, yes.' She swigged red wine from a fishbowl-sized goblet and sat up more formally. 'I do hope you're not going to spoil it.'

'No danger.' He, too, rose and pulled on a T-shirt over his shorts from a random pile of clothes while the radiator of D9 spewed out background heat. 'I was just wondering, that's all, whether you have any family.'

'The answer is no.'

'I'm sorry. Is that why you live in hall?'

'No; that is merely a temporary arrangement, until I find a house I like.'

'Dr Kovacs lives in Bramcote. He might be able to find you a nice property there—it's handy for the campus.'

'No doubt, but I prefer to do things my way.'

Morgan strode to the table and poured himself some wine. Magda had been right when she had intimated that a young man's dream was a sexual partner who could perform yet spare the commentary, but he was beginning to find her own excessive taciturnity a challenge. She knew a little about him—his Yorkshire home, his brother and sister, his old school—but the compliment had not been returned. He

125

found himself wanting to know.

'Magda...'

'Yes, lover-boy?'

'Did your parents bring you here, or did you choose to come?'

'I came with my mother after my father was killed in Prague...but she never got over his death, and never settled. I have fended for myself for many years now—and that is all I am going to say.'

'I think you should talk about it,' he said seriously. 'If not with me, then with Dr Kovacs. I'm sure his experiences must be similar to yours.'

He put an injudicious hand on her shoulder, but she slapped it away. 'That's just the point,' she burst out. 'You refuse to understand, don't you? I don't *want* to go over the past, with anyone! I am trying to make a new life. The past is gone—all that matters now is the purity of work.'

'Work...do you ever think of anything else?'

Deliberately she made a languid face, and eyed him from beneath lowered lids. 'How can you ask that when I am here with you?'

'You know what I mean. Do you have any other recreations?'

'I ride horses. Yes, Morgan—that surprised you! At weekends I drive out to a farm in Derbyshire and take a mount at a fast canter across the hillside. If only the fields were larger, I could gallop... You miss so much in a car—the biting air on your cheek, the thunder of hooves against the frozen ground, the unpredictability of the living beast you ride...'

'I think I'd prefer the car; at least it has brakes.'

'I expected that of you. Don't worry—I wasn't going to ask you to ride with me. I am not fond of chatter. I like to be alone, with the horse and the elements.'

'Garbo,' he muttered. Nevertheless, his imagination thrilled to the spectacle of Magda, magnificent in tailored jacket and gleaming black boots, thrashing the rippling chestnut flanks of a hunter as it powered its way towards some endless horizon. How had he failed to guess himself that she was a horsewoman?

'So that's your life when I'm not with you,' he said. 'Research and riding.' He frowned, suddenly remembering Dr Kovacs's letter bomb. 'Do be careful, Magda,' he urged. 'I know you do a lot of work out of hours in the physiology lab. Remember that there's a crank on the loose trying to murder scientists.'

The sun died out of her face. 'I don't think I could forget. Dr Kovacs came close to death, and the police have an enormous task trying to track down the perpetrator...'

Her expression became thoughtful. 'I'm not sure we should leave it entirely to them. Their methods take time—too much time. This person could strike again. Morgan, you're a student in a men's hall. Have you heard any talk which might help to pinpoint this lunatic?'

'Not exactly. There's a fairly rabid Animal Concern supporter on this very landing, but I've no reason to think he's the bomber.'

'Who is that?'

'Jason Gower in D6.'

'Have the police seen him?'

'I don't know.'

'They should. They should interview everyone of his persuasion.'

'He's a close character; he only rarely gives himself away.'

'All the more reason why he should be made aware that *he* is being watched.' Magda drained the last dregs of her Chianti, and musingly regarded the door. 'Perhaps I shall visit this Jason myself.'

In Wellington Hall, Fay unzipped her sponge bag, extracted the bottle of 'Endeavour' she had bought, unscrewed the top and inhaled the scent deeply. Muttering snatched phrases she then sprinkled a few drops of the aftershave across her pillow and turned down the lights before curling into a ball on the patchwork counterpane, her cheek inches from the damply aromatic patch.

'Every time,' she murmured. 'Every time.' First, her father. Then her kind friend from the Medical School's Physiology Department. Then Keith; now Morgan... Strange kitten-like noises came from her throat. Always they abandoned her.

She closed her eyes and tried to steady her breathing. The spicy citrus tang made Morgan seem very close. He had been so charming at the beginning, a true knight errant, salvaging that awful evening with Keith by his presence and his promise. When had it been? Medics' Ball, last March.

Memories flooded her brain. Keith in the Craft Club, hammering his pewter, darting those shyly speculative glances. The invitation to Medics' Ball—*the* campus event. Hours of shopping for the dress, experimenting with new make-up and buying a corsage (Keith didn't look the type who would think of something like that)—only to be made to feel unwelcome, scarcely tolerated, paraded in front of the high table then jettisoned at midnight.

She had stared out at the winking lights of south Nottingham from a balcony in the

Trencher Building, trying to subdue the churning humiliation before facing people again. Sounds of uninhibited hedonism rocketed through the keen night air, but she was alone...

A voice with a mild Yorkshire inflexion startled her. 'Taking a break from the dancing?'

She swung round; a tall, broad-shouldered silhouette stood between her and the balcony door.

'Er, yes.'

'I don't blame you; it gets pretty steamy.' He moved closer, and the light fell on his profile; she saw craggy but well balanced features, strong in the brow and chin. 'What do you think of our party?' he went on.

'Oh...it's got everything. Medics' Balls are renowned across the campus.'

'Really?' The side of his mouth twitched; there was a small scar near the lower lip. 'How gratifying.'

She realized why he was amused, and retreated in confusion. 'Sorry,' she said. 'I blurt out naïve things sometimes.'

'Nothing wrong with that. You're Keith's partner, aren't you? Shall I keep you company until he comes back?'

Hot embarrassment in the darkness. 'Actually—he's gone,' she whispered, hanging her head with the sharp shame of it.

'He said he had to get up early to revise for an exam.'

He snorted. 'What a little squirt,' he said. 'That isn't for a fortnight. I suggest you forget about him and come out for a drink with me next week.'

Disbelief... 'Aren't—aren't you with someone?'

'Not after tonight,' he said, and had moved forward to take her in his arms.

Fay sniffed, swallowed and tried vainly to stem the welling saltwater in her eyes by clamping the lids tightly shut. It wasn't fair! It wasn't fair! Painfully she levered herself to a sitting position; the damp patch on the pillow was larger—his aftershave, her tears.

Do something, she admonished herself. Be angry. You have a right: don't those magazines always say so? Let him know how you feel. Act now.

Chris couldn't sleep. His radiator had started to clank at odd hours, due to air in the system; he had reported it once, but to no avail. Now, despite the adverse weather, he would be forced to turn the radiator off altogether. He resolved to buy his own bleed key for the vent valve at the earliest opportunity if the hall staff weren't prepared to help.

Yawning, he padded to the window and twitched the curtain aside, albescent moonlight bathed his bare feet. The radiator was still in partial shadow, but he was confident of finding the lock-shield valve by sense of touch. First, though, he pressed his hand against the top; yes, it was cool here, warmer below. As he prepared to crouch down, he allowed his gaze to stray to the silent outer gardens of Calverton Hall, its silvered bushes and majestic trees...

His heart gave a jolt. Someone was out there, staring up at his window with almost palpable intensity. He stepped back, but the figure didn't move, and gradually he realized that his window was not the focus of interest, after all: it was Morgan's. With no leap of the imagination Chris identified the figure as Fay, despite the shawl or cape which thickened her outline. She stood motionless, and so did he until the pervasive chill finally drove him back to his bed. Sleep remained elusive; pity for Fay was wrestling with the beginnings of revulsion, and he felt an uneasy instinct that trouble was brewing for Morgan.

In the morning, Chris encountered Morgan in the corridor; his friend was puzzling over an envelope which had been thrust behind his name-plate on the door of D9.

'I was here last night,' he remarked,

slitting it open with his thumb. 'Why didn't they just knock?' He tapped, and the enclosure slid out: it was a photograph in two jagged halves, on one side Fay, smiling up at Morgan with all her blazing uninhibited affection, on the other side Morgan himself—bisected straight through the face.

Chris felt profoundly uncomfortable, as if he had witnessed a secret aberration. It was obvious that Fay had delivered this; what was less evident was whether or not she had intended to rip the photograph straight through Morgan's image, or whether in her fury she had been guilty only of inaccuracy. 'She must still be upset,' he muttered.

Morgan gave a heavy shrug and turned away. 'She's sick in the head,' he said.

'Thank you for agreeing to see me in your flat,' said Montgomery to Hubert Pomeroy later that day.

The lecturer's little nod of acknowledgement was scarcely a gracious one. 'It's my haven from prying eyes,' he said. 'I can't say I understand why you're here, though. Inspector Bayliss has spoken with all of us.'

'I know—but his area of interest is primarily concerned with the activities of animal rights groups. I'm trying to explore the question from the other side: why did *someone* try to kill *Laszlo Kovacs?* Do you have any opinion yourself?'

'I do. I think some anarchic campus hothead went too far, and Dr Kovacs was an obvious target because of his recent work with diabetes. It wasn't just reported in scientific journals, you know—it was blazoned across the tabloids, giving details not only of Dr Kovacs himself, but of his experimental methods.' His mouth turned down at the corners. 'Not the sort of fame I would countenance myself.'

Montgomery knew jealousy when he saw it. 'Did that give him ideas above his station?' he asked.

'No-o.' The denial was wrung out against much reluctance. 'But it's professionally unbecoming.'

Montgomery glanced round at the possessions in the rented tutor's flat where they sat. Apart from a good many books, they were a modest collection for an academic approaching forty. Perhaps Dr Pomeroy's achievements hadn't been attained as smoothly as he would have hoped.

'You say you subscribe to the animal rights theory, and I accept that,' he said. 'Let's just consider the possibility of another motive, though, however unlikely. Can you think of any enemies that Dr Kovacs might have?'

134

'Not really. His personality is too weak.'

'In what way?'

'He doesn't like to take initiatives himself. He prefers difficult decisions to be sanctioned from above, to relieve him of responsibility; it's rare for him to take matters into his own hands. His handling of the students isn't impressive where discipline is concerned. They take advantage of any hint of weakness—*I* grasped that fact long ago. It's hardly surprising: they're only schoolchildren two or three years on.'

'But Dr Kovacs is positive where work is concerned.'

'Anyone can stumble on a lucky break.'

'Do you think he deserves his position in the department?'

Hubert Pomeroy's nostrils flared. 'He's a foreigner who's come running to England just because of a spot of hardship in his own country. There's another one in the department, too: Magda Hepworth—perhaps you've met her? She has a physiology PhD like mine, but none of my medical qualifications—yet we're on the same salary scale. *She's* Czechoslovakian. It's insidious, you see...a few here, a few there. They never go back. Look at hospital medicine...they come over from India, from Sri Lanka, from Africa, from the Middle East, often on expensive grants from their own governments. They're supposed to train, then put their knowledge to use in their own country. But *they like it here*—so they stay.'

From what Montgomery had heard, overseas doctors had provided a vital lifeline in staffing the unpopular specialties like psychogeriatrics and ear, nose and throat surgery. Like women in hospital medicine, few of them were allowed to reach the really top posts... If Magda Hepworth was right about Hubert's personal paranoia, he should have sympathized with their difficulties. 'So his nationality may have given him enemies?' Montgomery asked ingenuously.

Hubert gave him a sharp look. 'Some of us may be unhappy about it, but we'd scarcely attempt to murder him for that reason.'

That was true enough. Montgomery decided that now was not the time to probe Hubert's attitudes towards discrimination against homosexuals. 'Returning to the animal rights theory, did Bayliss give you some advice on protecting yourself?'

'He did.'

'I found myself wondering whether this incident might have a connection with young Keith Mayhew's death.'

Hubert went rigid. 'Why do you say

that?' he enunciated after a pause.

'Well...it's a long shot, but Keith was purportedly considering visiting a member of the physiology staff for help with his work. You'll recall we discussed this at the time. One of those very same staff has subsequently been exposed to a letter bomb. It's remotely possible that someone was trying to leave a device near one of you when he was disturbed by Keith, and forced to silence him.'

'I—that's an idea, of course. Yes; I dare say it's just feasible. But I can't throw any light on the subject.'

'Have you ever received a threat, or had any of your belongings tampered with?'

'Here? No.'

'No one's ever tried to break into your flat?'

'No.'

Why did Hubert look so edgy? 'Just remind me where you were on the Saturday night that Keith died,' said Montgomery.

Hubert scowled. 'I went to town, not that it's any of your business. Suffice it to say I wasn't in the flat, and saw nothing to indicate terrorist activity when I got back. Now, if you'll excuse me, I have a lecture to prepare...'

'It would be helpful to know what you were doing in town,' persisted Montgomery politely.

137

'Enjoying a meal at Ben Bowers with a friend. Satisfied?'

'Thank you.' Montgomery inclined his head a minuscule fraction, and left.

9

'I know it shouldn't be my concern, but I'm worried about Fay.'

Eleanor looked at Chris in surprise as they ambled, hands in pockets, around the outside of the Medical School, filling their lungs with clear cold air between lectures.

'You've seen her?' she asked.

'Yes. She still comes to D Block, but now it's Jason Gower she visits. I don't know whether she's trying to make Morgan jealous or not, but Jason is a really odd character. He's quietly fanatical, and Fay has always struck me as someone who's easily led... I feel it's an unhealthy association, yet they won't thank me for interfering. Has Fay said anything to you?'

Eleanor grimaced. 'You're joking, I take it. No—I'm poison at the moment. She associates me with Morgan. However...' She stared up at the adjacent Chemistry

Building, her lips curled mirthlessly. 'If she felt I could be of use to her I've no doubt the bridges would be repaired.'

'Morgan *has* been a brute,' said Chris. 'I think it sent her off her head. There was a photograph... Sorry, I shouldn't be telling you this. Suffice it to say that I feel her judgement is impaired just now, and Jason might draw her into something she wouldn't normally involve herself with...'

'She's already joined Animal Concern.'

'That's just the kind of thing! Jason could even be in cahoots with this bomber. I'd like to talk with her, find out if she's simply trying to thumb her nose at Morgan, but of course she thinks we're all traitors and we're laughing behind her back.'

'I could try to have a word, if you like,' offered Eleanor.

'That would be really kind,' he said appreciatively.

'But if I come out with a broken jaw, don't be too surprised,' she laughed.

Eleanor pondered an appropriate subject to broach in order to restore links with Fay. If it wasn't for Chris, she wouldn't have wanted to make the effort; Fay was capricious and illogical, irritating characteristics for someone as clear-headed as Eleanor. The face-cream, an obvious choice of gambit, was a non-starter; she had seen it in the fridge only days before, duskily furred, a sorry mess. No—it was best to be general.

'Chicken fricassée,' she said with approval, looking over Fay's shoulder as she read the evening meal menu. 'That's one of my favourite dishes.'

'I did like it,' said Fay, regarding her with a wary eye, 'but now I think of the chickens, and I'm not so sure.'

Eleanor recalled reading a highly respected naturalist's comment that man was biologically designed to be a meat-eater, but kept quiet.

She fell into step beside Fay. 'What are Animal Concern's views?'

'They all seem to be vegetarian. I ought to become a vegetarian.'

'Is Jason?'

'Oh yes.'

'You're seeing quite a lot of him, aren't you? I bet Morgan's kicking himself.'

'You think so?' Fay tried to sound uninterested, but her heightened colour gave her feelings away.

'Oh, probably. But I suppose it's too late now, isn't it?'

'Far too late,' said Fay with anger. 'He could have apologized at any point, but he hasn't even *asked* if we can start again. Jason is a much more genuine person. I think there are few things more worthwhile than championing the helpless.'

They were nearing the back of the queue of girls which brightly hummed outside the dining-room doors.

'This recent attack on Dr Kovacs,' began Eleanor carefully. 'Is Jason worried about the organization getting a bad name?'

'Not if it stops what's going on!' cried Fay. 'If it achieves results, makes them stop torturing innocent animals, then nothing but good will come of it.'

The shock was momentarily paralysing. Then, when her faculties returned, Eleanor found herself stretching every nerve to combat suffocating revulsion and stand her ground two feet from Fay.

'He could have been killed,' she said through lips gone stiff.

'So what? Why should someone take the lives of defenceless creatures while expecting to retain a carte-blanche right to live themselves? Who do they think they are? God?'

A bell shrilled above their heads and the queue of girls surged forwards; new additions brought their own momentum from behind. Mouthing an excuse, Eleanor stepped smartly aside; as Fay was swept along in the press, Eleanor found that she could finally breathe.

Chris squeezed and pummelled his socks in the wash-basin of D block's bathroom. It was a larger basin than the one in his room, and conveniently situated for hanging small items on the clothes line stretching over the bath. Normally, he performed his domestic tasks in a kind of dreamy haze, taking time, creating a deliberate break from book-work. This evening, however, his senses were sharpened; he could hear a low female voice in Jason's room next door—presumably Fay—and found himself worrying about their relationship all over again.

His hopes of regaining his own room without an embarrassing meeting were foiled when Jason's door opened just as Chris was crossing the landing. To his surprise Magda emerged, looking worried and thoughtful. A sarcastic voice floated out from behind the door: 'Thank you for wasting your time on me, Dr Hepworth.'

Chris had always been in awe of Magda, and her liaison with one of his peers caused him to feel even more awkward, if anything. Nevertheless, they all fighting an unknown fanatic, and it made sense to join forces where possible...

'Dr Hepworth?' he asked tentatively.

She paused at the top of the stairs and seemed to notice him for the first time. 'Yes?'

'Would you like to come into my room for a moment?'

She raised her eyebrows. 'I seem to have heard those words before.'

'Please.'

Inside D8, Chris found it difficult to give voice to his anxieties.

'Dr Hepworth...do you know something about Jason? Has something been said by the police?'

She looked at him appraisingly, then decided to confide. 'Not by the police,' she said. 'By Morgan. He had suspicions that Jason might know the bomber. I thought I would speak to this student directly, tell him about our work, how important it is.'

Good God, thought Chris. She thinks a lecture will solve it.

'I hardly expected to convert him,' Magda went on, 'but there was a chance he would identify some validity in the other point of view. It was also possible that he would feel exposed, watched, and suggest that his friends lie low.'

'How did you get on?'

Her face grew sombre. 'I failed. He is intent on his own rigid creed. He openly expressed sympathy with the bomber. He boasted that the police had seen him and could pin nothing on him...' She wiped a dark strand of hair from her broad, pearly forehead and inhaled deeply. 'Christopher, I would not be surprised if he *was* the bomber.'

A centipede with very cold feet ran down the back of Chris's spine. 'Dr Hepworth,' he urged, 'do be careful. They might target you next.'

Sergeant Bird entered Montgomery's office in the wake of his brisk knock.

'I've made the enquiries, sir,' he said. 'The staff at Ben Bowers confirm that a table for two was booked in the name of Hubert Pomeroy on the night in question. There were no defaulters that night, but they were unable to describe the appearance of the diners—it was Saturday, and busy.'

'What time was the table booked for?'

'Nine fifteen.'

'Hm.' Montgomery fingered his chin. 'I can't see us acquiring a photograph of Pomeroy with any great ease; without solid evidence against him we can't take our own. What did Dr Hepworth have to say?'

'She has a tutor's flat in Beeston Hall, much like the Pomeroy arrangement, and says she was home that night because her car was undergoing repairs. It's true about the car: I checked just in case her memory was at fault. It was locked in Pemberley's garage with a camshaft problem. So there was nothing much for the bomber to attack at her place. She didn't see anything unusual inside the flat. Neither did Laszlo Kovacs at his home, where he spent the evening with Anna.'

'Thanks, Will.' Montgomery was polite, but he felt depressed. It had seemed like such a good idea at the time, a linkage via an unwitting member of the Physiology Department between Keith Mayhew and the bomber. It could have explained Keith's death and allowed them to close the file. But no substantiating facts had emerged, and his instincts about Hubert were just that—instincts. They were no further forward.

'Chris told me you've been speaking to Jason,' said Morgan to Magda as they lay warmly contiguous in the narrow single bed.

'I tried; he didn't want to listen.'

'It was certainly brave... I'm not sure that it was wise.'

'Are you criticizing me?'

'I wouldn't dare. No—seriously, I have a feeling about Jason. He's so committed to his cause, I think he could be ruthless.'

Magda pulled herself up on to her elbow. 'I had to do something,' she said. 'Just being on our guard isn't good enough. I thought I might be able to influence these people at source, as it were, by reason if possible, if not, by fear of being caught. It's worrying, Morgan. We are all in the firing line.'

Morgan could see the faint gleam of her teeth in the dark and feel the tension in her body: without another word he pulled her mouth down on to his own and changed the subject.

Hours later, Morgan woke up. Magda had given a little twitch in her sleep, and the back of her heel had caught his calf. She was muttering, too, strange words he couldn't quite identify.

'*Gyilkos, gyilkos.*' Surely that was a foreign language. He didn't know any Czechoslovakian, but he could always look it up in a dictionary.

'*Gyilkos...gyáva.*' There is was again. He would make a note of that and tease her later on...

'I was talking in my sleep?' she echoed incredulously in the morning.

'You were.'

'I don't believe you.'

Morgan poured steaming water into a mug containing a tea-bag, gave it a stir and pushed it towards her. 'You said, "Dilkosh, dilkosh." It's obviously a term of endearment.'

'You are entitled to your fantasies,' she said drily. ' "Dilkosh"? It makes no sense.

The word was probably "dishcloth".'

He laughed. 'Now *I* don't believe *you.* I shall find out. I'll go and ask someone at the language lab.'

'Please yourself, if you wish to look foolish. Now I must go.' She dressed neatly, drank half the tea and left. It was just before six; Magda never flaunted her presence in the block by using the bath. She coupled with Morgan in an almost businesslike way, then performed her ablutions elsewhere. Nevertheless, he smiled to himself and whistled a few merry bars. Two nights ago she had actually let him stay in her room; he suspected he was just beginning to break through her reserve.

At half-past eight Morgan locked his door and sauntered along the corridor towards the stairs. No scrabble for a cooked breakfast this time—all the medical students in his year had to fast today for Hubert's physiology experiment. It was a nuisance; he was hungry already.

Ahead, the door of D6 suddenly flew open. Fay stood there, one skinny shoulder bared as Jason's oversized dressing-gown slid down her upper arm. She turned slowly towards the bathroom, her carriage self-consciously erect. Clearly the signal for her egress had been the closing and locking of his own door, but she affected a start, as if surprised at his appearance.

Morgan saw only a silly little girl playacting. He felt nothing at all, not even pity. Offering her the most bored of 'good mornings', he turned the corner, pattered down the stairs, and left D block without a backward glance.

As he angled across the car-park *en route* to the Medical School, he thought again about the letter-bomb. It was an obscene, cowardly way of making a point. Behind the potential drama and shock lurked a dark, reptilian mind, a mind incomprehensible to one who relished the healthy aggression of the rugby pitch. *That* was the way to settle your differences with someone—meet them face to face and thump hell out of them!

Morgan was anxious on behalf of Magda, Laszlo and all the preclinical staff—even Hubert. Now they wouldn't know a moment's real peace. They would have to check their letters, their offices, their homes, their cars... Would they have to use those mirror devices, like politicians? This was a university campus, for God's sake!

He drew level with Hubert's decrepit Renault 5 and found himself wondering what sort of safety routine Hubert was now employing. Could you see enough simply by crouching down? Morgan paralleled the thought with action; he knelt on the cold tarmac and peered under the chassis. Wrapped round the exhaust was a handful of crushed twigs, but he could see nothing resembling wires or a suspicious box. He released the twigs—it would be a long time before Hubert bothered, judging from the neglected state of the car—and rose to his feet, contemplating them idly. He was no arborist, but the presence of fragments of a damp old acorn seemed to indicate that the twigs were oak. There were some more jammed in the front wheel-arch. Hubert must have been zipping carelessly through a forest...

A distant cough, prim and falsetto, made Morgan start: Hubert himself was approaching. Quickly Morgan scattered the twigs over the ground, and continued his journey to the Medical School. No point in asking for trouble.

The nine o'clock lecture took place as planned, but the ten o'clock session was cancelled. For most of the students, a single hour was barely enough time to return to hall and achieve anything worthwhile; residents of Calverton, however, did have that option since their hall stood near the fringes of 'Tech Town', the campus's main science area.

'We can't even have a cup of coffee,'

moaned Steve, pulling a doleful face as they passed the hot drinks machine. 'This stupid practical of Hubert's.'

'I'm going back up the hill,' announced Morgan. 'I want to see if my bank manager has deigned to write yet. Are you coming, Chris?'

'No—you go ahead.'

Morgan left with Brad and Steve, indulgently amused; Chris had developed a habit of going out for lakeside walks with Eleanor whenever they had any free time. Intense discussion was the only overt purpose—but who knew to what such proximity might eventually lead?

At Calverton, Brad and Steve peeled away towards T block, while Morgan crossed the quadrangle, entered the foyer and headed for the pigeon-holes.

'No letters for me, Taff?' he asked as he sifted fruitlessly through the mail in the 'B' section.

'Not today, boyo,' returned the day porter, a potbellied Welshman who took root behind his desk at nine and did his utmost to stay there for his entire duty period. 'You can do me a favour, though,' he continued. 'I've got a parcel here for Jason Gower. It won't fit into the pigeon-hole, so I'm keeping it behind the desk. You're in D block with him, aren't you? Perhaps you could tell him it's arrived.'

150

'I'll take it if you like,' offered Morgan. 'I'm off to the block now, and he may well be in. He only has one lecture on Tuesday mornings.'

Whistling, Morgan climbed the stairs of D block, moving lightly for a man of his size. The handrail gleamed and the air smelt of polish; somewhere in the distance he heard the rattle of crockery. Outside D6 he paused; the door was slightly ajar and a large bunch of keys hung from a single key inserted in the lock. Softly he tapped against the wood.

'Jason?'

No reply.

'Mrs Potter?'

In the continuing silence he pushed open the door and stepped inside. The bed was unmade and clothes were scattered across the floor: their cleaning lady must have made the wise decision to fortify herself with a break now. Impassively he deposited the bulky parcel on the desk, then frowned as a glint of metal winked at him from a tear in the packaging. Curious, Morgan picked the parcel up again and kneaded it between his large hands. The contents were well packed, almost obsessively so; he could discern nothing of their shape through the protective layers. He wondered if anything was broken. He wondered...

With a rapid glance over his shoulder

Morgan adroitly used his fingertips to enlarge the hole. Nestling in sheets of polythene were electrical items unfamiliar to him. They looked like connectors—or maybe some kind of sophisticated switch. Holding his breath, he pried as much as he dared, but could identify nothing further. The parcel *could* be innocent, and yet...

Postmark. Think, and act. You haven't got long. The letters were faint. B–R ...BRISTOL. Now Morgan was truly alarmed. It was one thing to *talk* about someone possibly being involved in violence: it was cosy gossip, vicarious horror. But stumbling across evidence was quite another thing. The word 'Bristol' was full of nasty connotations: a research department attacked, a veterinary surgeon almost murdered in her car, a department store down the peninsula gutted with fire... The people responsible weren't just hotheads looking for a cause and jumping on to a bandwagon: they *were* the bandwagon.

He strained his ears to listen, but the block remained uncannily quiet. Leaving the parcel, he began to riffle through the loose stacks of papers on the desk, the object of his search uncertain but its importance beyond any doubt. Deftly he checked inside the wardrobe and under the bed, sifted through drawerfuls of clothes and wrestled with a locked desk drawer until finally his roaming gaze alighted on the book-shelf.

One book had no title. Among solid chemistry tomes exuding academic virtue, one thin spine lurked grey, unmarked. In seconds Morgan had yanked it out of the row and was flicking through it, his breathing rapid now.

It was a scrapbook of cuttings, newspaper reports varying between brief 'filler' paragraphs and substantial articles. He saw illustrations of smashed windows and smoking, blackened shop-fronts. Another photograph showed a struggling mob, placards and fists aloft, faces contorted with hatred; some individuals wore hoods. The common theme was Animal Militancy and its various 'triumphs'.

Leaning closer, Morgan peered at one of the hooded activists in the demonstration. A scarf with a distinctive zigzag pattern was wound round the man's neck—a scarf very similar in design to one of Jason's. It wasn't proof, of course, but the very existence of the scrapbook indicated a more than passing interest in the subject of violent protest. Morgan replaced the book and turned his attention once more to the papers on the desk. If only there was some document, something relevant with Jason's name on it, he would go straight to the police...

A footfall behind caused his heart to lurch violently. Before he had time to straighten his back, the door flew open and Jason rocketed into the room.

'What are you doing here?' he demanded. 'What the hell are you doing with my papers?'

For a moment Morgan's brain felt like a cube of polystyrene. There were no nerve cells, no synapses, no rational thoughts. Jason looked fearsome in his fury—eyes glaring, teeth almost grinding at this invasion of his privacy. Any further provocation, and who knew what might happen.

'Keep your hair on,' Morgan managed to say after a pause. 'I was looking for a blank sheet, to write you a message. This parcel's been hanging around for you in the foyer, so I brought it over. Mrs P left your door unlocked.'

Jason took a step forward, his face changing as he noticed the package for the first time. The black eyes narrowed, and flicked a doubtful glance at Morgan. 'It's damaged,' he said.

'I know. Hope the contents aren't fragile. You'll have to complain to the Post Office if anything's broken.'

Jason's mouth tightened; Morgan felt that the invisible balance between suspicion and acceptance was tilting inexorably in the wrong direction, but when the chemistry student spoke, the aggression was gone from his tone.

'I dare say,' he said. 'Thanks for collecting it, but please don't bother in future.'

'No sweat,' answered Morgan, leaving the room with a show of nonchalance.

That was a lie. Morgan Brunt was a six-foot-three-inch rugby forward, an amalgam of Celtic creativity and Yorkshire grit; Jason Gower was a slimly built five foot seven with no known sporting interests...yet Morgan's hand, as he fumbled for the key to D9, was slick with moisture, the same moisture that meandered in chilly little runnels between his shoulder blades down, down towards the floor.

10

Hubert was in his element. He stood at the front of MDL2, his body adopting its usual subtly twisted stance, like a stunted tree, his pink eyelids blinking...yet his sibilant tones were charged with didactic sarcasm, and his audience had so far afforded him the respect of total silence.

He was delivering the preamble for the

second-year physiology practical.

'You're all hungry, and doubtless feeling very hard done by,' he said. 'The purpose of your fast, as you know, is to study how gastric secretion changes in response to various carefully controlled stimuli. In the absence of an Alexis St Martin, we have to use *indirect* means to obtain our supplies.' He held up a length of packaged thin rubber tubing, then slapped it against his palm, reminding the watchers of the kind of huntsman who is rather too free with his whip.

'This is a Ryles tube,' went on Hubert. 'When a certain proportion of your number struggle into your clinical years, you'll encounter these tubes in hospital wards on an almost daily basis. They play a part in the coarsely but aptly named "drip and suck" procedure which is employed when a patient's gut refuses to function, either because of blockage or ileus—that is, a temporary paralysis. Larger versions of the tube are used in casualty departments for stomach wash-outs following drug overdose, or cases of accidental poisoning.

'Thus—' he thrust the tube accusingly towards them—'those of you who succeed in swallowing one of these tubes in the next few minutes will be given the privilege of a brief period of empathy with your future patients.'

'I don't rate empathy for its own sake,' muttered Brad to Morgan. 'Why stop there? Why not have your leg chopped off just so you know what it's like?'

'You wish to make a point, Mr Pike?' asked Hubert icily.

'No, sir.'

'Then keep your idle chatter for later. Now, you'll have all studied the analytical details in the manuals... In the first instance the entire class will divide itself into pairs, *both* members of which will, in turn, attempt nasogastric intubation. From among those successfully intubated I shall choose a number of subjects for this afternoon's experiment. The rest of you will be allocated roles as supervisors and analysts.' He clicked his fingers towards a discreetly hovering technician, and the man darted into a side room to return with a towering pile of plastic buckets. A groan surged through the laboratory. 'I shall outline the method of intubation,' said Hubert, 'then you will each put it into practice. There shall be no exceptions.'

'First, you inspect the nose. You may find among our rugby-playing fraternity that only one nostril is fully patent. Lubricate the tube, and pass it slowly into the nasopharynx while your subject breathes quietly in and out through the mouth. As you proceed beyond this point, ask your subject to swallow; you may give a little water to help, if necessary. If coughing and retching occur, due to the gag reflex, you do not withdraw the tube, but hold it still until your subject is able to continue. When you consider that the tube has reached the stomach, you test its position as follows...'

Within minutes the air was alive with spluttering sounds, as purple-faced students heaved convulsively over the thoughtfully provided buckets.

'He's loving this,' whispered Steve, Chris's partner, casting a baleful glance in Hubert's direction.

'Don't attract his attention! We've done nothing yet. Let's try again...' Carefully Chris fed the slippery tube forward only for Steve to expel it with an explosive bout of retching the moment it reached the pharynx.

'This isn't going to work,' gasped Steve, tears pouring down his cheeks. 'Let's swap over.'

Chris thought it predictable that Steve had given up so easily. There was no real incentive to succeed: those who failed got their lunch, those who retained the tube became guinea pigs for the entire afternoon. But didn't the man have any *pride?*

Soon he discovered for himself that the

difficulties were real. How on earth *did* they manage in hospitals? How did the patient overcome the tickling, infuriating, all-powerful urge to—oops, sorry, Steve. You should have stood back a bit.

From the next bench snippets of accusation flew between Morgan and Brad.

'He said aspirate, not excavate!'

'The fluid's bile-stained...'

'Must be in my bloody gall-bladder, then.'

Chris wandered across with Steve. 'We can't do it,' he confessed.

'I say, why tamper with nature,' began Steve. 'If we've been given a gag reflex, it must be for a jolly good reason...'

'Yer pair of wimps,' pronounced Morgan. He and Bradley had both managed to swallow the tubes, and wore the anchoring tape across their cheek-bones like a row of military medals. Chris looked round the room at the other scattered couples and gave a rueful smile; almost all the successfully intubated students were women. Perhaps his two friends were more afraid of Hubert than of the Ryles tube.

He glanced at Eleanor, and she winked at him.

'Hey, you're cheating!' exclaimed Steve, pointing to the tube which led neatly out of Eleanor's mouth to end beneath a row of tape just above the jawline.

She strolled to join them. 'No, I'm not,' she said. 'It's a perfectly valid method.' Leaning forward, she added in a low voice: 'I did it myself. Bronwen's so cack-handed, I thought she was trying to perform a bronchoscopy.'

With his characteristic brand of unveiled contempt, Hubert flitted through the laboratory, selecting the requisite number of human guinea pigs. Morgan, Bradley and Eleanor were all included, while Chris was designated a supervisor and Steve an analyst.

'This is going to be boring,' said Morgan, scanning the schedule for the afternoon's experiments. 'You'll want me at intervals for samples of blood and gastric juices, but in between there'll be sod-all for me to do. I shall find a quiet corner and read this.' He reached into the pocket of his white coat and briefly exposed the title of a Wilbur Smith thriller.

'Don't let Hubert catch you.'

'I won't. By the way, I need to talk to you about Hubert; I found something very interesting under his car this morning.'

'What—a bomb?'

'No; nothing as exotic as that. The significance didn't strike me immediately, but...'

'Wait. He's coming this way.'

'I'll tell you later. Tonight. And there's

something even more important...'

With that Chris had to be content.

At one thirty Chris returned from a snatched lunch and ruled some lines in his notebook. 'Morgan's for pentagastrin, and Brad's for an insulin test,' he said to Steve. 'If I keep their samples fifteen minutes out of phase, will you be able to cope with them half-hourly?'

'I reckon so,' said Steve, 'if this pH meter behaves itself.'

'Good. Now, the first blood sample...' He broke off at the sight of a pale face peering through the glass of the laboratory door. ' 'Scuse me a moment.' He slipped across to the door and let himself out into the corridor where Fay stood looking strange and gaunt.

'Can I help you, Fay?' he asked.

'I—I wanted Morgan,' she mumbled almost inaudibly. 'He wasn't at Calverton, so I thought he might be here, but I can't see him in the lab.'

'He's downstairs, sprawled on the soft chairs by the coffee machine. You must have walked right past him.'

'No—I came along the admin corridor. Thanks, Chris. Does he...is he in a good mood?'

'Well, there's a tube up his nose and he's had nothing to eat since yesterday.'

'Oh.'

The sound of Steve calling his name drew Chris back into the laboratory. ' 'Bye, Fay,' he said hastily, and turned his attention to the intricacies of the experiment.

Morgan was dozing. In the beginning, he had closed his eyes to avoid silly questions from passing students, but he had soon found it expedient to cat-nap in between trips upstairs to be attached to a vacuum suction pump: nights had recently been too precious for sleeping.

The chairs were very comfortable—soft and deep, with no side-arms, so he had been able to push three together and create his own lounger. If it wasn't for the experiment, he could have a most profitable afternoon. As long as Hubert didn't cotton on, all would be well.

He heard quiet footsteps close at hand: slow, cautious steps as if someone was unwilling to wake him. It wouldn't be Chris, then; he always arrived with a patter, a hearty shake of the shoulder and some quip about stewing in one's own juices.

Morgan relaxed, kept his eyes shut and let his mind wander. For a moment he thought he could discern an infinitesimal tug on the nasogastric tube, but nothing followed and no one spoke. Good. Leave a fellow in peace.

Suddenly, a terrible sensation. His chest was squeezing tight, suffocating him... In a wave of panic Morgan sat up, clawing at the neck of his shirt. Dizziness assailed him; he tried to vomit, but couldn't.

The oppression was unimaginable. As his frantic heartbeat thundered in his ears, he knew that this was how it felt to die—recognized and rejected the knowledge. Surely somebody must help him. Surely...

He staggered two paces, then his legs began to buckle. Hoarsely he cried out; somewhere there was a calf bleating in agony.

The world had become a dark red blanket trussing him ever tighter... With a last choking gasp Morgan keeled to one side, crashed into the drinks machine and lay still.

'*What?*'

Montgomery's own ears told him that his reaction had been too vehement. The news was a gut-wrenching shock, and somehow the terse shout registered his protest. Clutching the telephone receiver in a hand gone cold, he clawed his professional integument back into place and issued a series of instructions:

163

'Don't let anything be moved, especially near the body... That's right. If you can manage to screen off the area, all the better. Try to ensure that no one leaves the building; anyone who insists should give their name, address and telephone number to the porter. We're on our way right now.'

As Montgomery hurried out of his office, shrugging on his winter coat, Sergeant Bird looked up from his desk in concern. 'Something happened, sir?'

'Yes. Another student is dead. He was killed in the Medical School less than an hour ago—with cyanide.'

William Bird, Brian Jackson, Robert Allen, Graham Smythe...each face mirrored his own shock and disbelief. In the end it was Jackson who spoke for them all:

'What the hell is going on down there?' he asked.

Laszlo Kovacs met them in the foyer, his face grey and etched with deep new lines, his thin fingers trembling.

'I'm so glad you've come,' he said with the relief of one who had suddenly found unwelcome authority thrust upon him. 'We didn't know what to do. This is dreadful—a tragedy.'

'The lady who rang said you'd asked for me by name,' said Montgomery. 'Are you in charge here, Dr Kovacs?'

'Yes. Professor Byrne is away until the end of the week.'

'Tell me about the incident. Who was the student?'

'His name is Morgan Brunt. He is—was—a second-year, a tall, outgoing man, the very last person you might expect to see—like this...' The lecturer's face twisted. 'The students were performing practical experiments on stomach secretions in the multidisciplinary laboratory on the first floor. Some individuals, including Morgan, had swallowed nasogastric tubes while others were analysing the samples. The procedures are disagreeable, but quite safe.' He looked at the ground. 'It seems that Morgan didn't stay in the lab with the others; for varying periods of time he made himself comfortable on some seats near the ground-floor coffee machine. That's where he was discovered, at half-past three.' Half an hour before the police were called.

'Were you overseeing this experiment?' asked Montgomery quietly.

'No...it was Dr Pomeroy.'

Montgomery felt Sergeant Bird's glance telepathically. Hubert Pomeroy again! The man who had humiliated Keith Mayhew, the man whose sulky aggression made seasoned police officers think that something, somewhere, was being hidden...

'Who actually found the body?'

'It was Jenny, a secretary in the Administration Department. She was taking a letter round the corner to Human Morphology, and...' Laszlo's voice tailed off; he swallowed.

'I see. Could you now show us the place?'

'Yes. Come this way.'

He preceded them through two pairs of glass swing-doors, then stopped by a hastily erected screen where a white-coated man did uncomfortable sentry duty.

'This is Bill Hathaway, from Biochemistry,' explained Laszlo. 'He tried to get hold of some chemicals to act as antidotes to the cyanide, but it was too late.'

One look down was enough for Montgomery to concur, but he forced himself to kneel by the body, to examine it with minimal disturbance, and to wonder what sort of depravity could lead one human being to kill another in this way.

The bitter almonds smell was strong. 'Tell me exactly what happened when Jenny made the discovery,' he demanded of the two scientists.

'She ran into MDL1 where the first-year students were doing a histology practical. Dr Farmer, who was in charge there, returned and told her to ring for an ambulance. The nearest casualty department, as you probably know, is at the Victoria Hospital. A student from the histology group was despatched upstairs to fetch Dr Pomeroy. Hubert sent the student on to my office, and we were both downstairs within half a minute. Hubert lifted Morgan's eyelids, felt for a pulse, then began to withdraw the tube, muttering about laryngeal spasm. I stopped him: the skin wasn't blue, it was a reddish colour, and as I leaned forward to examine the lips I suddenly smelt the characteristic cyanide smell.'

Laszlo spread his hands in a dazed gesture reflecting the confusion he had experienced on diagnosing the cause of death. 'This sounds foolish, but...I understood that cyanide had killed Morgan. All the signs were there. The whys and hows were in abeyance. We had to deal with the situation as we found it. So...I began cardiac massage, and asked Hubert to fetch chemicals from our lab and from Biochemistry. But all along, I knew we were too late.'

Laszlo shuddered, and Dr Hathaway took up the tale. 'It took me three or four minutes to find dicobalt edetate, so in the mean time they'd given him both sodium nitrate and thiosulphate. It was all anyone could do... We got an airway and some oxygen set up, but there wasn't a flicker of life.'

'This rubber tube was left *in situ*, then,' said Montgomery.

'Yes.'

'Were your chemicals given via the tube?'

'No—we injected them. There was already a cannula in the vein to meet the experimental requirements. If there had been any hope at all, we would have proceeded to gastric lavage, but...'

'Quite.' It was clear where the half-hour had gone to. 'Did the ambulance crew try any further resuscitation?'

'No. They could see it was hopeless.'

A light female voice broke in from the other side of the screen. 'Excuse me. They're in our office just now. They want to know whether you'd like them to take the body away.'

'Not yet,' said Montgomery. 'Go and get their story,' he instructed Jackson, then turned once more to the two lecturers. 'Is Frobisher coming?'

'He's just finishing a PM at the Victoria,' supplied Hathaway. 'Then he'll be straight over.'

'Good. Now, I want a room. An office, a lab, anywhere as long as it's quiet. We need to interview every second-year student from that physiology practical, and anyone who may have used this corridor since lunchtime, be they student or staff. But first—please send me Dr Pomeroy.'

Hubert Pomeroy looked even less physically appealing than before. Freckles stood out like a scattered galaxy on his waxen cheeks, and a tic bunched the skin below his left eye at erratic intervals; his expression, though, held sullen defiance.

'Dr Pomeroy,' said Montgomery gravely, after offering a seat in the small library he had commandeered, 'what can you tell us about this afternoon?'

'He should have been in the lab.' The lecturer's breathy voice sounded almost angry. 'He should have been in the lab.'

'When did you last see Morgan alive?'

'I can't tell you precisely. How would anyone know, with sixty students in the room? I suppose it would be two thirty, or maybe three o'clock. Christopher Shallet was having difficulty getting blood out of the cannula in Morgan's arm, so I checked that it was patent. It was.'

'Where was this?'

'In the lab, of course.'

'Did you at any time see Morgan downstairs by the coffee machine?'

'Only when the tragedy had already occurred.'

'Did you notice him going missing for

parts of the afternoon?'

'I told you, there were sixty students to organize. The experiment calls for frequent samples of gastric juices, blood and urine, so it would have been reasonable to assume that any student not immediately apparent was in the lavatory.'

'So you didn't particularly notice that Morgan wasn't with the others?' pressed Montgomery.

Hubert gave a cluck of annoyance. '*No.*'

Montgomery steeped his fingers and regarded the physiologist appraisingly. 'I understand that a first-year student burst into your lab to tell you what had happened. Do you recall his exact words?'

'No.'

'The gist, then.'

'He said something like, "Dr Pomeroy, come quickly. Morgan Brunt has collapsed." I looked round the room, puzzled, asked where he was, and was told he was down by the coffee machine.'

'What did you do then?'

'I asked the student to bring Dr Kovacs, and ran downstairs.'

'What were you expecting to find?'

Hubert frowned. 'What sort of question is that?'

'I'm asking you for your understanding of the situation at that point from the information you had been given.'

'Oh...I don't really know. I thought Morgan had been taken ill.'

'So you didn't know at that stage he was dead.'

'No; the student was only acting as messenger, passing on what Dr Farmer had told him.'

'Right... So you thought Morgan might be ill. A strapping lad like that, suddenly.'

'Listen, Mr Smart Detective Montgomery. The students were giving each other injections of substances like insulin and histamine for the purposes of the experiment. As long as all the proper procedures were followed, this should have been perfectly safe—but once you get students wandering off on their own, not giving their full attention to the matters in hand, then accidents become possible.'

'Is that what you thought had happened?'

'I didn't think anything!'

'I was just curious,' said Montgomery mildly, 'as to why you called for Dr Kovacs *at that stage*—before you had seen Morgan.'

Hubert looked stunned. 'I—I've no idea. I must have been seeking moral support.'

'Were you expecting to find a situation you couldn't handle alone?'

'I—I really can't say.' He shook his head vacantly then blinked, narrowing his eyes at Montgomery so the pale irises glinted

171

like chips of glass. 'I responded to the urgent tone of the student who came with the message,' he said, articulating each syllable with precision. 'The presence of a colleague seemed advisable.'

Montgomery nodded noncommittally. 'What occurred when you reached the ground floor?'

'I found Dr Farmer, fussing with the boy's collar but not really achieving very much. I saw straight away that Morgan wasn't breathing, and for some reason I imagined that his tube had become misplaced. I began to undo the tape on his cheek preparatory to withdrawing the tube, but Dr Kovacs, who arrived mere seconds after I did, told me to stop. He then felt for a pulse, and instructed the young lady from Administration, who was hovering and wringing her hands, to send for an ambulance immediately.'

'It sounds as if Dr Kovacs was decisive.'

'Yes,' Hubert conceded sulkily. 'For once he managed to be.'

'Did you think the boy was dead at that point?'

The tic jumped below Hubert's eye. 'Yes,' he said slowly. 'But I couldn't let myself believe it. He'd been in my class...'

'What happened then?'

'The first-years started spilling out of

their lab, all agog, so Dr Farmer had to herd them back again. Dr Kovacs began cardiac massage on Morgan, then leaned towards his mouth and withdrew looking shocked. He said, "I can smell cyanide," so I bent over, and I could smell it, too.'

'What were your thoughts at this time?'

'My "thoughts"?' mimicked Hubert angrily. 'I didn't have any. I could smell bitter almonds—fact. There wasn't time to think of why. My mind was on antidotes and resuscitation measures.' He paused, and continued more musingly. 'Administration had had the presence of mind to send another girl to us: she was quaking behind the coffee machine like a terrified rabbit. Dr Kovacs was asking for certain chemicals. I said I would go up to Biochemistry for the edetate while the girl obtained the other things from Physiology, which was nearer. I found Dr Hathaway in Biochemistry; it took him two or three minutes to lay his hands on the agent, and so we were the last to return. All possible antidotes were given, to no avail.'

'Morgan was dead,' said Montgomery.

'Yes; Morgan was dead.'

Montgomery let a few seconds of silence elapse, then calmly asked: 'How do you think it happened?'

The muscle under Hubert's left eye twitched and fluttered.

'I don't know. It's not for me to say.'

'Come, now.' Montgomery leaned forward persuasively. 'Everyone's entitled to an opinion. You've known these students for fifteen months, so your ideas are particularly valuable. Morgan seems to have been a strong, physical kind of chap. How does someone like that end up dead from a dose of cyanide?'

'It's obvious. It was squirted down the nasogastric tube.'

'I don't mean practical aspects, the method. I mean, what circumstances could bring about this effect?'

'I don't know.'

'Did you see much of Morgan away from the Medical School?'

'No. I live quietly.' Hubert's lip curled. 'All I can tell you is that Morgan was one of the rugby set. They aren't my type at all. They're loud, aggressively macho: rucking and rutting are all they live for. Luckily for Morgan he was bright enough to keep up with the course work.'

'Ah: he was a successful student?'

'Yes.'

'Could he conceivably have taken his own life?'

'Him? Never.'

'That leaves us with accident and—deliberate action on the part of another person. Tell me, Dr Pomeroy, is cyanide

174

available in the Medical School?'

'There are various forms of cyanide, Inspector, as any schoolchild would know. Which did you have in mind?'

Montgomery felt annoyed. Hubert Pomeroy was in no position to be 'clever'. 'Considering that we are not yet aware which form killed Morgan Brunt, such comments are unhelpful,' he answered. 'I'm asking about the general principle—are forms of cyanide open to common access in the Medical School?'

'Possibly. Scientific procedures are taking place on all floors every day.'

'But you don't know for sure?'

'No.' Hubert gave a little smirk, and Montgomery tried hard to clamp down on his gut detestation of this man.

'Returning to your own practical experiments,' he said coolly, 'whose responsibility was it to keep an eye on the students who were acting as subjects this afternoon? Was there a system, or were the arrangements fairly random?'

'Are you trying to imply that I failed in my duty?' Hubert's hands were clenched into tight little fists.

'I wouldn't dream of implying anything.'

'Yes, you would! I repeat that the experiment was carefully organized. Every pair of students being tested had another allocated to take samples and generally supervise what went on. Christopher Shallet was looking after Morgan and Bradley Pike. They all knew that the subjects were to stay in the laboratory area at all times.'

'You stipulated this?'

'It didn't need to be stipulated; it was obvious!' Hubert's left cheek, leapt into spasm, completely beyond his control. He pointed a shaking finger at Montgomery. 'I know your game!' he shouted. 'You're looking for a scapegoat, just like you were before—and I fit the bill! If you and your band of clodhopping incompetents fail to find the perpetrator, you've got a ready-made smokescreen: just blame Hubert Pomeroy! He was negligent! Well, I'm not having it. You might think your warrant cards give you power over your fellow citizens, but we all know what sort of bullying blockheads find their way into the world's police forces! I *won't* take it, and...'

He broke off at Montgomery's icy stare.

'I'd strongly advise you to refrain from insulting us, Dr Pomeroy,' he said in flat tones. 'Thank you for your time. We may well be in contact soon with further questions.'

Brian Jackson chucked unnecessarily loudly as the physiologist left the room. 'You rattled *his* cage, all right!'

Montgomery swung round on him. 'Go and see what Graham's up to,' he said, referring to Smythe, Jackson's young partner. 'He was supposed to be directing the SOCO boys when they arrived. Then I want you both to address the first-year medical students *en masse,* and ask if anyone saw anything relevant this afternoon—in particular last sightings of Morgan alive. Ditto the administration staff, and the people working in the Human Morphology Department.'

'Why Human Morphology?'

'Because that's on the ground floor, just beyond the coffee machine.'

Jackson groaned. 'It's nearly knocking-off time.'

'It was. Just think—all these people are going to be very grateful to you. Until they've been seen, they can't go home either.'

Jackson left with a disgruntled tread, and William Bird, who had been sitting quietly in the background, ventured a comment. 'We get the second-years, right?'

'Yes—at least, until reinforcements arrive. What do you make of friend Hubert, Will?'

'Hm...he was on the defensive, as ever. Full of bluster. I think he's genuinely frightened that the blame will somehow fall on him.'

'That begs the question: *is* he to blame? Has he just coldly murdered a student, and if so, why?'

'The coincidences are mounting up,' said William Bird soberly. 'Two deaths and one close shave—and the Physiology Department is linked with all these events. I'll tell you something, sir: I thought that tweaking the tube sounded a bit doubtful. Dr Kovacs said they might have proceeded to wash out the stomach if there'd been any hope—perhaps Pomeroy wanted to remove the tube to preclude that.'

'What a mind you've got, Will. That didn't occur to me, but I did wonder why he wanted to involve Kovacs before he'd even found out what was wrong. I felt he wanted to blur the responsibility, avoid any period of time when people might point out that he was alone with the body...'

'Dr Farmer was there.'

'Yes, but he soon had to take control of his class. And the admin girl wouldn't have been able to swear that Hubert's ministrations were clinically sound. There's another thing, too...that delay in getting hold of one of the antidotes they needed. I wonder if it was *all* down to Dr Hathaway? Or did Hubert drag his feet on the way to Biochemistry?'

Montgomery shook his head slowly from side to side, frowning. Now wasn't the time for speculation and analysis; they were here to gather data. He took a piece of paper, briefly noted down the points they had made in his own personal shorthand, then looked across at William Bird.

'Bring me Christopher Shallet,' he said.

11

Christopher Shallet shuffled into the room like a zombie, gently propelled by the bulk of Sergeant Bird at his elbow. He hardly seemed aware of his actions as he sank down stiffly on to the chair provided; only the eyes were alive with a raw pleading look, as if begging to be told that it wasn't true.

Montgomery envisaged his own son Justin sitting there. 'Christopher,' he began, 'I'm sorry we have to meet again like this. I've been told that Morgan was your friend.'

'Yes.' The voice was a hoarse whisper.

'You were in D block together, I think?'

'Yes; next-door neighbours.'

'And you were also together this afternoon at the start of the physiology practical experiment?'

'Yes. We were in a group with Bradley

Pike and Steven Listerfield.'

'Had you been expecting to do this particular experiment?'

'Sorry?' Chris started and was more alert in his puzzlement.

'Had this exact practical been scheduled for some time?'

'Oh...yes. Since last term.'

'I see. And was there any pre-selection of the individuals who would swallow the tubes?'

'No, we were all to try. Some of us just couldn't manage it, while others had no trouble. Morgan called it "a doddle".' Chris winced and turned his head away.

'So the subjects for your experiment were chosen from among the successfully intubated students?'

'Yes. Dr Pomeroy said he was looking for volunteers, then went, "You—and you—and you." ' Chris managed to produce the ghost of a smile.

'You were to take samples from Morgan and from Bradley Pike, I understand. Did that leave you with much free time?'

'No. I had to label things and chart them, and liaise with Steve Listerfield, who was doing the analyses.'

'Whose idea was it that Morgan should relax away from the lab when he wasn't needed?'

'His own.'

'You'd have found it easier if he'd remained within sight?'

'Yes, but...it was no big deal.'

'Did he return to the lab at the requisite times?'

'The first time, yes, but then he kept falling asleep so I had to go down and give him a shake.'

'I see. When was the last time you saw him alive, Christopher?'

Misery on the young man's face. 'Three o'clock,' he said. 'Or rather, just after. Those were the last recorded samples.'

Montgomery paused; this was very difficult. 'You've heard what happened? The details?'

Chris blinked and gave a jerky nod.

'Can you think of any reason why someone should do that to Morgan?'

'No.' The voice was like a cracked bell trying to toll. 'There are people around with—little grudges, people who've had disappointments, but nothing to justify sheer evil.'

'I'm sorry, Christopher. I know this is upsetting. Just one more question for now: during your travels between MDL2 and the area of the ground-floor coffee machine, did you ever see anyone alien to the building? Someone who didn't belong in here?'

A flicker in Chris Shallet's brown eyes

told Montgomery that he had hit home, perhaps for the first time.

'Er, no,' came the answer.

'Christopher?' They had been here before. That subtle evasiveness following Keith Mayhew's death, which Montgomery had finally put down to guilt for not having helped the lad more... 'Any non-medical personnel,' he persisted. 'We need to eliminate them, so as not to clog up our enquiry. You saw someone, didn't you?'

'Yes, but she can't have been involved.' Chris sounded distant, reluctant.

'Tell me anyway.'

Silence while Chris flicked his gaze to William Bird and back again.

'Please, Christopher.'

'Well...' Chris clasped his hands and took a deep breath. 'Fay came by earlier. She's Morgan's ex-girlfriend.'

'Fay who?'

'Fay Gillingham. She's not a medic; she does Social Sciences. But it was half-past one.'

'Did she speak to Morgan?'

'I don't know. I told her he was downstairs, but when I next saw Morgan we were too busy with the samples to discuss anything else.'

'Do you know when she left the building?'

'I'm sorry, no.'

182

'*Ex*-girlfriend, you said?'

'Yes. They broke up about three weeks ago and there was some bitterness, but now she's going out with another chap from our block, so even though she was fond of Morgan, I think she's getting over it.' Suddenly he looked appalled. 'She won't have heard!' he exclaimed. 'Somebody's going to have to tell her!'

'Little grudges', Christopher had mentioned earlier. 'Disappointments'. His was a nature that either saw no evil or saw it late, with disbelieving awe. Montgomery himself had encountered too much viciousness in life to exempt anyone without due process. 'Leave that to us,' he instructed Chris, and noted the faint sag of relief. 'I'd be obliged if you'd say nothing.'

'Whatever you think is right,' said Chris. His energy was visibly fading, and Montgomery decided to let him go.

'Thank you for your help, Christopher,' he said. 'We will need further words, perhaps tomorrow, but this'll do for now.'

The chair scraped across the floor as the young man stood up and trudged to the door. Just before he left he turned once more to face them, and they caught a glimpse of the pleasant, sincere personality he would display in normal circumstances.

'Call me Chris when we next meet,' he said. 'Morgan always did.'

'I thought you might ask him more about Morgan's character,' said Sergeant Bird when Chris had gone.

'The other boys will supply that, I'm sure,' replied Montgomery. 'Any gaps can be filled in tomorrow.'

'We'd better check on that ex-girlfriend. The name "Fay Gillingham" rings a bell with me, but I can't recall the context.'

'Same here. I wonder if Morgan had a more current girlfriend? The usual cause of break-ups is...' A tentative knock on the door interrupted him. Through the thin glass panels they could see the shoulder and hip of a stout individual wearing a white laboratory coat. 'Come in!' he called.

There was a brief hesitation, then Magda Hepworth stepped into the room, putty-faced under the unkind fluorescent light.

'Ah, Dr Hepworth,' said Montgomery. 'This is timely. We were hoping for a few words with you when we'd seen the students.'

'Inspector Montgomery,' said Magda in a badly executed parody of her usual crisp tones, 'I had to see you. There is something I must tell you...'

When Magda had divulged the story of her affair with Morgan, Montgomery's first reaction was one of surprise. It wasn't the age gap which gave him pause, it was more the concept of prickly, workaholic Dr Hepworth embroiling herself with a student of Morgan's stamp. 'You say you've been lovers for three weeks,' he reiterated carefully. 'Were you friends for some time before?'

'No; we had hardly exchanged a word.'

'How, then, did the relationship begin? Who was the initiator?'

The pale lips lifted slightly at the corners. 'It happened very simply. Morgan asked me to his room one night for a drink. Events took their turn and I stayed. The willingness was equal on both sides; a need in both of us was met.'

'Would you say it was mainly physical?' Montgomery read Magda as one who would not find such a question embarrassing.

'Unquestionably,' she said. 'In many ways we were strangers. We were not in love, but recently...there were the beginnings of a closeness.'

'When did you last see Morgan?'

'This morning, about six o'clock. He couldn't have his cup of tea because of the experiment.'

'How did you spend this afternoon?'

'I was not lecturing, so part of the time I was in the laboratory with Dr Kovacs and

Michael Chan, and part of the time I was in this library. I also visited the small lab at the end of the corridor for pieces of equipment.'

'Were the two colleagues you mentioned in the laboratory the whole time you were there?'

'I couldn't say for certain.'

'Did you see anyone who didn't belong in the Medical School out in the passages, or anyone acting suspiciously?'

'I'm sorry, no.'

'What about Dr Pomeroy? Was he wandering the corridors?'

'No; he would have been in MDL2, overseeing the practical.'

'You're quite sure? We're particularly interested in the period between three and three thirty.'

Magda frowned. 'I was here in the library then, researching an article. No—I didn't see Hubert at all.'

Montgomery was aware of William Bird stirring restlessly in a seat diagonally behind him. 'Would you like to ask some questions, Sergeant Bird?' he invited.

'Er, no, sir. I was just thinking...we'd better find out from the porter if he saw the Gillingham girl leave the building, before someone lets him go home. We need to know that before we visit her ourselves.'

Concern leapt into Magda's eyes. 'Do

you mean *Fay* Gillingham?' she asked. 'Was *she* here today?'

'So we've been told,' said Montgomery. 'Do you know the girl?'

'We met briefly in rather unfortunate circumstances. She probably feels that I've usurped her position with Morgan.'

'Did you—yes do go, Will—did you and Morgan ever discuss Fay?'

Again a strange, self-deprecating smile. 'No; we didn't talk a lot.'

'Did Fay make threats to either of you?'

'No.'

'Candidly, do you think she could have been involved in Morgan's death today?'

Magda looked anxious. 'I don't know her—but surely not. She's just a young girl—and so tiny and fairy-like. I can't imagine it.'

'I know you say you didn't speak a lot with Morgan, but there must have been *some* conversation. Can you remember anything he said last night?'

Her lips tightened. 'We were discussing the letter-bomb which was sent to Dr Kovacs. We were wondering if a student from D block was responsible.'

'What's this?'

'We spoke of Jason Gower. He is a member of Animal Concern, a dogmatic individual who seems to applaud violence on the flimsy pretext of saving animals. I am a physiologist. Like Dr Kovacs, I too look under my car every time I wish to drive it. Inspector Montgomery, I know this may not be your province, but we are all very frightened, and—I don't know, perhaps, just perhaps, Jason Gower has done this thing today.'

'Tell me again about those sightings of Fay Gillingham,' said Montgomery to William Bird as the library clock registered ten thirty p.m.

'The Medical School porter saw a girl answering her description enter the foyer from outside just before one thirty; it's lucky for us that she has such distinctive long hair. That observation tallies with Christopher Shallet's story, and also information received by Sergeant Allen from another student, one Eleanor Ransome.'

'What's this?' Montgomery made a quarter-turn to include Robert Allen in the discussion.

Allen drew up his chair. 'Eleanor is a second-year medical student,' he said, 'but she's also a resident of Wellington Hall, where Fay lives, so she knows her by sight. She saw Fay through the glass doors of MDL2 at half-past one; her attention had been caught by Christopher Shallet suddenly abandoning a conversation with Steven Listerfield and opening the door to talk to Fay. Apparently they spent less than two minutes in the corridor, then Christopher returned alone. Eleanor didn't see Fay again.'

'I asked for her opinion of the girl's character, and she gave it most forthrightly. According to Miss Ransome, Fay fashions an identity for herself by following trends: she picks up ideas and slogans from others, and peddles them with uncritical fervour. Miss Ransome credits her with neither original thought nor logic; I gather logic plays little part in Fay's choice of dogma, and likewise she will stubbornly defend her creeds in the face of logic.'

'Did she think Fay capable of murder?' asked Montgomery.

'She stalled a bit when I put that question to her, but I could see it in her eyes. Her actual answer was "In the right circumstances—possibly." '

'Not what Dr Hepworth thought,' murmured Sergeant Bird.

'No,' said Montgomery, 'but she hardly knows Fay. Go on, Robert—what about Fay and Morgan?'

'Fay had caught Morgan and Magda Hepworth virtually *in flagrante delicto*, it seems, and she was naturally angry and upset. But within a fortnight she'd got herself involved with a chemistry student from the same hall as Morgan: a chap called Jason Gower.'

'Jason Gower!' Montgomery's tired mind clicked up a gear. The Animal Concern activator, teaming up with Fay...

'The porter didn't see Fay leave again,' said William Bird obliquely. 'Perhaps she went out the back way to the Chemistry Building.'

Cyanide...Montgomery's brain was now racing. 'Supposing she saw Morgan the first time, but he was asleep, or occupied with someone else,' he suggested in hushed tones. 'Supposing she left the Medical School at the rear, went to see Jason, then returned...' Irritably he shook his head. 'There's no evidence for this,' he said. 'None at all. We haven't even been able to interview the people concerned, because they're both out somewhere. Let's be canny in the morning. We'll start our enquiries at the Chemistry Building before we approach Jason directly. Who knows—we might catch him out in a lie.'

'You mustn't feel guilty,' insisted Anna Kovacs that night as Laszlo stared into the fire, battered by the events of the afternoon. 'You did everything you could. No one could have saved the boy.'

But he did feel guilty. Like a woman,

he endured it as a constant state. And new guilts stirred up old ones...

'Time for bed,' she said, holding out a hand as if he were a child.

Laszlo both longed for, and dreaded, sleep. His body craved its healing, but his mind would be allowed no merciful oblivion; old torments would resurface: whether wearing their true face, or some grotesque new guise, they knew where to find him, and all that unmanning fear of violent death would once more shake his bones into jelly...

'Stop him! Stop him!'
The roar of the crowd... Pain in his shoulder... Panic and horror.

Laszlo's limbs shot out in a wrenching convulsion and he woke up palpitating. For a few moments he was confused, unable to orientate himself, then the reassuring softness of Anna's thigh brought him back to reality. Miraculously, she was still asleep. He moved as close as he dared; slowly, his muscles relaxed and the sharp edge of the nightmare dulled to the familiar ache of self-reproach. 1956 had taken his innocence away. People with opposing views had clutched at the age-old 'solution' of weapons. Atrocities, mistakes, families ripped apart, many never to see each other again... Cousin Szusza lost with her little daughter...

Laszlo sighed and buried his face against his wife's shoulder; gradually all coherent thought slid away.

Eight miles away in Carlton Montgomery, too, was reviewing violent events, only this time events of the more recent past. It had been a demanding day, gruelling even, yet as he so often found, his brain was jammed in 'hyperalert' mode just when he needed to sleep. So much data, most of it probably useless but maybe, just maybe, a hidden treasure waiting to be revealed, like a Bronze Age torque prised from a muddy field.

They had been excited about Fay Gillingham, but now Montgomery was less sure: the pressure to provide an early solution engendered its own enthusiasms. Here in the calm of his own bedroom, with only Carole's quiet breathing to punctuate the stillness, he judged the theory too pat. The 'treasure' they had glimpsed was probably the edge of a cheap twentieth-century door-stop.

Restless, he turned on his side and heard a muffled protest beside him.

'Richard!' Her voice was slurred with sleep. 'Do leave me some quilt. You just pulled it away again.'

'Sorry.'

She adjusted the bedding and he sank into his new position, holding it for all of three minutes before rolling on to his back again.

'For God's sake!' Carole exploded. 'Can't you count sheep or something?'

He didn't reply.

'I'm sorry,' she said, immediately contrite. 'It must have been awful seeing that student. But if you don't switch off at night you won't have the energy and clear thinking you need to solve the case. Why don't you concentrate on something totally different? Last week's squash game, for instance, when you thrashed Patrick Lord?'

'I'm trying to remember something,' said Montgomery.

'All the more reason to focus on another subject: what you're after might suddenly spring to mind.'

He made a brief noise of assent, but ignored the advice. He *was* trying to remember something, but recall was being made doubly difficult by the fact that he didn't know what it was he needed to remember. An item of relevance to the case, that was all he knew.

In the background Carole was speaking, her voice drowsy again. 'By the way,' she murmured, 'I'll be out tomorrow night.

Heather will be cooking, if you find you've time for supper.'

'You're out with Joan?' The response was merely automatic.

'No: Mark. He wants to discuss one of his new schemes with me.'

'Right.' What *was* this thing he had thought might be significant? Montgomery prided himself on having taken no medicines since an altercation with a villain had left him needing painkillers ten years earlier, but occasionally he envied the nitrazepam-poppers, their ready resort to the oblivion provided by a neat little pill or capsule. His brain was active, charged with energy, but a confined, futile energy, a hamster endlessly treading its exercise wheel. It was going to be a long night.

Christopher Shallet was very cold. He had been sitting motionless on the hard chair in his small dark room for three hours now, facing the bare window with mind and body in a state of suspended animation while all around him Calverton Hall prepared for sleep.

Morgan, dead. Chris found he couldn't believe it, even though the room next door was silent. Not big, hearty Morgan. Careless, intelligent Morgan. Arrogant yet such fun to be with. An epitome of life—an oak tree...

Across the garden he could just discern another tree, the chestnut in silhouette against the last of the lighted windows in his field of view. Someone in the room below Hubert's flat was still awake—reading, or perhaps just listening to music. Someone innocent and uninvolved, not like the boy who had climbed that chestnut tree only a handful of weeks ago—weeks that now seemed like years.

Once more he could see Keith Mayhew lying on Hubert's bed, his glasses neatly stowed on the bedside chest-of-drawers, his face only partially visible, but quite enough to recognize him. Unhappy Keith, whose sense of failure and self-disgust had led him to suicide—*or had it?*

What had Morgan been trying to say during the physiology practical? Something about Hubert's car... Frightening suspicions began to claw at Chris's consciousness, ideas absent in the numbness immediately following Morgan's death. He didn't know what it meant, but one thing he did know: the police would be asking for him again, soon—perhaps tomorrow. They would sense that he was hiding something. But information once divulged to them could not be credibly retracted. Supposing he was wrong? Then a sordid episode would have been disinterred for no useful purpose, and both Keith and

Morgan would have had their names sullied thanks to him.

Chris shivered as the room grew even colder, but he made no move towards the radiator valve or the wardrobe where his jacket hung. Dimly he knew he needed someone to talk to, but who? Not Brad and Steve. They had gone out that evening to get very determinedly drunk. No, not Brad and Steve...

Downstairs, the main door to D block creaked furtively; half a minute later he heard light footfalls in his own corridor. A scarcely audible knock sounded at the door.

Chris didn't move.

Again, a gentle knock. He clenched his fists and teeth. Go away, he thought. I'm not ready yet. Whoever you are, I don't want to see you. Just go...

As he sat in cramped rigidity a low whisper reached him.

'Chris; it's Eleanor. Are you still awake?'

He drew in a startled breath. Eleanor! The one person he felt he could trust. He didn't speak, but rose stiffly from the chair and hobbled towards the door, his muscles protesting. The footsteps outside began to recede; he fumbled with the handle, lurched outside and leaned over the banister bounding the stairwell.

'Eleanor!'

She stopped half-way down the flight below; he saw the pale oval of her face as she glanced upwards, made a turn and retraced her steps without fuss.

'Were you sitting in the dark?' she asked as they entered D8.

'Yes.' Chris flicked on his Anglepoise lamp and closed the door behind them.

'I'm sorry to come so late.'

He saw without surprise that it was midnight. 'I'm glad you did,' he said, and discovered that he meant it. He motioned her to sit down on the bed. 'May I take your jacket?'

'Er...not just yet, thanks.' She gave him an odd, appraising look. 'Do you know that it's freezing in here? Nearly as bad as outside?'

'Oh.' As swiftly as he could Chris drew the curtains together and unscrewed the radiator valve as far as it would go. 'I was thinking,' he offered by way of explanation.

'Me, too.' She seemed to understand exactly what he meant.

'Morgan...'

'Yes.' Eleanor knitted her fingers together uneasily as he encouraged her to continue. 'I've been going over it in my head all evening, and in the end I had to come. Chris, do you think Fay killed him?'

He had almost forgotten Fay, so pre-occupied had he been with Hubert. 'Fay?' he repeated stupidly. 'No, I don't think I do.'

'But she came to the lab this afternoon. You were the one who spoke to her. What did she want?'

'To see Morgan.'

Eleanor's eyes were eloquent. 'You don't think *that* was significant?'

Chris shook his head and tried to marshal his thoughts. 'No. I know it looks bad, but—Fay's just a confused little girl. She had an upsetting shock from Morgan three weeks ago, but I can't accept that as a reason for murder. Why now? And are we suggesting that she just happened to have a dose of cyanide in her pocket?'

'No.' Eleanor gave a rueful half-smile. 'It's funny, but people often find it difficult to dissociate their estimation of someone's capacity for evil acts from that person's physical appearance. Fay is fragile and petite, with hair like Rapunzel, so she can't possibly be involved...' Her expression became grave. 'Unfortunately, I've spoken to her myself quite recently, in Wellington Hall, and to be honest, she frightened me. There seems to be a new hardness under her usual obduracy, and I feel that Jason could well be the cause. You know Fay—malleable until someone plants an idea, then stubborn as they come. What if he's acting like a Svengali, using her, her disposition and her knowledge of the Medical School, to further his own ends? If he's been cleverly playing on both her sense of personal grievance *and* her new-found idealism, then the two together might provide sufficient motive.'

'I don't know...' Chris had to acknowledge to himself that something within Fay had repelled him recently. But frightened him? No.

Eleanor was regarding him solemnly. 'Last week, Chris, you suggested to *me* that her judgement was impaired, that Jason had undue influence. There had been some incident—to do with a photograph. I'm not asking you to tell me about it, just to remember.'

'I don't mind you knowing. What the hell? Morgan wasn't bothered, so she didn't achieve anything. It was a petty gesture: she sent him a photograph of the two of them torn down the middle. No, sorry—correction: torn through Morgan's face. But I'm sure it was just a temporary upsurge of spite.'

Eleanor sighed. 'Perhaps,' she said at length. 'You could be right. My reason for coming tonight, Chris, was to be square with you. I told Detective Sergeant Allen about Fay's visit to the lab. He asked me various things about her: her character, her friends...I was completely frank. We covered much the same ground as you and I have just covered, but I didn't offer him any theories or interpretations. If the facts support Fay as a murder suspect, the police will make all the necessary connections themselves. If they ask you about her, though, will you be honest?'

'I already have been, more or less...' His voice trailed away, and he knew from the hammering of his heart that he was on the point of divulging the shameful secret.

'You're not convinced, are you?' Eleanor was saying, her eyes still troubled. 'I don't like the idea myself, but I can't think of anything better. *Someone* murdered Morgan, someone with no soul. Chris, tell me straight: do you know something which exonerates Fay?'

Chris took a deep breath. 'No,' he said in a rush. 'Not that. But I know something else...'

When Chris finished his story, he could see that Eleanor was deeply shocked.

'I thought it would do more harm than good to speak up,' he went on as she digested the information, 'but now I'm not so sure.'

'It's horrible,' she said slowly. 'We all thought Keith committed suicide because he couldn't cope with the medical course; even though the circumstances were mysterious we felt that that was what he'd done. But Hubert's role changes everything!'

'Do I tell the police? I still don't know whether or not this is significant.'

'Oh, yes. They've got to know. Even if it was just an accident, it will tie up a loose end for them. And if it wasn't, if it *did* have any bearing on this afternoon...'

Chris suddenly found himself shuddering violently. In his mind he was once more gripping the rough bark of the chestnut tree, staring appalled through Hubert's window at the figure on the bed, only this time he recognized that the body was dead, and it wore not Keith's face, which he *had* seen, but Morgan's, which he hadn't.

'Chris?'

Keith had been dead *then;* not later, not in Sherwood Forest. Now Morgan was as cold as Keith. It was really true.

'Oh God,' he croaked, and closed his eyes.

He heard a rustle as Eleanor covered the four feet which separated them, then felt the strong circle of her arms. The lapel of her winter jacket rasped against his cheek, but behind it he could just discern the faint, warm scent of perfume on her throat. He lifted his own hands and clasped them together behind her back; the circle tightened: he wished he could be petrified right there, for ever.

'Chris,' he heard her whisper, 'may I stay here tonight?'

12

'You know, I can accept one coincidence in this tangle, but not two,' said William Bird to Montgomery at eight thirty the next morning as they walked briskly down the campus hill towards Wellington Hall.

Montgomery paused in his stride. 'That's just what I was thinking,' he said. 'There have been three events, linked in many ways, yet sufficiently different to make one wonder if the connections are spurious. Take the *modi operandi*, for instance: asphyxiation in the case of Keith Mayhew, an attempt to blow up Laszlo Kovacs with a letter-bomb, and the callous yet opportunist murder of Morgan Brunt using cyanide...they're all different! The obvious mismatch is the letter-bomb, yet if Keith's death *was* an accident, or suicide, then we're back with our two coincidences.'

He bunched his shoulders against the

dank January chill. 'I feel very strongly that Morgan's death follows one of the other two incidents. From what we've heard, he was an intelligent and popular student with no enemies except possibly a jealous girlfriend. I have to admit I'm less enthusiastic about Fay Gillingham as a possible suspect than I was yesterday. Unless she's actually unbalanced, murder by cyanide seems an extreme reaction to being disappointed in love, especially since she found someone else straight away.'

'They say a week's a long time in politics,' mused Sergeant Bird. 'I bet a lot can happen in three weeks on a university campus.' He looked around him at the long tree-lined avenue where they had stopped, at the gunmetal lake to one side and the wide stretch of dun winter grass on the other. 'It must be lovely here in spring, when everything's budding. Imagine taking your books out and sitting under that chestnut tree...'

'Yes, well,' Montgomery cut in impatiently; his sergeant was prone to making horticultural digressions. 'Returning to the new boyfriend, I wonder if we're making too much of the fact that Jason Gower has sympathies with Animal Concern, and also happens to be a chemistry student?'

'I doubt it,' said William Bird. 'It sounds

pretty damning to me.'

'But where does Keith Mayhew fit in?'

'Perhaps he doesn't. Perhaps he *is* the odd one out. Suicide for reasons best left undisclosed.'

'Don't be flippant, Will.'

'I'm not. Don't *you* think that's more likely than our unproven theories of him surprising a prospective bomber near a physiologist's home?'

'I suppose so,' Montgomery sighed. 'Damn it, this has even got me wondering again whether someone *other* than an animal rights activator might have sent that bomb to Kovacs!'

Sergeant Bird resumed his heavy stride. 'As if things weren't complicated enough... Come on, sir, let's catch the Gillingham girl unprepared and see if she can clear a way for us through this jungle.'

Fay Gillingham yawned as she opened the door, and peered at them through hollow, reddened eyes. She wore a baggy jumper over a calf-length Paisley skirt, and the remarkable hair straggled untidily across her upper torso like battered corn. Montgomery felt a pang of resigned annoyance at this first sight of his quarry: her ravaged face, whether representing grief or a late, late night, was a token of knowledge; she would confirm this, and

204

her acting abilities would not be put to the test.

'You've heard the news?' he asked after the briefest of preambles. She nodded. 'Do you mind telling me from whom?'

'I was out with my boyfriend last night,' she said in a light, childish voice. 'When we got back to his hall, Calverton, the other boys in the block told us.'

'When did you last see Morgan yourself?'

She eyed Montgomery warily, as if assessing how much he knew. 'Yesterday,' she whispered.

'What time?'

'After lunch. I tried to find him in Calverton, but he wasn't there, so I went down to the Medical School.'

'Why did you want to see him?'

This time her gaze avoided his, and applied itself to the clutter of ornaments on the window-sill. 'I suppose you know about me and Morgan,' she went on slowly. 'We were together for nearly a year, and it only went wrong recently. I was angry, and I did something rather silly. Then I regretted it. I wanted to tell him I didn't mean to be so stupid.'

'I see...but why did you choose the middle of a working day? You wouldn't get much privacy in the Medical School.'

'*That's* why I went to Calverton first, but he never came back for lunch. Why then? Because I didn't want to run into *her*, and the danger would have been too great during an evening.'

'Did you get to speak to Morgan?'

'No. Chris told me he was in the middle of an experiment, and when I found him he was lying on some chairs joking with a group of students, so I knew my timing was awful. I decided to try again another day.' Her lower lip wobbled and she bit it, almost breaking the skin, at the same time looking mournfully towards Sergeant Bird.

'Did he see you?'

'No. I crept past and left the Medical School by a back way.'

'Why?'

'Because I thought since I was at that end of the campus I might as well say hello to Jason. The Chemistry Building is just behind the Medical School.'

'At what time, exactly, did you leave the Medical School?'

Fay's face showed alarm. 'How can I tell you that? I don't know myself. It was the end of lunch—perhaps ten to two.'

'All right. Did you find Jason straight away?'

'Yes; he was working on an experiment himself. We spoke for a few minutes, then I came back to Wellington.' Her chin came up with an air of infantile defiance, an indication that, for her at least, the interview was over.

Montgomery rubbed the side of his jaw. 'Was that via the Medical School again, Fay?'

'No.'

'You're sure?'

'Absolutely. I went up behind the Trencher Building and over the hill.'

Montgomery glanced at his watch. 'If you'll excuse me for five minutes, I have to make a telephone call. I've been expecting a report.' He abruptly left the room, and William Bird smiled deprecatingly at Fay.

'I hope we're not keeping you from your lectures,' he said. 'What's your subject? Is it English?'

'Geography.'

Under the bulky overcoat his back stiffened, but he made his face assume a genial expression. 'Do they call that an Art or a Science these days?'

'A Social Science.'

'Ah. Everything seems to be high-tech now,' he mused. 'Don't they use satellites to assess crop yields and such?'

'Yes,' she answered flatly, then began to thaw. 'The course is more mathematical than I expected; we have to understand statistics, and computing.'

'Do you get much time off?'

'A reasonable amount.'

207

'That's good. Make the most of your years on this splendid campus. Are there clubs and groups for people to join?'

'Yes.' She threw the weighty curtain of hair back over her shoulder, and he saw the first flush of animation on her cheeks. 'I used to crochet table-mats in the Craft Club, but now I've joined a much more worthwhile organization: Animal Concern.'

He hadn't expected her to be so brazen. 'Aren't you afraid of getting a bad reputation from Animal Militancy?'

'Oh, no. They have their own methods, but our mission is education. Then intolerable public pressure will be put on all these cruel scientists.'

'Did Jason tell you what was going on?'

'Yes. I hadn't realized...isn't ignorance terrible! They say silence implies consent, or something like that, so once I'd heard the facts I knew I had to play my part.'

'Which is...?'

'We're working on an information leaflet. It'll be distributed all over the campus and later, I hope, in schools.'

'Have you spoken to the scientists, to get a balanced view?'

'There's no need: we *know* what they're doing. Students from all kinds of faculties have told us. The worst offender is the Medical School.' Her face fell, and she kneaded the Paisley skirt between her small fingers. 'Oh dear. For a moment I'd forgotten.'

'I'm sorry,' said Sergeant Bird. 'Were you very fond of Morgan?'

'Yes...no, more than that. For a long time, I loved him. I did, I did.'

Montgomery was waiting impatiently in the foyer. 'Did you get anything?' he asked, immediately leading the way through the stout wooden doors to avoid any possible eavesdropping, inadvertent or otherwise, from the bored-looking porter.

'Yes and no. She waxed evangelical about Animal Concern, quite spontaneously. It was odd, sir; she's got to be either hopelessly naïve or a clever little cookie. I could feel my guns being spiked before I had a chance to fire any of them. But she let slip the most important thing without realizing... You know we thought we'd heard the name Fay Gillingham before? We had. She was the girl who went to Medics' Ball last year with Keith Mayhew.'

Montgomery slapped a fist against his palm in a paroxysm of irritation. 'Of course! I knew the name was familiar, but there were so many immediate matters pressing that I couldn't bring it to mind.'

'I only remembered when she said she

was studying geography. I believe it was Colin Haslam who interviewed her in connection with the Keith Mayhew case. She was only seen the once, because her information related solely to last March.'

'Where's Colin now?'

'On leave.'

'Typical. Well, that settles it. As soon as Jackson and Smythe have reported on their interviews in the Chemistry Building, we target Fay Gillingham and Jason Gower. I don't know what they're up to, but this is where it stops!'

'Gower was in the chemistry lab for most of the afternoon,' stated Brian Jackson as the detectives met over a snatched cup of coffee two hours later. 'He was continuing an experiment he'd started in the morning. Our witness can't swear, however, that he didn't leave for a short period of time, because they all took their breaks as and when they got the chance.'

'Did they see Fay Gillingham?' asked Montgomery.

'Yes. One of them knows her by name. She came to find Jason at around quarter to two, and stayed no longer than twenty minutes. Their demeanour was serious, but this lad volunteered that Jason doesn't have a sense of humour, so that might be normal for them.'

'They were in his sight all the time?'

'Yes, then Fay left.'

'What about the cyanide?'

'There are several forms of it available in the Chemistry Building, from powders to liquids.'

'Hm. Did he see Jason hand anything to Fay during their conversation?'

'No.'

Montgomery's brow furrowed in a contemplative frown.

'Sir,' put in William Bird, 'they may have been making a rendezvous for later, while other people were taking these staggered breaks. Perhaps he supplied Fay with the poison elsewhere, or he might have done the whole thing himself, on the basis of her information. It could have taken as little as ten or twelve minutes if he was lucky to catch Morgan dozing.'

'Indeed... Where's Smythe, by the way?'

Jackson used his thumb to indicate the door. 'Just out there,' he said. 'Some student wanted a word—wouldn't talk to me. Graham's cursed with a sympathetic face.'

Almost immediately Detective Constable Smythe's sympathetic face appeared in the doorway. 'Sir,' he hissed to Montgomery, 'there's a young man here who specifically wants to speak to you.'

'I'm busy; you find out what it's about.'

'He won't say, expect that it's confidential, may or may not be relevant, and concerns Hubert Pomeroy.'

Montgomery rose from the chair in an instant, abandoning his half-drunk coffee. 'Who is this student, Graham?' he asked.

'His name's Christopher Shallet; he says you saw him yesterday.'

'I did; let him come in... Hello, Chris,' he went on as the boy hovered uncertainly on the threshold. 'I understand there's something you want to talk about. Will you join me in the corner?' He indicated a small table set apart from the rest of the room.

'No,' said Chris, very firmly.

'I could try to find a private office.'

'No; what I have to say is confidential. I don't want anyone else to hear.'

'Fair enough. What do you propose?'

'Let's walk round the lake.'

'If you like.' Montgomery reached for his coat and escorted Chris out of the Medical School, ignoring facetious mutterings from Jackson. Outside, the grey chill gnawed even more deeply; the lake and its environs looked singularly uninviting. The youth and the detective walked in slow synchrony, heads slightly lowered, hands thrust into their pockets.

They had doubled back by the time Chris finished his story, and were standing across the water from the dominant Clock Tower Buildings. A flotilla of dejected mallards paddled past as Montgomery experienced mixed emotions.

'You say Morgan told you he found something interesting under Hubert's car, but hadn't realized the significance at the time? Did he specify in any way?'

'No. I asked him if he meant a bomb, but that was a silly question: obviously, he'd have been telling Hubert, not me. He said no, then we had no further chance to speak.'

'Why have you told me this now?'

'Morgan died only hours later. It brought back all the business with Keith I've just outlined.' Chris struggled to express his complex shifts in thought. 'When Keith was found dead, none of us had any difficulty perceiving it as suicide: most people thought his academic worries had been the cause, while Morgan and I reckoned it was self-reproach for involving himself with Hubert. We couldn't see any virtue in making our knowledge public—on the contrary, it might have done a lot of harm.' He sighed. 'That probably sounds like an excuse, but it was the way we felt. We didn't imagine anything *criminal* had happened—consenting adults, and all that—but now...' He lifted his head to look squarely at Montgomery. 'I think

Keith might have died in Hubert's flat.'

'You were certain it was Keith you saw?'

'Absolutely.'

'You said the face was turned away.'

'But it was him.'

'Did he move at all?'

'No—but I only peered in for a few seconds. Light was coming from the doorway, and I was afraid Hubert would discover us.'

'Did you spot Hubert himself in the flat?'

'No.'

'Did you see him anywhere in the vicinity of Calverton that evening?'

'No. His car wasn't in its usual place; that's why we'd thought it was safe to hunt for the exam papers.'

'Hmm...how well illuminated was the part of Keith's face that you saw?'

'It was dimly lit by indirect light from the door. I couldn't see the skin colour, or anything.'

'So it's fair to conclude that you don't know whether he was dead or alive at that exact moment.'

'Yes, but—I feel now that he was dead.'

A jackdaw chacked thinly in the trees. Cold ate through Montgomery's lined greatcoat and burrowed deep into his bones. 'Thank you for your information,

214

Chris,' he said. 'I won't disclose this beyond selected colleagues unless it's strictly necessary, but you must understand that if it turns out to be pertinent, I might have to.'

Chris gave a reluctant nod. 'I know; that's why the decision to speak was hard. But if it helps you find Morgan's killer, then I did the right thing.'

Awareness of his responsibilities pressed down a little more heavily on Montgomery's shoulders. The Mayhews had been on the telephone that week, pleading with him for permission to bury Keith... now there were two corpses. Nevertheless, he attempted to reassure Chris. 'That's what we're here for,' he said.

'Phew!' whistled Jackson when he and Smythe had been told the news. 'You were right to hassle that little git Pomeroy.'

'Nothing is proven yet, remember,' warned Montgomery with some asperity; if Brian Jackson had not been already substantially involved in the Mayhew case, he would have excluded the sergeant without a qualm. 'I want absolute discretion. I can't pretend to understand what's going on, so we need data, in particular evidence of the manner in which Morgan spent yesterday morning—every minute of it if possible. We've got to identify the trigger for his death.'

Robert Allen chipped in with a cautious question. 'Do you believe the Shallet boy?'

'Yes,' said Montgomery, 'I do. He may remotely have been mistaken, but he wasn't lying.' He looked at his watch. 'You three have some lunch, then go to Calverton and try to find out how Morgan spent the first part of the morning before lectures, and also the hour between ten and eleven. Bradley Pike and Steven Listerfield should be able to help you. Or the cleaning lady, or the hall porter. Do what you can and report back before five. William and I shall carry on with enquiries in the Medical School—with especial reference to Hubert Pomeroy and his practical class.'

' 'Course I knew Morgan,' stated Owen 'Taff' Hughes, Calverton's daytime porter, in response to the question from Jackson. 'He was a great lad: one of the best. I don't understand what happened at all; they shouldn't mess about with dangerous chemicals at the Medical School.' He shook his head despondently.

Jackson decided to let that comment pass. 'When did you last see him?' he asked.

'Yesterday, man! He stood tall as that doorway there. It's as if a great oak has been chopped down by mistake.'

'What time was this?'

'Why, let me see... The post must have been because I gave him the parcel. I'd say ten o'clock. No, maybe quarter-past. The middle of the morning, anyhow.'

'Did he say anything unusual, or act out of character?'

'No, he was breezy as ever.'

'So you just gave him a parcel, and that was that.'

'Pretty much.'

'Did you see where he went to when he'd left you?'

'Well, no, but I imagine it was straight to D block, because he thought Jason might be in.'

'Jason?' Brian Jackson leaned ominously across the desk towards the porter. 'What's this about a Jason? Do you mean Jason Gower?'

'That's him. The parcel was his, see, but it was cluttering up the foyer here, so Morgan offered to take it to D block.'

'Describe this package.'

'Well...it was bulky, well packed but beginning to split at one end...brown paper, a Bristol postmark...' He shrugged. 'Nothing remarkable.'

'Thank you,' said Jackson brusquely. 'What number is Mr Gower's room?'

'D6.'

Jackson turned to go, but Smythe

lingered to address the porter himself. 'What's your opinion of Jason Gower?' he asked. 'Are we likely to get a friendly reception?'

'No...I'd watch your step with him. He's a dark one: secretive. Not like Morgan; you should have seen him play rugby—he was an inspired forward. His mother was Welsh, see, so he might have been allowed to play for the national team eventually...*that* would have lifted them out of the doldrums. It's a tragedy...' They left him to his doleful reminiscences, his jowls drooping like a St Bernard dog, and angled smartly across the quadrangle to D block.

'He won't be in,' predicted Smythe as Jackson's knock echoed throughout the stairwell.

'We'll make sure first...' Jackson hammered even more loudly, and they heard a furtive rustle on the other side of the door. Moments later the lock disengaged with a click; a slightly built young man stood in front of them, the sleeves of his tatty denim shirt rolled up, veiled hostility in his stance.

'No need to shake the block to pieces,' he said. 'Who are you? What do you want?'

'CID,' said Jackson, treating their suspect

to a glimpse of the unflattering picture on his warrant card.

'Again? Are you with that Bayliss chap, or is this something different?'

'Your neighbour,' said Smythe with unexpected harshness, 'Morgan Brunt. Have you heard what happened to him yesterday.'

'Of course.'

'Then you won't be surprised to hear that we're speaking to anyone who knew him, however superficially. We're trying to piece together his movements yesterday morning, and we understand that he came to bring you a parcel.'

'That's right; we met on the stairs and he handed it over.'

'Did you speak for long?'

'No; I just said thanks.'

'What was in the parcel?'

'Mind your own business.'

'It's better if you answer, sir,' said Jackson with undertones of menace.

'It was a winter woollie from my great-aunt, but I still don't see why you need to know that.'

'Where does your great-aunt live?'

Jason Gower's eyes flickered with a brief suspicion. 'Bristol,' he said after a pause.

A door clanged on the ground floor. 'Look, sir, may we come in?' asked Jackson. 'We have some more questions which could be described as delicate.'

'I was *trying* to get my lab report finished,' grumbled Jason, retreating into the room with an ill grace.

'I'm sure we appreciate the sacrifice of your time,' said Jackson, who could quell his innate vulgarity and emulate the smoothness of Montgomery when he chose. He strode to the desk and scrutinized the papers there. They did indeed relate to laboratory data, but bore signs of having been scattered randomly across the surface for appearance's sake, perhaps minutes earlier.

'You said you had some questions,' said Jason, tapping his foot.

'That's right. We wanted to ask about your girlfriend, Fay Gillingham. She came to visit you at the lab yesterday, so we've been told.'

'So? Is it a crime?'

'Not at all, but we'd like to know the substance of your conversation.'

'I don't believe this! Are you serious?'

'Please answer the question.'

'God knows; it was some general waffle.'

'Mr Gower, why should Fay take the trouble of seeking you out in the Chemistry Building just to speak "general waffle"?'

'You tell me. You know what women are like. I could have done without the interruption.'

Jackson sighed. 'Did she mention Morgan Brunt at all?'

'Yes. She was rambling about a photograph she wished she hadn't given him. I really wasn't listening.'

'Are you and Fay very close?'

'We screw, if that's what you mean.'

Jackson abandoned his own attempts to be subtle. 'Obviously, she got together with you on the rebound from Morgan,' he said rudely, 'but perhaps you can tell me how you met?'

'We have common interests,' said Jason with a shrug, 'and I'd seen her around anyway.'

'Animal Concern.'

'That, and other things. Have you asked all your questions now? Do you mind if I get on with some work?'

'Very shortly... May we see the wrapper of your parcel, please?'

'I'm afraid not. I threw it away yesterday; you can't keep clutter in a room this size.'

'The letter, then. Your great-aunt must have sent a covering note.'

'Ditto. Dear Sarah is quite dotty, and her writing resembles the tracks of an inebriated crab.'

'Can't say I've met one of those. I suppose you didn't throw the jumper away?'

'No. It's in here.' Jason opened a drawer and pulled out a chunky russet pullover, hand-knitted in Shetland wool. Whatever the calligraphic deficiencies of the sender, the knitting was deftly done.

Jackson nodded. 'Do you mind if we have a little look round the rest of your room, sir?'

Tension was palpable in the air as Jason made up his mind what attitude to adopt. 'I do mind,' he said quietly, 'and I dare say you have no search warrant. But I also imagine that if I refuse you'll draw your own conclusions.'

'That is a possibility, sir.'

'You can drop the "sir". I know it sticks in your craw. Go on, then.' He gestured expansively with his right arm. 'Search away!'

Jackson and Smythe complied with brevity and little heart: the student had acquiesced too easily, which probably meant there was nothing to find.

'Just one last question,' said Smythe with simulated carelessness as they prepared to leave. 'Did you see anyone acting suspiciously in the Medical School yesterday?'

'Now what would give you the idea that I was in the Medical School?' asked Jason with an unpleasant leer. 'I never went near the place.'

'Not even to use it as a cut-through?'

'Not even to use it as a cut-through.'

'Thank you for your time,' Jackson said gravely.

Jason Gower snorted. 'I won't say you're welcome.'

Montgomery was concerned when he heard the story nearly two hours later.

'You should have either left him alone, or torn the room apart from top to bottom,' he said. He walked to the window of the small, overheated library and stared thoughtfully at the rolling campus beyond; a freezing fog was developing as the light faded, and the windows of distant buildings glimmered ever more hazily. 'There's no choice,' he continued, 'we'll have to get a warrant tonight. In the mean time, D block must be kept under surveillance.'

'From outside?' gasped Smythe.

'Of course from outside. There's plenty of cover in the quadrangle; if you see Gower leaving the block with barrow-loads of stuff, you know what to do.' He reached for the telephone. 'I want Jack Bayliss in on the search. I suspect he's not going to be too pleased about this.'

At ten o'clock exactly, Jason Gower's study-bedroom was expertly ransacked.

Its occupant remained serene and philosophical throughout. Not even a pamphlet was found. Half a mile away Fay Gillingham stood tearful as her den in Wellington Hall was similarly combed. Aside from a modest collection of anti-vivisectionist literature, the searchers' haul was little better.

13

'Today we concentrate on Hubert Pomeroy,' decreed Montgomery as his detectives gathered round for a briefing the next morning. He allowed his gaze to rest frostily on Jackson and Smythe before continuing: 'We'll keep a low profile at first, and see what we can build up against him from the evidence of witnesses. Already we know that he was intermittently absent from MDL2 during the afternoon of the murder, so he had opportunity. Christopher Shallet's story hints at a motive: did Morgan discover something to connect Pomeroy with the death of Keith Mayhew? Perhaps Morgan challenged Pomeroy in the Medical School, and desperate measures were called for...

'There's the question of Pomeroy's car.

Christopher said that he and Morgan considered it safe to break into the flat because the car wasn't in Calverton's car-park—yet the flat had at least one occupant, Keith Mayhew. We have it on record that Pomeroy was seen by witnesses driving away from the car-park just before seven that night, a time when Keith was known to be still in his room. So what happened then? Did he come back from a short trip, find the car-park full and put his vehicle elsewhere? Unlikely, since there tends to be extra space at weekends. Did he take a short trip, then deliberately park in an unusual place in order to give the impression that he was out? Perhaps he didn't want to be disturbed... Or did he not even leave the vicinity of Calverton, but simply park round a corner and return surreptitiously to the block? Remember it had long been dark by seven o'clock.

'We have another possibility which might explain the discrepancy: supposing Keith was already in the habit of visiting Pomeroy? He might have been given his own key... So perhaps Pomeroy *was* out when Morgan and Christopher saw Keith, and Keith was simply inside waiting. Christopher couldn't be certain if he was dead or alive when they spotted him in the bedroom around nine thirty.

'Now, nine fifteen is the time of the

225

restaurant booking; we know that a table was reserved at Ben Bowers in the name of Pomeroy. Two people did eat there that night, but we have no real proof that one of them *was* Hubert Pomeroy. All we can say is that it is likely.

'So where does this leave us? Frobisher was only able to place the time of death within broad limits, namely between seven and eleven o'clock. Pomeroy drove away before seven, but may have returned quite promptly. However, we know from stomach contents analysis that Keith hadn't eaten for several hours before he died, so it seems unlikely that *he* accompanied Pomeroy to Ben Bowers, unless he had no appetite when he got there.'

'When was the booking made?' asked Robert Allen, his eyes sharp and interested.

'Tuesday. It's a popular venue.' Montgomery regarded all his officers in turn. 'Does anyone have any points they wish to raise?'

Smythe raised his hand a few inches, flushing. 'Sir, I—I'm not quite sure what we're suggesting here. Say we prove that Dr Pomeroy could have been in his flat at the appropriate time, and could have murdered Keith. What motive did he have, and why didn't he hide the body properly?'

'Perhaps it was an accident,' proposed

Jackson. 'You know—little games with Keith that got too rough. Then he panicked and just wanted to get the body away from his patch.'

'I accept that,' said Smythe, 'but if the first death was an accident, why was the second one so cold-blooded? We're postulating that the two are connected, but it seems wrong *psychologically.*'

Jackson wrinkled his nose. 'I don't know,' he said. 'Once you're on the slippery slope, you'll do anything to protect yourself if the stakes are high enough.'

'He's forty and an ordinary lecturer,' commented Allen. 'Before he came here he worked in London, at the same level. I wonder why he made the move?'

'That's one of many things we need to find out,' agreed Montgomery. 'Will you take that on, Robert? Brian and Graham—I'd like you to try and track down sightings of that car, and also examine its underside as discreetly as you can. William and I shall see if any of Pomeroy's immediate neighbours remembers hearing cries or sounds of violence coming from the flat on the night in question...I must say, though, that after seven weeks the chances are slender.'

Hubert Pomeroy's flat was, like D block, in

the mellow, ivy-clad portion of Calverton Hall. To one side were locked storage rooms full of old furniture, but the other abutting rooms housed resident students.

Montgomery knocked softly on the door of the appropriate first-floor room. The name 'Dez' was splashed across it amid a collage of racy posters. Montgomery was not sanguine about the likelihood of success; the other residents had been so far either absent or unhelpful.

'Come in,' called a casual voice. He entered with Sergeant Bird to find three young men lounging around the study with their books, one tipped back on a hard chair, his trainer-clad feet planted solidly on the desk.

'Are you, Dez?' Montgomery addressed the owner of the feet.

'That's me. What can I do you for?' Under an upswept thicket of blond-streaked hair the student looked vaguely curious at the advent of two middle-aged visitors.

'We're from the CID: Detective Inspector Montgomery, Detective Sergeant Bird. Could we have a few minutes of your time?'

Startled and embarrassed, Dez dropped his feet to the ground and sat erect in the chair. 'If it's about the poor guy from D block, we don't know anything.'

'It's true that we're gathering evidence concerning that incident,' said Montgomery, 'but we were also involved with the death of Keith Mayhew seven weeks ago, and that's our focus of interest today. We have received information indicating that he was in this block on the Saturday night before he was found dead in Sherwood Forest. Did you know him by sight?'

They all shook their heads. 'Not really,' said Dez. 'We'd seen him around the hall, but we didn't even know his name until his picture appeared in the paper.'

'Were you in this room that night?'

He looked ominously vague. 'Probably. I wanted to get some written work finished before Christmas, so I was here most weekends.'

'You say you'd seen Keith "around the hall". Did you *ever* see him in this block?'

'Not that I can remember.'

Definitely uphill work, thought Montgomery. 'Dr Pomeroy, one of the tutors, lives above you, doesn't he?'

Dez pulled a face. 'Doesn't he just. Any music over ten decibels and he's down here knocking on the door. But if *he* wants to play his Noel Coward classics, then that's all right.'

'We have information that there may have been a disturbance in Dr Pomeroy's flat on the night we were talking about. Did you hear anything from this room?'

'Oh, it was *that* Saturday, was it? Yes, I heard a sort of scuffle, then a loud thump. I thought he'd dropped a book from a high shelf, or fallen over himself.'

'Did you go up to enquire?'

'No; he doesn't welcome interference. He looked all right when I saw him the next day, so I ventured a joke. I said something like, "Were you having a boxing match last night?", but he just glared and told me to mind my own business.'

'He didn't ask what you meant?'

'No.'

'Did he say he'd been out?'

'No.'

'What time did you hear the sounds?' This was all so hopeful that Montgomery hardly dared expect precision.

'Lateish,' said Dez after a pause for thought. 'Nine, or not long after. I always knocked off work to go to the bar at half-past.'

'You're sure?'

Another pause. 'Definitely.'

Hallelujah!

'No one recalls seeing Pomeroy's Renault in the vicinity of Calverton after seven that night,' supplied Smythe a few hours later, 'but we did get one positive result.

We examined the underside of the car ourselves, as you suggested, sir—and this is what we found.' He drew from his pocket a transparent bag containing a nondescript-looking mulch, and passed it across the table.

Montgomery peered inside. 'Twigs,' he said slowly. 'Leaves.'

'They were impacted under the front nearside wheel-arch.'

'So?'

Sergeant Bird leaned forward. 'They're *oak* leaves,' he said.

'He could have picked them up any time, anywhere.'

'There aren't so many places where tracks might be so narrow that a bunch like that gets caught up under your car.'

'The ground was frozen,' said Montgomery. 'That's why there were no tracks.'

'Yes, but that wouldn't affect the undergrowth, and anything which had fallen into it.'

'We'll never prove these are from Sherwood Forest.'

Sergeant Bird met Jackson's look with a wicked eye. 'No, but Hubert Pomeroy doesn't know that, does he?'

'I don't know why you keep asking to see me!' expostulated Hubert, his whispery voice quavering with suppressed rage. 'How am I supposed to get on with any work? Professor Byrne isn't here, and Laszlo Kovacs is doing little enough to cover the gap!'

'I'm sorry,' said Montgomery, not sounding at all contrite. 'We have some supplementary questions regarding the recent student death.'

'But I've told you *everything I know* about Mr Brunt,' hissed Hubert. 'Everything!'

'Oh? That's very thorough of you. But I wasn't referring to Mr Brunt. I was talking about Keith Mayhew.'

They all saw the horror leap into Hubert's pale eyes. The tic in his cheek immediately ignited, so uncontrollably that he had to press against it with three of his fingers to quell the arcing muscles.

'We'd like to know,' went on Montgomery, 'how your car managed to pick up half of Sherwood Forest in its front nearside wheel-arch.'

Hubert swallowed, speechless for several seconds before he gasped, 'I went to the Visitor Centre to look at the Robin Hood exhibition—just before Christmas.'

'What an odd time of year to choose. Perhaps you've got a leaflet to show us?'

'I don't keep things like that.'

'That's unfortunate.' Montgomery said nothing further, but subjected Hubert to his most glacial stare, reducing the physiologist to a pitiable state of agitation.

'What is it you want from me?' he asked, almost in tears before groping for the familiar prop of anger. 'I'm here, aren't I? Ask your bloody questions! Get on with it!'

'You told us you went out with a friend to Ben Bowers restaurant on Saturday, December the twelfth—that is, the night before Keith Mayhew was found dead. In the light of new evidence, we need you to be more precise about your movements that evening from, say, six o'clock onwards.'

Hubert was pale, but still fighting. 'I decline to speak,' he said thickly. 'This is a charade.'

'Dr Pomeroy...' Montgomery leaned forward earnestly. 'If you were in town as you claim, it will help you immeasurably—but we must have details, and the names of people who can vouch for you.'

'Why, just because you've found a few twigs?'

'No.' Montgomery's voice was very soft.

Hubert visibly stiffened.

'We have information from a witness that Keith Mayhew spent part or all of that Saturday evening in your flat,' went on Montgomery.

Something seemed to die in Hubert's face. 'It's a lie,' he muttered tonelessly. 'It's a damned lie.'

'Then tell us the truth.'

Hubert paused, his sunken eyes fixed to the desk in a gaze of dull torment. 'I can't.'

'Just your movements from six o'clock.'

Another pause, then a cynical snort. 'All right. Much good it'll do either of us... At six I was having a bath in my flat. At five to seven I drove into town and parked in the multi-storey behind Maid Marion Way. I met a friend by appointment in the Playhouse bar, where we had drinks for the next hour and a half, before walking up to Canning Circus where Ben Bowers is. We had our meal, then went on to a club. I had a nightcap at my friend's place, then drove back alone to Calverton in the small hours.' Hubert raised his head and gave a bitter smile. 'Was that what you wanted?'

'The gist,' said Montgomery neutrally, 'but it can't be verified without the details. Will you give us the name of your friend?'

'No; it's out of the question.'

'We might be able to keep this confidential.'

'I said no!'

'What about the name of the club?'

'Likewise. We aren't members anyway.'

A lie, thought Montgomery immediately. Whatever else might have been false, that certainly was.

'What time did you return to Calverton?'

234

'Around two o'clock.'

'Was Keith Mayhew in your flat?'

'I'm not answering any more questions.'

'Did Keith have a key? Was he there, waiting for you?'

Terror flared in Hubert's eyes. 'No more!' he shrieked. 'No more! Arrest me if you have to, but I'll say nothing!'

They could smell his sweat, the sour sharp scent of fear, but Montgomery found that his store of compassion remained resolutely padlocked. 'We aren't arresting anyone,' he said, 'but it's our duty to see if the allegations can be substantiated. I have a warrant here which gives us due licence to search your residence in Calverton Hall, including your personal possessions. Officers will accompany you to the flat now in order to effect this search; I'm sure you appreciate that your cooperation will make things easier for everyone.'

Hubert Pomeroy sat stricken and mute.

'Sergeant Bird is still up there with the forensic biologist,' said Jackson to Montgomery some hours later. 'They're taking fibre samples from the carpet, the bed, the settee—everything.'

'And the car?'

'Especially the car.'

'Good,' said Montgomery. The forensic results might well produce vital proof linking Keith Mayhew with Pomeroy's flat and the Renault. In the mean time, though, there were great gaps in the circumstantial evidence which needed to be filled.

'You got me in trouble with Bayliss regarding your handling of Jason Gower,' he continued conversationally.

'Oh?'

'Big trouble,' confirmed Montgomery. 'So now it's time for your penance.'

'I don't believe in penances,' said Jackson hastily.

'Ah. Well, I always think it's the very people who don't believe in them who have most need of them...so here's your brief: I want you to take Graham Smythe to the Lynx Club tonight, and see if anyone can remember seeing Hubert Pomeroy on December the twelfth.'

'The Lynx Club?' echoed Jackson, his face twisting in disgust. 'That's Vice Squad territory. We can't go there!'

'Yes, you can. Here's a photograph of Pomeroy I got from Security. Use it to find out who his friend is, then we can work backwards and see if the friend confirms the Ben Bowers alibi.'

'Why the Lynx Club?'

'Chris Shallet mentioned it. Apparently Morgan Blunt went to the club once for a lark, and saw Hubert there—hearsay, of course, at this stage, but *you* can turn it into solid evidence. I gather they open at ten, so why don't you and Graham have a few hours off, first?'

'Mind your backs, won't you!' chortled DC Grange as Jackson clumped mutinously out of the room. The gesture he received in return was not inappropriate.

' "Lynx" is a play on words,' murmured Smythe that night as they approached the club's green neon sign, a garish illumination in an otherwise darkly sinister alleyway between tall buildings. 'I've been doing some research: it's a club for gays to meet and form couples—forge links, you see?'

'It's also a haven for rent-boys,' growled Jackson. 'Let's make this as quick as possible.'

They bypassed two Neanderthal bouncers with a flash of ID, traversed a narrow lobby and found themselves in a cavernous room decorated almost entirely in black and silver. At one end, a barman stood idly wiping glasses while a handful of clients sat at nearby tables sipping their drinks; at the other end, the deserted dance-floor gleamed beneath an assortment of strangely shaped objects: with grudging amusement Jackson identified them as gauntlets and suits of chain-mail—another, less subtle connotation for 'links'.

They sidled up to the bar, and the warrant card was again quickly aired, the barman's craggy features remaining imperturbable throughout.

'We'd appreciate your help in trying to trace the movements of this man,' said Jackson in a confident voice, exchanging his warrant card for the picture of Hubert Pomeroy. 'Were you working here in the middle of December?'

'Maybe.'

'Can't you remember?'

'I said maybe.'

'I see... Well, we have reason to believe that he came here at least once during December with a friend—on a Saturday night. Do you recognize him?'

'We get lots of people in on a Saturday,' said the barman, continuing his polishing and barely glancing at the photograph.

'Is he a member?' persisted Jackson.

'It's not for me to say.'

'But have you seen his face here?' Jackson was keeping his own cool with some difficulty.

'Maybe.'

'You're not being very helpful.'

The man leaned forward. Jackson suddenly became aware of his height, the truculent jaw, the breadth of his shoulders, the gnarled fists—not only gnarled, but tattooed...

'Listen,' said the man. 'We don't want trouble. People come here to be themselves, you understand?'

'There won't be any trouble for the club,' said Jackson, resisting the urge to step back a pace. 'We just want a few words with his friend, that's all...'

While Jackson was engaged in increasingly fruitless conversation, Graham Smythe nervously assessed the clientele. It was well before pub-closing time, hence the club's sparse occupancy, but the handful of people here probably represented a reasonable cross-section. Two men sat together, all bared chests, leather and manacles. One wore a lot of make-up. Another couple entered from the lobby: without much surprise Smythe discerned that in this club chain-mail didn't only hang from the ceiling. At one of the tables a thin, pale youth watched the doorway with an aura of mock casualness, taking shallow puffs from a cigarette. By the bar a man of fifty-five or so watched the youth in his turn.

Smythe was just craning his neck to see what sort of musical arrangements the place had when the man at the bar caught his eye. He held out his glass, nodded towards it and raised his eyebrows at Smythe. The detective was horrified and embarrassed. He shook his head, but the

239

man winked encouragingly at him and began to move closer, along the bar.

Smythe turned and clutched Jackson's arm, interrupting a sentence in mid-flow and making him jump violently. 'Don't *do* that!' snapped Jackson. The man was now barely five feet away, advancing with gleaming eyes and a moist smile on his loose-lipped mouth. Desperate, Smythe held out his own warrant card like a shield, then swung round to involve himself in Jackson's increasingly testy interrogation of the barman.

Jackson had resorted to threats. 'That young lad over there,' he was saying. 'I suppose he gives you backhanders so he's got a nice dry place to work from?'

'We don't comment on individual clients,' said the barman distantly.

'One pick-up and he won't be the only one in schtuck,' snarled Jackson.

'No,' broke in Smythe, firmly, 'there won't be trouble for the club. That was our undertaking.' He looked straight into the barman's face. 'We're investigating a very serious crime,' he said. 'It didn't take place near here, and the man in the photograph may not have been involved. His friend is entirely free from suspicion. So, you see, if we can only find out who the friend is, we might through him be able to eliminate our man from the enquiry altogether. We have no interest in the club beyond that.'

The barman pursed his lips consideringly, and flexed his scarred knuckles. 'All right...' he said at last. 'I might be able to find someone who knows something...'

Jackson and Smythe escaped two hours later with headaches and a valuable lead. Smythe's admirer had long since bolted, but strains of a Queen hit pursued them out into the alleyway, where rain fell drearily from the blackness above and clones of the green sign glared up at them from a matrix of spreading puddles.

'That bastard Montgomery!' said Jackson quietly.

'I wonder if the barman would have taken a bribe from *us,*' mused Smythe.

'He might, but Mr Holier-than-Thou would never have sanctioned it.' Even if you'd kept your mouth shut, young Graham. 'That bastard Montgomery!' he repeated.

'Well done,' said Montgomery the next morning. 'You've got the boy's name and description, and he comes regularly to the club on Thursdays...there's your next bit of overtime.'

'Did Forensic find anything in the flat?' asked Jackson.

'Nothing obvious, but of course the tests will take days. In the mean time,

241

we concentrate on all relevant aspects of Pomeroy that we can think of. We've enough manpower to make a clean sweep—unless something else happens.'

14

Anna Kovacs saw the muted glow of the landing light as she slowed her car preparatory to turning into the driveway. Good! Laszlo must be home. They could potter in the kitchen together while she chopped vegetables for the meal, and share some of the minutiae of their respective days.

She pulled on the handbrake, switched off the headlamps and climbed out of the vehicle, reaching across to the passenger seat for her bag of books. Most of the class had managed to attend tonight's German lesson, even though it had been held an hour earlier than usual. They were a keen group, she had found, despite their widely differing backgrounds and abilities. Adults were in some ways more rewarding to teach than children; they had actually chosen the subject themselves, not had it forced upon them. Conversely, however, it was difficult to insist that a rugged construction engineer hand in his homework on time!

Locking the car, Anna approached the front door, her lips curving into a reminiscent smile at the thought of Mrs Westerley, a large, well-travelled lady who had decided to polish up her German in anticipation of a forthcoming trip to Koblenz. She had confided to the class an unfortunate gaffe from a previous holiday bedevilled by rain: striding into the shoe department of a store, she had demanded *gummiboots,* not realizing that *boot* in fact meant 'boat'. The mystified staff had been unable to provide her with rubber dinghies.

Yes, thought Anna, they were nice people. She was always sorry when the summer term ended and they went their separate ways.

She closed the front door behind her and walked to the foot of the stairs, where the hall was partially illuminated by the light from above. 'Laszlo?' she called. A faint creak sounded on the upper floor, but there was no reply.

She climbed a few stairs and called again; the silence persisted.

Bemused, Anna stood still for a moment. She *knew* Laszlo was near, yet why wasn't he answering? A stealthy scraping sound from the landing increased her puzzlement before the light was suddenly extinguished. An explosion near her shoulder made her gasp. Running feet thundered down the stairs; something heavy slammed into her, wiping her grip from the banister and sending her crashing into the hall. Her head struck the telephone table: fireworks seared through her brain.

Anna stirred. It was dark, quiet—and very cold. A vicious draught snaked across the hall floor, coiling round her ankles, nipping at the hem of her skirt: the front door was ajar. Hooking her fingers into the carpet's rough pile, Anna cautiously heaved herself into a crouching position before pausing, head down, gripped by vertiginous nausea.

Outside, a car with a familiar engine note was approaching the house; as it slowed and swung into the drive, a bar of light from the headlamps momentarily flashed through the open doorway and lay across the hall.

Laszlo...

When an agitated Laszlo ushered them into the warm sitting-room, Montgomery and Sergeant Bird were relieved to see that Anna, though pale, looked both *compos mentis* and unbowed.

'Mild concussion, that is all,' she said in

response to their enquiry. 'I have a thick skull.'

Montgomery accepted the seat he was offered. 'Tell us everything,' he said.

When Anna had finished, he painstakingly examined the hallway and staircase; tiny fragments of glass were scattered over the lower stairs. 'It wasn't an explosion Anna heard,' he commented to Laszlo, 'it was an implosion. Someone threw a light bulb at the wall here—to destroy fingerprints, I would guess.' Carefully they climbed to the landing and found, as expected, a side-light deprived of its bulb. 'Your intruder either didn't know where the switch was, or he didn't want Anna using the switch in the hall,' Montgomery reasoned.

'He got in at the back,' said Laszlo as they returned to the ground floor. 'He forced the french doors to the dining-room.' The detectives appraised the damage as he held aside a heavy velvet curtain: it was a crude, unprofessional job.

They sat down again with Anna, and Montgomery thought over the details of her story. 'Your German class was an hour early,' he said. 'Why?'

'Oh, they needed the building for a conference. This happens about once a year.'

'I see. Did anything seem unusual to you when you drove back to the house?'

'No. The landing light was on, so I assumed Laszlo was home. He puts his car in the garage; I always park where the driveway widens. When I went inside, everything still seemed normal. It's as if something was reassuring me...' She turned towards Laszlo, her expression oddly speculative. 'Forgive me, my dear, but even when I was knocked down, instinct was still telling me that the person was *you*...'

'There must be a reason for this,' said Montgomery crisply as Laszlo gasped at his wife. 'Did you glimpse a coat like Laszlo's, perhaps—or hear a similar cough?'

She frowned in puzzlement. 'No.'

'The footfalls?'

'No.'

'What about a scent? Cigars? Aftershave?'

Her handsome face lit up. ' "Endeavour"!' she cried. 'That was it! How clever you are, Inspector.' She turned to Laszlo and laid a spontaneous hand on his knee. 'I could smell your aftershave, so I was sure you were in the house.'

'Is that the type you habitually wear?' asked Montgomery.

'Yes,' affirmed Laszlo.

'Do you know anyone else who uses it?'

The physiologist gave a wry smile. 'Many people. There was a promotion in the Union shop at Sherwood last year, and both staff and students took advantage of this. It is a nice tangy fragrance.'

'Does Dr Pomeroy, perhaps?'

'I don't recall... No, I'm not sure. When you wear something yourself it is harder to discern on others.'

'Surely the scent doesn't last all day?' Montgomery turned back to Anna.

'No,' she answered, 'but when Laszlo comes home he washes his face and sometimes re-applies the aftershave.'

Montgomery slowly nodded. Anna watched him, her mouth firm, her eyes blue and clear. 'Inspector,' she continued, 'do you think this was meant to be another attack on Laszlo?'

'I do,' he said frankly.

'That is what we thought... Is this the work of animal activists? Do you have any idea at all who is behind it?'

'The straight answer is we don't know.' Montgomery addressed them both. 'That letter-bomb had all the hallmarks of Animal Militancy, and at least one student on campus is under suspicion. But we have also had reason to focus our enquiries on one of your colleagues: Hubert Pomeroy. Could he have any possible motive for harming you?'

The two Hungarians were clearly taken aback. 'Hubert?' echoed Laszlo faintly.

'Yes. Do you stand in his way professionally, perhaps, or—do you know something about his personal life which he might consider incriminating?' Montgomery mentally held his breath as he watched the consternation on Laszlo's face transmute into concentration. He knew it was much to hope for, the possession of secret knowledge by Laszlo, but the prize was inestimable: the potential linkage of four disparate events.

It was Anna who answered him. 'The Lynx Club,' she said steadily; Montgomery wondered if Sergeant Bird's startled face mirrored his own.

'Anna...' Laszlo remonstrated, but without much conviction.

'We have been asked, so we shall tell what we know.' Her chin rose. 'At the beginning of December, Laszlo and I went into town for a meal,' she said to Montgomery. 'On our way back to the car-park we took a short-cut through a narrow street which turned out to be most unsalubrious. A club was situated half-way down; it had a green sign. From an upper window there came music and ribald laughter. We tried to pass by quickly, because two drunken couples were arguing in the doorway—four men. As if to confirm

248

our sudden insight, two more men emerged from the club, entwined like lovers. We both recognized that one was Hubert Pomeroy.'

'Did he see you?'

'No; at least, we thought not. He was too—engrossed.'

'Dr Kovacs, has Dr Pomeroy given you any reason to feel that he knows you spotted him that night?'

Laszlo seemed to sag. 'I told him myself,' he said. 'I felt it was only—fair—to give him a friendly warning.' He spread his hands in appeal. 'He is a tutor to the boys in Calverton! I suggested he reside away from the campus...'

'How did he receive this advice?'

'Badly. He felt it was none of my business.'

'Did you discuss the matter with any other members of staff?'

'No. I didn't want to make trouble for Hubert. I wanted to give him time to see for himself that the situation was undesirable.'

'So you promised him secrecy?'

Laszlo nodded heavily. 'I did.'

Anna moved the bedroom curtain aside and looked at the squad car in the dark street below. The dining-room window was now boarded up, and all the bolts in the house had been engaged. 'They are still there,' she said in comfortable tones. 'Do come to bed, dear.'

Laszlo paused in his restless pacing. 'Not yet. You should have agreed to go to hospital. What if an extradural haemorrhage develops?'

'I'd rather stay here with you. Hospitals are all fuss and noise.'

'But there is danger here!' His face contorted, and he clenched his fists. 'God, Anna, it's me they want. Why don't you leave until it's over? They will find a way.'

The wildness of his tone chilled her heart. 'Who are "they", Laszlo?' she asked. 'Blinkered students desperate for a sense of purpose? Are you afraid of *them?*'

The chill deepened as she waited for a reply.

'No,' he said at last. 'It is the old enemy; I feel it. Escape was an illusion...we have never been really free.'

A sense of irony and bitter nostalgia clamped her throat, but she lashed at him with all the energy she could muster. 'Laszlo, this is paranoia. The enemy you speak of *no longer exists,* except in your mind. Like the Stasi they are gone, and the events of long ago are forgotten.'

'Simon Wiesenthal does not share your concept of time.'

'Laszlo—there is no connection! He seeks cold-blooded killers; we were freedom-fighters, embroiled in the violence and heat of a one-sided war.'

'They have their ways,' he went on as if she hadn't spoken. 'Secret police murdered Georgi Markov with a poisoned umbrella—they inserted a pellet containing the plant toxin ricin into his thigh.'

'That was 1978,' she retorted. 'We still had a Cold War then. Markov broadcast openly from the West against the communists of Bulgaria. You, Laszlo, are happily much less important. You take no political stance here, and neither do I. Listen...why don't we *both* go away for a while? Let us visit Agota in Paris.'

'I cannot leave until Professor Byrne returns.'

'When is that—next week? Then we'll go next week. What do you say?' Her eager smile belied the deep anxiety she felt for Laszlo. He was cracking up; long-buried nightmares were distorting his judgement, threatening to overwhelm him, destroying him as surely as if that letter-bomb had exploded. Her head began to ache again in earnest; the effect of the painkillers was wearing off.

'Very well,' said Laszlo at last. 'If Inspector Montgomery agrees, we shall go.'

'Are you going to give the Kovacses permission to leave?' asked Sergeant Bird when he heard of the proposal.

'Yes,' said Montgomery, 'but they can't go as far as Paris. They're important witnesses, and we need access to them.' He toyed irritably with his pen; on the other side of the scales hung Laszlo's physical and mental welfare, permeating all Montgomery's thoughts with a sense of urgency. 'I've asked Laszlo to keep quiet about last night's incident among his immediate colleagues. If Pomeroy was involved, he might just blurt something out; at the very least he'll be puzzled. I'm hoping Forensic will come up with something very soon, then we can take him in.'

'Supposing they don't?' tendered Jackson through a mouthful of coffee.

'That's what I like, positive thinking.' Montgomery sighed. 'We'll be in deep water. Pomeroy is the only person who fits the bill for *all* the crimes, whereas the Animal Militants seem to have no connection at all with Keith Mayhew. If Keith had found them planting a bomb at Pomeroy's flat and been silenced, I can think of no reason whatsoever why Pomeroy shouldn't have informed us himself. However sordid his own alibi, divulging it would still be preferable to being suspected of murder.' He looked round at his detectives, all present except Robert Allen, who was in London, and invited their comments. 'Are we missing something?' he asked. 'Are there other people we should be investigating?'

'I've wondered about the Hepworth woman,' said DC Grange. 'She was linked with Morgan Blunt, and she's from eastern Europe, like Dr Kovacs.'

'True enough. But she was the one who warned him about the letter-bomb.'

'I know. I thought perhaps it was a clever trick to throw us all off the scent.'

'Interesting idea...but how do we connect her with Keith Mayhew and Pomeroy's flat?'

'Her car was out of service over that weekend,' remembered Sergeant Bird.

'Anyone can hire a car,' said Jackson. 'Neither Jason Gower nor Fay Gillingham has their own transport, but I wouldn't exclude them on those grounds.'

'What about Michael Chan?' put in Smythe. 'We've said before how the Physiology Department seems to be the hub of these incidents: shouldn't *all* Laszlo Kovac's colleagues be put under the microscope? There could be any number of dark grudges simmering away within the department itself.'

Montgomery gave a tight smile; lack of ideas was certainly not a problem, but streamlining the investigation was. 'I think we're agreed that Laszlo is the current target for our killer,' he said, 'and the points about the other physiologists are well made. Our best approach, then, is to re-examine the letter-bomb incident, see what people's reactions were to this attempt on Laszlo's life, and find out exactly how each of them spent that day. Some of this is ground already covered by Jack Bayliss, but he took the Animal Militancy angle from the beginning. Our perspective will be different, so who knows? Maybe we'll strike lucky.'

'Yes, I still remember that day,' said Magda Hepworth, folding her hands across her lap and giving Montgomery her full attention. 'Very clearly...every detail. I have never been so close to a bomb before.'

'Tell us what you, did—from the morning onwards.'

'That is easy. I was lecturing until eleven, then I went up to the lab to work on my project. Lunchtime tends to be the most productive period, because interruptions are few, so I try to work through it, if I can. I make sandwiches in Beeston Hall in the mornings...

'Michael Chan and I stayed in the

lab until two. I recall the porter coming through to place something brown in Dr Kovac's office, but as I told your Inspector Bayliss, I didn't notice the exact time. It was around one o'clock.'

'Was Michael Chan in your sight from eleven onwards?'

'Yes. He too brings sandwiches.'

'What about Dr Pomeroy? Was he in the department when the porter came?'

A fleeting expression of contempt crossed Magda's face. 'No. He had gone to Calverton, as usual, for another of his two-hour lunch breaks,' she said.

'And Dr Kovacs?'

'He had left for the Tech Town cafeteria a few minutes before.'

'I see. Tell me what you did after two.'

'Oh, our secretary called in and asked if I would sign some letters. When I got to her office, I became embroiled in dictating some more. One of them was tricky; it concerned an application for new funds for equipment, so I tried to get the wording just right. I was in the middle of this letter when Michael Chan came to say Dr Kovacs needed me. It was nothing urgent, but I didn't know that, so I told the secretary I would be back shortly, and returned to the lab.

'Dr Kovacs was inside the glassed-in

office, sitting at his desk. Through the open doorway I could see him pulling staples from a package on his knee. Michael stood just outside the door, holding a print-out; he was shifting his weight from foot to foot and looking impatient. As I drew close to Michael, Dr Kovacs began to tilt the package so the contents could slide out: suddenly I saw wires. For a moment, I didn't understand, then a small cylinder like a battery appeared. I shouted to Dr Kovacs to stop.'

The pupils of Magda's eyes were large with the memory; her chest rose and fell with accelerated breathing.

'You organized an evacuation of the immediate area, I believe,' said Montgomery.

'We all did; the three of us took charge because Professor Byrne had gone across to Immunology.'

'Did Dr Pomeroy help with this?'

'Hubert? No. He was still in Calverton. He told us later that the warden had asked for his assistance regarding a homesick boy.'

Montgomery nodded noncommittally; behind him, Sergeant Bird scribbled copious notes.

'Inspector,' Magda was regarding him with a level stare. 'These questions about the letter-bomb... You were investigating

Morgan's death. Do you think the two are connected?'

'I don't know,' he answered. 'Anything is possible.' He signalled the end of the interview, but as she rose to leave, he added a final question. 'Just one more thing,' he said. 'Your surname, Hepworth...is your father British?'

'My father is dead, but no, he was a Czech, like my mother. I have found the name "Hepworth" is easier for people here to deal with than the name I was born with.'

'Perhaps she's an illegal immigrant,' murmured Sergeant Bird when Magda had left. 'The technicians say she mixes as little as possible with her colleagues, and if you consider who they are, that's quite understandable. Kovacs might want to compare his experiences with hers, and as for Pomeroy...he's xenophobic in the extreme.'

'Ripe for mutual blackmail, though,' grinned Montgomery. 'No, I'm not serious. Magda's description of events has been very useful for elimination purposes. If Michael Chan knew anything at all about the bomb, he wouldn't have been hanging around just outside the office while Kovacs was grappling with the package. At the very least he would have been gouged by flying glass when the bomb went off. Neither he nor Magda could have left the package in the foyer between twelve forty-five and one, when we know it was deposited there. But Hubert Pomeroy was conveniently absent right through lunch and beyond.'

'An innocent courier could have been used.'

'Yes, but I'd have expected such a person to have come forward once the news broke on the campus—and the incident *did* cause a stir. No, Will, if Magda or Michael Chan decided to use a bomb, either as a serious effort to kill, or as a cover for a future attempt—which seems pretty daft to me—they'd have either sent it to Laszlo's home, where the blast couldn't affect them, or made sure that they were well out of the way until he'd opened it. Dangerous lunatics are usually well versed in the art of self-preservation!'

Michael Chan clearly relished a chance to speak his mind. His face, despite the oriental paradox of a sinister smile around the eyes, was mobile and intelligent, and he waved a vehement forefinger at the detectives whenever he considered a point required emphasis.

'Yes, it was a shock,' he said. 'We had no warning letters. It takes a lot to upset Magda, but I can see her expression now, first puzzled, then horrified, as the fiendish device slid into view. Anyone in the lab could have been hurt, or even the porter, who never experimented on an animal in his life—but these Animal Militancy people don't care. Their view is emotive and empirical, and I dare say they would regard an "innocent" victim as simply an unfortunate casualty of war.

'I wanted to speak out, Inspector, but Dr Kovacs wouldn't let me. The scientist is in a hopeless position...if he justifies his work, he attracts a stream of abusive letters and phone calls, his family are threatened, a bomb is put under his car. If he keeps quiet, the argument is lost by default. And that default is growing daily. You probably knew about the Anti-Vivisection League, the acceptable face of animal rights protest. They are allowed to send "information packs" to thousands of our schools. Some of that information comes from articles in medical journals, which they subject to a lay interpretation. Other material is bought from groups like Animal Militancy, thus swelling *their* coffers for those same violent activities the AVL claims to eschew. Naturally, the scientists are given no opportunity to address the schools themselves.

'So what's the result of all this? False facts are peddled. The protesters affirm that cell and tissue cultures are adequate for all experiments. That isn't true. Without complete physiological systems, much important work would stop, or never be started. Transplants, research into child blindness, gene therapy...'

'And Dr Kovacs's work here on diabetes.'

'That's right. I think his very success brought him to the attention of these people.'

'What exactly is he doing—can you tell me in a nutshell?'

'Gladly. It's a kind of transplantation. You know what diabetes is, don't you: certain cells in the pancreas aren't producing insulin properly, so sufferers have to inject themselves with insulin, sometimes three times a day, in order to make good the deficit. Without it, they would become ill and die.

'Well, for many years insulin from cows and pigs were the mainstay of treatment, but some people developed allergies to these, or became resistant. Also, world-wide supply shortages were projected. Genetically engineered human insulin seemed to answer these problems, but there's been recent concern among clinicians that patients using this type of insulin may be less aware of falling blood-sugar levels, which lead to "hypo" attacks. And, of course, the inconvenience of injection continues.

'For a long time scientists have been trying to transplant insulin-producing cells successfully into diabetic rats, but the cells have always been rejected. Dr Kovacs found a way to overcome this problem, by siting them in the thymus, a gland which is to do with immunity, under cover of a single immuno-suppressive injection. Thereafter, he found that the body didn't treat the cells as "alien", but accepted them, even when some of them were subsequently transplanted to other areas.'

Montgomery just about understood the significance of the finding. 'A real break-through if it works in humans,' he said.

Michael Chan nodded eagerly. 'Yes.'

'Is this the only laboratory carrying out such work?'

'No. Parallel studies are going on in America—but we are the first British lab to be involved.'

'Was anyone here jealous about the publicity which surrounded Dr Kovacs last year?'

'I don't think so. Prof Byrne, as head of department, tried to filch some of the credit, but it was definitely Laszlo's work, in conjunction with immunologists whom he very properly acknowledged.'

'What about any *other* grudges within the department?'

'There's Hubert,' said Michael airily. 'He hates us all for being foreigners, and thinks he should be paid more than Magda, but apart from that, no.'

Montgomery stood up. 'Thank you for your time, Mr Chan,' he said.

The student gave a small bow. 'My pleasure,' he replied. 'I give you notice, Inspector, that when I am a free agent, I *shall* speak out. These people who campaign against us will grow up one day. I'm talking about the young idealists, not the psychopathic anarchists who organize them. They'll have a baby of their own, very precious to them, and that baby might have a serious problem: cystic fibrosis, let's say. Suddenly, they'll turn to medicine, and expect someone to have devised a cure. Indeed, research workers are trying to do so right now. But what if all those scientists have been driven away by violence, and no one has been prepared to endure the danger, harassment and sheer unpleasantness of the campaigns? Then there'll be nobody out there to help them...they'll be shouting in the dark.'

He turned on his heel and left the room.

'He's right, you know,' said Montgomery soberly. 'If Heather was dying, and medical science could offer something to save her life, I wouldn't be too squeamish as to how it was developed.'

William Bird agreed but said nothing: he was thinking about his fine black and white cat, Sam.

'Someone had better provide Michael with a long-handled mirror,' went on Montgomery.

'Actually, he has a bicycle,' said his sergeant.

They relaxed into muted laughter. 'He'd be advised to stick with it,' said Montgomery. He stretched. 'I'm thirsty. Let's go and get another coffee.'

'They'll bring us one.'

'No; I need the exercise. We can walk up to the Trencher Building.'

They left the Medical School and began to climb the hill towards the centre of the campus, William Bird doing his best to slow Montgomery's crisp strides into a gentle amble. For once, the air was mild, and the morning was so well advanced that the prospect of food being served in one of the Trencher's cafeterias was pleasantly realistic.

'Poor Laszlo,' he mused. 'He didn't want to stick his neck out, yet he was still targeted. Michael Chan seems to be in no doubt that it was an animal rights attack.'

'Mm,' concurred Montgomery. 'If it was,

though, we're back with our coincidences. How many do we accept? Was the incident in Bramcote a follow-up to the letter-bomb, or does it link in with the student deaths?'

Sergeant Bird nudged him. 'Isn't that Pomeroy over there? If it is, his road will intersect with ours in half a minute. Do we want to interview him again?'

'No. Let's see the Calverton warden and wait for some forensic results first.'

They expected the physiologist to acknowledge them then continue on his way, but instead he blocked their path, arms folded, face low-browed and venomous.

'It's cat and mouse to you, isn't it?' he hissed. 'You've got the evidence, but you're in no hurry to charge me, are you? Oh, no. Why go for the little one when you're after the big one? You see...I know the way your minds work. But you can't prove the big one, can you? You'll never be able to prove it.'

'Is there something you want to tell us, Dr Pomeroy?' asked Montgomery sternly. 'Would you like to make a statement?'

'What, do your job for you? No... If I were you I'd settle for what you've got. The other one isn't what you're thinking.' Abruptly his lips trembled, and anguish stared out of his eyes. 'Let it lie,' he whispered. 'For God's sake, let it lie.'

Montgomery made as if to detain him, but Hubert pushed blindly past, and stumbled towards the Medical School.

'Has he gone off his rocker?' asked Sergeant Bird, amazed.

Montgomery watched the lecturer's shambolic progress, his own steely eyes narrowed. 'No,' he said, 'but for the first time he's let on that he knows something.'

15

In the Trencher Building's basement cafeteria, Eleanor negotiated her way between the tables with practised ease, holding her laden tray aloft.

'In the corner,' suggested Chris. She began to comply, but suddenly changed direction and angled towards the opposite side of the room, to an unappealing table which awaited clearing.

'I just saw Inspector Montgomery,' she explained as she piled away the used crockery. 'Near the window, with Sergeant Bird.'

'*Here?* Good heavens.' Chris carefully deposited his bowl of soup and plate of salad on half of the available space, and carried both trays to the nearest stack. He was glad that Calverton had adopted a 'pay as you eat' scheme: it meant that he wasn't obliged to return to hall every lunchtime.

'I'd love to know what they're saying to each other,' said Eleanor when he came back. 'When Fay's room was searched, I thought she must be the prime suspect...but nothing has happened since.'

'It's the same with Jason,' said Chris. 'Presumably there's no proof—or they didn't do it.'

'Do you believe that, Chris?'

Chris tore a piece off his bread roll, and tried to define his thoughts. 'I'm confused,' he said at last. 'Only Morgan's death counts with me, and I simply don't know whether it was linked with what we saw in Hubert's flat, or not. If it was, then Hubert's guilty—but he's still walking around Calverton, free as a bird. If it wasn't, then Fay did it, but to kill someone because they've ditched you is just *mad.*' Angrily he destroyed the rest of the roll, and buttered the multifarious fragments. 'Real people don't do that sort of thing.'

'Oh, sometimes they do,' countered Eleanor. '*They* perceive their motive as adequate, even if we don't.' She glanced towards the corner where the two detectives were finishing their meal. 'Sergeant Bird

266

enjoys his food,' she said, 'though I don't think the inspector has had much more than a cup of coffee.' Her gaze returned to Chris. 'I've been wondering,' she said awkwardly. 'We've always looked on Fay as being Jason's tool. With good reason, I should add. But suppose she used *him* for her own ends, to supply her with cyanide... What if she gave him some spurious tale, said that Morgan was a danger to the animal rights people? I'm only guessing, of course...'

'I don't know. This whole thing's a nightmare. It's so vindictive, she'd have to be raving mad.'

'You told me about a photograph,' said Eleanor. 'That—didn't sound very sane to me.'

Chris froze, a spoonful of soup half-way to his mouth. 'I've just thought of something,' he said. 'Magda and Fay have met before.' He related the brief dialogue they had exchanged on the morning that Fay had discovered Morgan's infidelity. ' "Professional confidence", that's what Magda called it. Fay was terrified of Morgan getting to hear whatever it was—so terrified she'd even discuss the subject with his new girlfriend.'

'Fay told me once she'd been in hospital,' appended Eleanor. 'That's in the days when we were speaking. She didn't specify, though.'

'Morgan was always very impatient with talk of mental disease,' remembered Chris. 'You chaffed him once about it—said he'd change his tune when he reached our clinical years. Do you suppose Fay's been a psychiatric patient?'

'It's possible...yes, very possible. But we can't go asking her. Whoops—keep a low profile. The police are just leaving.' Eleanor turned her face towards the wall and Chris shrank down lower in his seat. She flashed him a shamefaced smile when they sat straight again. 'I wonder why we did that? Guilty consciences, I suppose.'

'That's it exactly,' said Chris. 'I feel riddled with guilt: guilt if I speak up, guilt if I keep quiet; guilt for having seen and heard things not meant for me—for being in the wrong place at the wrong time!' *But most of all, guilt for being alive when Morgan isn't.*

Eleanor reached across the table and grasped his wrist. 'No, Chris—the right place at the right time. The police need information—we can't expect them to do the job without it. I only wish we could help them further: they seem to be stuck.'

Chris pushed aside the remains of his soup but made no attempt to start on the cheese salad. 'You said we can't ask Fay about her past history,' he said slowly, 'and I agree. But speculation is no good to Inspector Montgomery—only facts.' He swallowed. 'I'll see if Magda can be persuaded to tell me.'

'How was yesterday's London trip?' asked Montgomery when he met up with Robert Allen at the library door.

'Fruitful, sir. I was making some follow-up enquiries this morning, and—I think you'll find the results interesting.'

'We're all ears.' Montgomery signalled to Jackson, Smythe, Grange and William Bird; they convened in a circle as Allen began:

'Pomeroy was a clinical researcher at the Thames and National,' he said. 'That's a similar salary scale to his current post. Five years ago there was some rather sordid episode with a male student: like Elizabeth Tudor at the time of Wyatt's rebellion, it was a case of "much suspected...nothing proved..." yet his superiors felt confident enough to ask him to leave. Pomeroy didn't contest the decision.'

'What, no tribunal and compensation?' sneered Jackson.

'No. His status as a homosexual was in much less doubt there than it is here at Sherwood. He'd already been attacked in a "queer-bashing" episode near a gay club;

he and his friend were struck with baseball bats by a gang of youths sporting British Movement tattoos.'

'Ironic,' mused Sergeant Bird. 'He has sympathy for some of their views.'

'So it seems he was glad to leave London,' concluded Allen.

Montgomery gave a brief nod. 'Indeed... What about references?'

'They weren't withheld, in view of the nebulous nature of the evidence against him.'

' "Go thou and sin no more"—but not in our district!' snickered Jackson.

'Yes, that's the overall flavour. He was out of work for a while, then finally got the post at Sherwood.'

They discussed the findings at some length, and when a particular telephone call came through to the Incident Room, Sergeant Bird left the group reluctantly at the behest of the duty constable. He was back within minutes, however, glowing with enthusiasm.

' 'Scuse me, sir, that was the liaison sergeant at Forensic...they've got a match! Fibres from a carpet lining the boot of Dr Pomeroy's Renault have been found on Keith Mayhew's woollen trousers. They've also identified some fluffs from the bedspread on the trousers and gaberdine jacket.'

'Was there anything of Keith's at the scene?' asked Montgomery.

'Yes.' Sergeant Bird's plump cheeks drew in, and his tone became more reverential. 'Saliva, sir, on one of the cushions we took away. It's consistent with Keith's blood group, and matches only six per cent of the general population.'

Brian Jackson gave a low whistle, but Montgomery felt strangely dispassionate. 'In that case,' he said, 'our Dr Pomeroy has some explaining to do.'

Chris hovered nervously behind the Medical School, waiting for Magda Hepworth. He knew the route she used whenever she walked back to Beeston Hall, but on certain evenings he had seen her climb into a Vauxhall Astra, presumably to go late-night shopping or some such activity. His position near the car-park would cover all options.

He had no idea how he was going to broach the subject of Fay even if he did encounter Magda. The only certainty in his life just then was a sense of obligation towards Morgan. Even if he failed with Magda, he had to try.

He shrank into the shadows as two biochemists he knew drifted past, chattering. It was already five thirty. Magda might be planning to work on in the lab for another three hours, but he didn't intend to check until at least six o'clock: it would be highly undesirable to run into Hubert.

Above and beyond, the lights of Tech Town blazed out into the darkness, and Chris could see a few miniaturized figures in white coats behind the windows of the Chemistry Building. Perhaps one of them was Jason... He shuffled his feet as a wave of damp chillness seemed to sweep up from the concrete beneath them; rain had fallen during the afternoon.

Suddenly, there was Magda just ahead, walking briskly towards the car-park. Chris started after her, his head emptied of introductory platitudes in the relief of seeing that she was alone.

'Dr Hepworth!'

Magda swung round.

'It's Chris Shallet,' he said, slowing down so as not to startle her.

'Oh...Christopher.'

As before, she was leaving the conversational burden to him—not unreasonable, he thought, considering that he was the supplicant.

'May I talk to you?'

'About medical matters?'

'No. Morgan's death.'

'Oh...I was just about to leave the campus, but you can have a few minutes. Shall we sit in the car?'

'Please.'

She led the way to the Astra and opened the passenger door for Chris.

'Well?' she said when they were both settled inside.

'This is difficult,' he began. 'The fact is, a friend and I think that Fay, the girl who used to go out with Morgan, has been behaving very oddly. We suspect that she has a history of mental illness, and if this is true, then we feel the police ought to be told. I—I know you had dealings with her once, some time ago...was it in a psychiatric hospital?'

Chris was looking out through the windscreen, but he could feel Magda staring at him. 'Did Fay tell you this?' she asked sharply.

'No.'

'Then how do you know?'

This was a question he had hoped would not occur to Magda. 'I'm sorry,' he said, 'I heard something I wasn't meant to on the morning you and Fay met in D block.'

'I see...yes, I imagine you did. The row must have alerted people all over the block.'

'I was in the bathroom and you were both on the stairs; I'm sure no one else heard.' He turned to assess her expression; in the gloom her face was very still.

'I understand,' she said after a pause,

'but you must realize that I *can't* divulge information which is—privileged, confidential. It would be wrong.'

'I understand it might be wrong to tell *me,* but surely the police need to know? Would you speak to them?'

She sighed. 'Christopher...I follow what you've said, and your reasons for thinking Fay might be involved, but take it from me—she's not capable of that kind of thing. Empty gestures, perhaps, but not positive action. If we misdirect the police, it means time lost from their real enquiry, and misery for Fay. I feel I've caused her quite enough misery already.'

Guilt...how Chris could empathize with that! But Magda didn't know the whole story.

'Dr Hepworth,' he said, 'I don't think you realize what we may be up against. Fay's now in cahoots with Jason Gower.'

'Jason Gower!' Magda's confident voice was shocked into a whisper. 'You're sure?' she added. 'Oh dear. That *is* bad news.'

'You see how that changes things? Please help us,' he urged. '*Was* it a psychiatric hospital?'

Magda bit her lip unhappily. 'Perhaps,' she said at length.

Chris was about to probe for more when she abruptly consulted the dashboard clock. 'I must go now,' she said. 'Can I

274

give you a lift to your hall?'

'Are you going off campus?'

'First to Beeston Hall, and then outside to an engagement.'

'Then please drop me off at Beeston.' He would see Eleanor in nearby Wellington Hall.

'Very well.' Magda drove expertly along the campus roads, negotiating the bends and speed-humps with unselfconscious skill, finally to park beneath a bright lamp in Beeston Hall's staff car-park.

'Thank you,' said Chris as a small 'clunk' sounded under the car. 'I—I'm sorry if I've seemed impertinent. I just wanted to do what was right for Morgan.' He unclipped the seat-belt and began to open the door. 'I miss him,' he added quietly.

'So do I.'

On an impulse, he leaned over and kissed her smooth left cheek, then scrambled out, faintly embarrassed by his action. He walked round to Magda's side as she activated the central locking mechanism.

'I wonder what that noise was just now,' she murmured. 'I hope my exhaust isn't coming loose.'

'Shall I have a look?' The car was well illuminated, so Chris began to crouch down, but before he could fully kneel a paralysing wave of horror rendered him immobile and almost speechless.

'Magda!' he croaked as she approached him, casual and oblivious. He pointed to the ground.

On the glistening tarmac lay a dark plastic box, packed with magnets and cylinders, and trailing a wire.

16

Chris was so terrified he thought he would vomit on the spot. In the unnatural light Magda's face was a garish mask of shock; for several seconds, neither of them moved, then she barked at him, 'Get away from here!'

'I said *go!*' she repeated as he stood his ground, then roughly shoved at him before reaching into her pocket and producing a torch. As he cowered astonished in the middle distance, he saw her kneel by the side of the car, examine the sinister collection by torchlight, and extricate something from the pile.

'It's a hoax,' she said wonderingly.

'What?'

'A few sticks of plasticine and some old wires—like this one.' Magda held out her trophy towards him, and gave a broken laugh. 'God, I was scared. I normally check my car, but...'

'I distracted you,' finished Chris. He too felt like laughing out loud. 'I'm sorry. Are you *sure* it's not live?'

'Of course. There's nothing there—no detonator or whatever. The box is an old sandwich box—it must have become dislodged when we went over the speed-humps.'

'Who would do such a perverted thing?' asked Chris.

Magda's face, relaxed in relief, instantly became sober. 'I think we know,' she said.

Empty gestures...

'Fay!'

'If what you told me is correct; if she is an associate of Jason Gower, then I think we have our answer. She wanted to punish me for taking Morgan.'

'What will you do?'

'I don't know. If this was her catharsis, then perhaps it should end here. Perhaps I'll do nothing.'

'What if it wasn't Fay?'

She gave a mirthless smile. 'If it was anyone else, I doubt the device would have been a dummy.'

'Do you mean she's not going to tell the police?'

Eleanor was incredulous, and Chris

suddenly felt very weary. It struck him that she was inevitably as willing to convict Fay as Magda was to protect the girl, while his own attitude fell somewhere in between the two.

'She might,' he said, struggling.

'You could have been *killed!*'

'Only if the device had been a real one,' he reminded her with an impatient sigh.

Eleanor gritted her teeth. 'Look, you've spoken of gestures... That photograph you told me about—yes, I can see you regret it now, but nevertheless I know—that could be regarded as another one. But it wasn't empty, was it? *Morgan died.* So one could more validly describe these things as warnings. If Fay put that sandwich box under Magda's car, what will she do next?'

'I don't know.'

'The police should be told.'

Suddenly Chris had had quite enough of female bossiness. Half of his mind was uncomfortably recalling how it was *Magda* who had knelt down and examined the device...by all the rules of manly conduct, it should have been him. But she had been so forceful. Only someone like Morgan could have overruled her.

Now Eleanor was haranguing him, and his legs were trembling with delayed reaction, and he wanted to be in Calverton, quite alone...

'I don't think we've any right,' he said, 'but if you do, go and see them yourself!'

With a muffled 'Good night' he turned and walked out of the door.

'I'm sorry,' said Sergeant Bird to the young female student who approached him the next morning, 'but both Inspector Montgomery and DS Allen are at Head-quarters, and I expect they'll be there all day. Can I be of assistance?'

'Yes—can we talk somewhere privately?'

She didn't look as if she'd slept much, he reflected as he led the way to a small office adjoining the library.

'Now, then,' he said encouragingly when they were seated.

Ten minutes later the circuitry in his mind was busily humming. 'Let me just reiterate,' he said. 'You tell me that Fay was in hospital once, and you have reason to believe that it may have been a psychiatric hospital. You say she sent a torn photograph to Morgan Brunt days before he died, and there has been another unpleasant incident in which she might have been involved, but you're not certain. Is that the sum of it?'

'Eleanor nodded.

'And you can't give me any more details?'

'I'm afraid not.'

'Fair enough. Thank you for coming forward...'

When she had gone, he returned to the Incident Room, musing. Montgomery was at that very moment grilling Hubert Pomeroy, and he very much wanted to be there. Nevertheless, this new angle on Fay could be very important. She was still a suspect; a psychiatric history could explain many things.

How to find out? Wellington Hall, or the Geography Department...Fay's home address...her parents.

'My husband died very suddenly seven years ago,' said Mrs Gillingham. 'A heart attack. It was a great shock.'

Sergeant Bird nodded sympathetically as he studied the woman seated on the chintzy sofa opposite. Aside from the insidious slackness of age, her facial features were identical with her daughter's: small and neat, with an upturned nose and eyes which were just a little vacant. Her hair, light brown shot through with grey, was wound into a bun at the back of her head; a few wispy strands spiralled over her ears.

'Fay was only twelve,' she went on. 'It affected her very badly...she had a nervous breakdown two years later.'

'How long was she in hospital?' he asked.

'Oh, quite a few months. It was all voluntary, of course, and towards the end she attended as a day patient.'

'Did she fully recover?'

'Yes...well, almost. She's been—*vulnerable* ever since. There were only the three of us, and suddenly her daddy was taken away. She was afraid to go to university, but I thought she should. A good career would make her more secure. Losing her company has been my sacrifice.'

Sergeant Bird began to understand.

The same eyes, but younger. Naïve, but with disconcerting flashes of shrewdness...

'What was I doing on December the twelfth?' repeated Fay. 'How will that help you find out who killed Morgan?'

'Another student died that evening.'

'I know; Keith committed suicide. Your Constable Haslam asked me questions, but I couldn't tell him anything. I'd had no contact with Keith for months.'

'We aren't certain that it was suicide. We feel there may be a link with Morgan's death, so we're trying to track down where *he* was that night. He may have seen something... You were his girlfriend at the time; were you with him?'

'No, sergeant, I was out singing carols for charity. I did go looking for Morgan after my throat got sore around eight

281

o'clock, but I didn't have any success. He was drinking somewhere with the rugby club. I tried their favourite pubs: no one was there. I imagined they'd all gone into town, but I called by Morgan's room in Calverton, just in case. He wasn't in.'

'What time was this?'

'Maybe half past nine.'

'Did you meet anyone you knew in D block?'

Fay frowned at him suspiciously. 'No. Should I have?'

'What did you do then?'

'I went back to Wellington. I wasn't very pleased.'

In other words, no alibi, thought Sergeant Bird. He wondered how Montgomery was getting on with Hubert Pomeroy.

The knock at Chris's door roused him from a slumped torpor; laying aside his anatomy book, he crossed the room and fumbled with the handle.

Eleanor stood on the threshold, half concealed behind a luxuriant poinsettia plant. 'Hello, Chris,' she said as he invited her in. 'I bought this for you; I thought it looked cheerful.'

'Thanks,' he said, placing it on the desk. 'I'd better warn you, I'm not much good at keeping the leaves red. One season, then they're green for the rest of their days.'

She gave a hesitant smile. 'I'll go now, and leave you to your studies. But I just wanted to say sorry for last night. I was so overbearing and insensitive...I've been kicking myself ever since.'

'*Did* you see the police?'

'Yes, but I only mentioned the photograph, and said we suspected Fay had a psychiatric history. I said nothing to compromise either you or Dr Hepworth.'

'Good... Hell, I'm bored with this book. Neuroanatomy drives me barmy. What say we go and watch some television in the common room—forget our woes for a while?'

'Why not?' she said.

As Chris locked the door of D8, they heard raised voices coming from the end of the corridor. 'See what I mean about hearing things?' murmured Chris as they hurried past D6. 'It's impossible not to round here.'

They heard Fay speak, the actual words inaudible behind D6's stout wooden door. Jason's reply, however, was vibrant with contempt.

'You *stupid* little cow!' he shouted. 'You're nothing but a liability. You're no bloody use to anyone!'

Eleanor's raised-eyebrow glance met Chris's; as they padded discreetly down the stairs, she leaned towards him and whispered, 'Dr Hepworth's car: could this be *quod erat demonstrandum?*'

William Bird slid softly into the Interview Room, where Montgomery was interrogating Hubert Pomeroy. Robert Allen made a brief gesture of acknowledgement before resuming his note-taking.

The air was acrid with smoke; blue swirls of it wreathed the small pale man sitting across the table from Montgomery, and the ashtray at his elbow told its own tale.

'One of your neighbours heard nocturnal thumps,' Montgomery was saying in very deliberate tones. 'When he joked about this the next morning, did you answer, "I don't know what you're talking about?" No; you said, "It's none of your business"—because you knew perfectly well what he was talking about.

'Then there were the twigs under your car. We suggested to you that they came from Sherwood Forest. Did you say, "I've never been there," or "I haven't been there recently"? No, you immediately came up with a story which might explain their presence. What was it? Ah, yes—a sudden urgent desire to follow the Robin Hood trail in the middle of winter.'

Hubert Pomeroy lit another cigarette with trembling fingers.

'You are a scientist, Dr Pomeroy,' went on Montgomery. 'I've already told you that we have irrefutable scientific evidence to show that Keith Mayhew, whether dead or alive at the time, was in the boot of your Renault. What is your explanation?'

The tic on Hubert's cheek twitched and quivered. All bluster had long gone; he looked trapped. 'I—I didn't take the car into town that night. It was low on petrol. I went on the bus instead.'

'Strange new-fangled things, petrol stations.'

'I...I don't like town-centre parking.'

'I see. So where did you put the car?'

'I just left it in its usual place.'

Montgomery half-rose from his seat. 'Dr Pomeroy, you are *lying*. On the night in question someone made a specific search for your car, and it was nowhere to be found in Calverton's car-park.'

Hubert's eyes rolled, and he stared dumbly at Montgomery, an oily film of sweat oozing from his pasty face.

Montgomery thrust his own face forwards, the mouth now narrowed, the features granite-hard. 'We also have forensic evidence which clearly links Keith Mayhew with your flat. In addition, a witness states that he *saw* Keith there on the night of December the twelfth. How do you account for that?'

Hubert Pomeroy gave a strangled sob and buried his head in his hands.

'The *truth*, Dr Pomeroy!' demanded Montgomery. 'That'll save a lot more grief.'

Slowly, Hubert looked up at them, the hands falling into his lap. His eyes still glinted redly, but behind the tears was the dullness of defeat. 'All right,' he said in lifeless tones. 'On your head be it.' He took a deep inhalation from his smouldering cigarette. 'I did use my car to get to town. I spent the evening in the way I described before: drinks, a meal, the club...I got back to the flat at two o'clock. A light was on in the kitchen. I thought I must have forgotten to switch it off. I went in there...

'Keith Mayhew was sitting upright on the floor in the corner, with one of my plastic bin liners over his head. Inspector, he was very dead.'

17

'Do you believe him?'

Montgomery flung himself into the chair in his own office, glad to be out of the Interview Room's fetid, fume-laden atmosphere. Revelations had come thick and fast during the previous hour, plausible details which he was tempted to believe: now, more than ever, he needed the sound common sense of Sergeant Bird.

'Pomeroy looks a broken man,' said the sergeant. 'My gut says yes: he's a homosexual, says he thought Keith was the same and tried it on with him in the first year, but was rebuffed. He punished Keith publicly ever after, magnifying his intellectual deficiencies to such an extent that Keith was eventually driven to take his own life. But the boy got the final revenge, by doing the deed in Pomeroy's flat. Pomeroy was suddenly faced with a body in the middle of the night, and knew he was morally culpable. Even though Keith had killed himself, the scandal would have been enormous and Pomeroy would never have been employed again. So his instinct was to take the body to somewhere unconnected with the campus, and hide it. When it came to the crunch, however, he had enough compassion for Keith's family to leave the body in a place it could easily be found.

'Yes—overall, I think it rings true. And the story accounts for Pomeroy's outburst to us yesterday—the "big" charge being murder, the "small" one associated with concealing a body. But I have to say one or two of the details don't quite fit.'

'That's my opinion too, Will. What about the saliva on the cushion? I haven't mentioned it to Pomeroy. Why was Keith seen on the bed? And how did he get into the flat? Pomeroy's suggestion that he might have left the door unlocked by accident sounded a bit weak to me.'

William Bird nodded. 'I reckon they *did* have a relationship, but Pomeroy doesn't want to add to the scandal by making that known. He probably gave Keith his own key—and has now hidden it for ever.'

Montgomery fiddled with his pen. 'There's going to be pressure on us to accept this suicide story. The Super's been pushing me for a result for some time...damn it, *we* want this case tied up so we can concentrate on other matters. But consider the opposite angle...Pomeroy has lied to us before. He's a clever man. Every time we've laid facts before him he's come up with an explanation to fit. The student Dez hearing thumps, for instance. Pomeroy claims he thought Dez meant noises at two fifteen, when he was trying to get the body down the stairs...

'But his stories don't fit the facts we *haven't* told him. Chris Shallet saw Keith *lying on the bed*. If Keith came that night to commit suicide, it seems an odd thing to do—unless he was thinking things over. If

288

Pomeroy murdered him, though, it makes sense. He left Keith hidden in the bedroom just in case someone called round, then hurried off to town to establish an alibi.'

'Two flaws there, sir... Pomeroy has been extremely reluctant to give his alibi, and the meal at Ben Bowers was booked four days in advance.'

'So it was a prior arrangement? I don't see any problem with that. Perhaps Keith came round unexpectedly sometime after seven, when Pomeroy had returned from his first outing. Perhaps he even threatened to blackmail Pomeroy—we don't know. But Pomeroy kept to his later plans, knowing that we'd find out eventually.'

Sergeant Bird pulled a face. 'So it's still wide open?'

'Yes.'

'Oh, well...tomorrow's Thursday, sir.'

'That's right. Jackson and Smythe go back to the Lynx Club. If we're very lucky indeed, they might get Pomeroy's friend to talk.'

'I don't see why we have to be landed with this,' grumbled Jackson the next morning, as he and Smythe sat in the Medical School discussing their strategy for the night-club.

'It's got to be us: we've already met the barman and established a rapport.'

'I meant in the first place.'

'Perhaps he thought we were the best men for the job,' suggested Smythe hopefully.

'Do me a favour! No, Montgomery's punishing us for making one mistake. He thinks Jason Gower hid the stuff between our search and Bayliss's. But he might well have got rid of it the day before, when Fay Gillingham was first questioned. I don't see why we should have to take the flak for that.'

'Fay Gillingham told Will that they'd been working on educational pamphlets,' said Smythe. 'Don't you find it suspicious that there was *nothing* relating to animal rights issues found in Jason's room?'

'I certainly do. I think he made a clean sweep, and overdid it. *Somewhere* on this campus is a cache of goodies, which might be plastered with his sticky little fingerprints.'

'Bayliss didn't find anything.'

Jackson snorted. 'Bayliss! He's not as convinced as we are that Gower is the one to focus on. No...if you want something doing, you do it yourself. I've got some ideas, Graham. Shall we slip over to Calverton while the cat's away?'

Information from Taff Jones coupled with their own topographical survey gave the detectives a good grasp of the layout and functions of Calverton Hall.

'...So each block has its own trunk room,' pondered Jackson, scratching his chin as he prowled the garden behind D block. 'Not on the ground floor as you might expect, but on the first floor, where room 10 would otherwise be.'

'They searched every nook and cranny of D block,' said Smythe. 'Behind the bath panel, in the cistern, everywhere—including the trunk-room.'

'I know—but look at it from Gower's point of view. He had stuff to get rid of, but didn't want to be spotted either by us or by anyone else. How would he go about it? Where would he put it?'

'Are we assuming that he wanted to preserve the things for later use?'

'That's my guess. He's a cocky little so-and-so: that would put him one up, wouldn't it? So there's a cache here somewhere. He hasn't any transport of his own.' Jackson ran his eye along the line of windows set in the ivy-clad wall. 'That's Morgan Brunt's window, D9,' he said, pointing, 'with the trunk-room to the left and D8 on the other side. Keep going right, and we've got D7 then D6 before that drainpipe which demarcates D block from E block. What does that tell you, Graham?'

'E block's trunk-room is immediately adjacent to Gower's room!' Smythe's enthusiasm flowered and faded in almost the same moment. 'That's no good,' he said. 'The trunk-rooms are all securely locked, and anyway the blocks aren't linked internally. He'd have had to step out into the quadrangle with all his things, and risk being seen.'

Jackson patted his head fondly, a moderate feat since Smythe's height was several inches greater than his own. 'Infant,' he said, 'why are we standing here in the outer garden? Don't you understand—he could have swung across from his window to E block. These ivy tendrils are really strong—they're glued to the wall with suckers. And the drainpipe would give added purchase.'

Smythe looked horrified. 'I call that desperate. How would he hold on to the things he was trying to hide?'

Jackson exhaled impatiently. His own brain was clear and crisp that morning, while Smythe seemed to be wallowing in a fog of obtuseness. 'Every student has a rucksack,' he said.

'Oh!'

'Shall we put our theory to the test, then?'

'What—climb up there? Certainly not.'

'I meant, let's get hold of the master key.'

292

'Ah...yes.'

'Here you are,' said Mrs Potter, the cleaning lady, looking both nervous and flattered by the attentions of two police officers. She threw open the trunk-room door and they stepped into its musty interior.

'Thank you, Mrs Potter,' said Jackson in tones of finality; taking the hint, she left them to it.

Trunks and suitcases were stacked against every wall, their labels disclosing origins from Nigeria to Cornwall. A miscellany of sleeping-bags, car roof-racks and sports equipment filled each space between the larger items. The sash window moved easily and had no lock.

Smythe began to check labels. 'We're looking for "Jason Gower", aren't we?' he said.

Jackson rolled his eyes. 'Do wake up, Graham,' he said. 'Gower's own trunk will be in D block. He'll have hidden the stuff in someone else's.' He snapped the locks on the nearest trunk, opened the lid, peered inside and closed it again. 'This is going to take some time,' he murmured.

'Can't we tell from the weight?' Smythe was eager to make amends. 'We can restack the trunks between us, and jiggle them a bit to make sure they're empty.'

'Graham—we're talking about *explosives* here. We treat every trunk as if it's going to blow us to kingdom come.'

Gingerly, Smythe lifted down a suitcase on the opposite wall, and made a methodical examination. With dust tickling their nostrils and a clanking radiator for company, they repeated the process with every one.

Jackson eased his back forty minutes later, and thrust out his underlip peevishly. 'Nothing,' he said. 'Not a sodding thing.'

'They're probably back in his room by now,' chirruped Smythe, keen to show that this time he was alert and functioning. 'He knows we can hardly search it again without new evidence...' One glance at Jackson's face silenced him. He crawled to a corner and unzipped an anonymous-looking sports bag. It was crammed with books and papers.

'Brian!' he gasped moments later. 'Have a decco at this lot!'

The hoard, which included a damning cuttings album, represented an accurate cross-section of Animal Militancy literature. One leaflet, 'Instructions to Members', continually referred to a 'Methods' booklet which the detectives were unable to find.

' "How to make a letter-bomb and blow someone's hand off",' murmured Jackson as he riffled through the papers. 'That's what their "Methods" book will be about.'

Smythe attacked the remaining zipper bags with renewed vigour, but remembered the virtues of caution when his fingers discerned an unnatural firmness within a rolled-up sleeping-bag. 'There might be something here,' he whispered, untying the retaining cord and slowly unrolling the bag. 'Yes—definitely...' The zip sounded loud as he held his breath; he turned back a flap of quilted polyester, and whistled softly.

A neat block of plastic explosive nestled in the padded depths.

'Yes, sir, we're relocked the door,' said Jackson down the telephone. 'No—no detonators or tilt switches. Just plastic explosive... Yes, according to Mrs Potter, the cleaning lady, he usually comes back for lunch... Right you are, sir.'

He replaced the receiver and joined Smythe, who had been pulling faces across the room in a mixture of relief and jubilation. 'Montgomery's coming over,' he said. 'Jack Bayliss, too. They're going to pull in Jason Gower and take his fingerprints. About time.'

Montgomery gave Jackson all due credit for the find, though he half wished it had been any other officer from the squad. Much of Jackson's work was sloppy, and the blend of insolence and discontent he so often displayed threatened both discipline and morale among his colleagues. Yet he *could* be sharp and imaginative, if sufficiently motivated. Everyone needed motivation; in Jackson's case, however, the chance to spite Montgomery was too often the spur.

With Bayliss, Montgomery examined the hoard, careful to disturb it as little as possible, before rejoining Jackson and Smythe in the hall of E block.

'Jason Gower's just gone in next door,' said Jackson.

The four officers quietly followed, but paused when a rattle of keys echoed along D block's ground-floor corridor.

'I'm not entirely happy with the concept of Gower using the windows,' said Montgomery in a low voice. 'Did you say the cleaning lady's name is Mrs Potter? Just hold on a moment while I have a word with her.' The sight of the trunk-room cache had given him a sudden hunch; ignoring Bayliss's impatient frown, he padded down the corridor to confront the floral-aproned figure emerging from D4.

'Does your master key relate only to doors in D block?' he asked her politely after introducing himself.

She shook her head solemnly. 'No, Mr Montgomery. This key opens all major doors in the old part of the 'all—A block to E block, and the tutors' flats. These other keys are for cupboards and areas like the attics; some of them are spares.'

'I see. Didn't you lose the master recently?'

She stared at him as if he were a wizard. 'I don't know how you know that, Mr Montgomery,' she said. 'It weren't for long; I found it again the next day.' Alarm suddenly registered on her worn face. 'Don't tell the bursar!' she pleaded.

'That's most unlikely. How did it happen?'

'Well, I finished early and went to chat with Peggy who does the common rooms, and I left the keys hanging from one of the doors, in case the supervisor came by—to show I was still on the job, you see. When I got back, the keys were on the floor. They'd slipped out of the lock, you see. I took them and hung them up by the ring as usual in the bursar's office, and it weren't till the next day I noticed the master'd gone.

'But it 'adn't gone far,' she added defiantly. 'It were lyin' in the corridor just near where the keys'd fallen. It must've come off the ring.'

Believe that and you'll believe anything, thought Montgomery. 'Is that why you didn't report it?' he asked.

'There were nothin' to report.'

'Of course. Did this happen before Mr Blunt died, or after?'

'Oh, well before. Poor Mr Morgan—'is room were always that untidy...the places 'is socks used to end up! But 'e were such a nice lad. Do you know, 'e gave me a big box of chocolates at Christmas...'

'Do you remember the day of his death?' interrupted Montgomery.

'I certainly do.'

'Did you see Mr Morgan on the stairs, talking to Mr Jason?'

'No, but I heard them quarrelling in Mr Jason's room. 'E's a nasty piece of work, that Mr Jason...'

'*Inside* the room—you're sure it was inside?'

'Mr Montgomery—I remember it perfect.'

'For Christ's sake, come on!' hissed Bayliss as Montgomery rejoined his colleagues. 'Gower will be coming out for his lunch at any minute!'

'He lied,' said Montgomery. His unruffled gaze moved to Jackson and Smythe. 'He lied to you two. Morgan Blunt was in Gower's room on the day he was killed. The cleaning lady remembers.'

Bayliss was suitably mollified. 'Great!' he said with a victorious gesture. 'Let's go get him.'

They started up the stairs towards the first-floor landing, Bayliss and Montgomery in the lead, Jackson and Smythe a few steps below. The door of D6 loomed above, stout and unwelcoming.

Suddenly—a deafening crack of sound. The door blew outwards on a massive concussive blast as the block trembled violently, and the officers were swept down the stairs as if by a giant toddler's hand to lie in a tangled heap at the bottom amid the echoing rumble of the explosion's aftermath.

18

Somewhere behind the ringing tinnitus Montgomery heard a groan from Smythe. Painfully he rose to his hands and knees; with considerable relief he saw that the majority of the groan represented effort as the constable pulled himself out from beneath Bayliss's weighty form. Bayliss looked dazed, but intact; Jackson, too. Along the ground-floor corridor the door of D3 opened: a wary student face peeped out like a terrapin emerging from its shell; the idiot expression of alarm would have been comical in any other circumstances.

'Get the students out of here,' ordered Montgomery as he staggered to his feet. He clapped a hand to the back of his neck. Was his head still in place? Yes. He grasped the newel post and began to climb the stairs. Dust swirled around him, making his eyes water. Down below, Mrs Potter had started up a low background keening, and Jackson was giving colourful vent to his feelings, but above there was nothing but an uncanny silence.

As he approached the gaping entry to D6, the choking cloud thickened. Gagging and spluttering, he unclipped a fire extinguisher from the wall and painstakingly advanced, scarcely able to see. The room was almost totally destroyed. If Jason *had* been inside...

His hands knew the truth before his eyes. Even before the ashes of devastation had softly settled in a pattering parody of healing rain, he found that which he had most dreaded to find.

Jason Gower would be telling them nothing.

'You ought to go home, sir, like Brian and Graham,' said Sergeant Bird much later.

Montgomery sipped his afternoon tea; he

shook his head in a very cautious gesture of abnegation. 'No, Will,' he answered. 'I'm staying. They only went because I insisted, and guess what? They're determined to go to the Lynx tonight. They've really got the bit between their teeth—I'm proud of them.'

'Has Bayliss come to any preliminary conclusions?'

'It's difficult; the forensic team are still working on the room. The epicentre of the blast was definitely at or near the desk, so the odds are that Jason was working on the bomb that killed him—but a booby trap can't be entirely ruled out at this stage.' Montgomery gave a wry grimace. 'That missing "Methods" book was on his shelf. A step-by-step guide to crude amateur explosive devices. Perhaps it didn't give quite enough information about potential pitfalls.'

'Mm...I was asking, sir, because a student from D7 called Peter Craig says he heard a particularly nasty row between Jason and Fay last night—or rather, Jason was doing the shouting, calling her things like a stupid bitch. Less then twenty-four hours later this happens...'

'Would someone like Fay have known what to do?'

'She would if he'd been teaching her. And there's that manual.'

Montgomery's head still felt muzzy. With effort he collected his thoughts, focusing first on Mrs Potter and her ring of keys. It was Jason whom he had envisaged stealing the master key, getting a copy cut then returning it the next day, but really there was no reason why someone else shouldn't have done so: Hubert Pomeroy, for instance, or even Fay. Had Fay crept back that morning and left a deadly trap for Jason?

'We'd better wait until Forensic can tell us more,' he said. 'In the mean time, though, let's look at Fay's role in all this. You found out some interesting things while I was interrogating Pomeroy.'

'Yes. I know it's circumstantial, but it does seem that a pattern is emerging with respect to Fay. She gets involved with someone; they let her down; they die.'

'Are you counting Keith Mayhew?'

'Yes. He took her to Medics' Ball, got her hopes up then abandoned her half-way through the evening.'

'But the timing, Will...'

'I know. That was last March. Supposing, though, the worst trauma acted as a kind of trigger, bringing on the other incidents in a cascade—a spree of revenge, if you like. Morgan's dumping her must have sent her over the top.'

'Nice, Will, but Keith's death and

Laszlo's letter-bomb both predated the killing of Morgan.'

'Okay...the trigger was earlier. Something in December. Perhaps one of them didn't send her a Christmas card.'

Montgomery took another sip from the cup, then pushed it away; the tea had gone unpleasantly cool. 'Remember what we said about these cases only two weeks ago?' he began. 'We agreed that one coincidence was acceptable, but not two or more. Nothing that's happened since has changed my mind. If the attacks on Laszlo Kovacs are the odd factor, and you think Fay might be responsible for the rest, then Hubert Pomeroy is lying about Keith Mayhew's suicide—and why should he do that? If Keith Mayhew is the odd one out, then you're saying Fay had it in not only for Morgan and Jason, but Laszlo too—and we've no evidence for that. We're looking at personal grudge now, not idealism. You understand the problems?'

Sergeant Bird nodded dolefully. 'I do. But it *feels* right. There's a *feel* of grudge in all this. Somehow we're letting peripheral issues confuse us.'

'I've a proposition,' said Montgomery, steepling his fingers. 'Let's find out more about Fay's stay in hospital. The term "nervous breakdown" is a vague euphemism. We need to know more. Was it neurotic or psychotic? Did she have dangerous delusions?'

'I'll do that, sir. I'll drive over there tomorrow.'

'Good. Then tonight you might perhaps like to come with me.' The expression in his eyes grew sharp. 'I shall call on Laszlo Kovacs to enquire if he's ever met a petite, long-haired geography student called Fay Gillingham. He may well be surprised. We've always assumed there's no link between them, but the fact is—*we've never asked.*'

Anna Kovacs turned to her husband. 'Your little admirer!' she said lightly.

'Yes—but what is this?' The physiologist faced the detectives with a puzzled frown. 'You were asking about Hubert before. He was arrested...'

'No,' contradicted Montgomery. 'He came back to Headquarters to help with our enquires. He's back on the campus now.'

'Why are you interested in Fay?'

'She was involved with Jason Gower, the student who died in the explosion at Calverton Hall today.'

Laszlo looked sick. 'We heard, of course, but no one knew all the details...'

'We wondered if he was the Animal

Militancy bomber,' cut in Anna. 'Can you tell us?'

'There seems little doubt.'

'Then I cannot in all honesty express any sorrow,' she said. 'We have lived in fear of another attempt on Laszlo's life ever since the parcel bomb.' Her mouth hardened. 'Was this girl an accomplice, then?'

'It's possible that she was his tool. There's a chance, however, that she used him and his evil devices for her own ends, selling him an ideological justification while using him as an instrument of vengeance.'

'For what?' asked Laszlo, thoroughly bewildered.

'That is what we're trying to find out. Would you care to explain your acquaintance with Fay?'

'I—yes, if you think it will help. Er...please sit down...' He settled into a chair, then began haltingly. 'It was a year ago last October. I was going for my lunch in the Tech Town cafeteria when I saw a young student trip and fall on the path near Mechanical Engineering. I went to help her up; she'd grazed her knee, nothing serious. She told me she was a fresher studying geography, and she was exploring the campus. She accompanied me to the café, and I felt it was only courteous to offer to share my table.'

Montgomery glimpsed the faint sardonic curl of Anna's lips.

'She talked a lot that first time,' Laszlo went on. 'Her father was dead and she was an only child; she found it overwhelming to be on this campus with five thousand other young people, making her own decisions on so many matters. She felt ill prepared.

'Well, to cut a long story short, Fay developed a habit of meeting me at the café. Or sometimes she would wait outside the Medical School for an hour or more in order to join me at lunch. It was difficult: sometimes I had to stay in the building, other times I wanted to talk with colleagues, but subtly she tried to make me *accountable* to her. It was "Where were you?" if I didn't turn up, and the threat of tears.

'Anna knew all about this, of course. She said it sounded unhealthy, but if I was sorry for the girl the best recourse was to invite her to dinner at our home, where she would see me in my own family setting. Fay declined.'

'That would have meant acknowledging my existence,' commented Anna with a grim smile.

'She sent me a very foolish Christmas card,' continued Laszlo. 'During the spring term I did my best to let her down gently. There was never any impropriety, you understand, but the situation was claustrophobic: it was as if she was trying to make me into a substitute father, or big brother.

'At last, she seemed to accept my attempts to create distance. She told me she had been invited to the Medics' Ball, and I was happy for her, because it meant friendship with someone her own age. I rarely saw her after that.'

'Do you still have the Christmas card?' asked Montgomery.

'No,' said Laszlo at the same instant as Anna said, 'Yes.'

'We were going to throw it away after one year,' explained Anna, 'but I decided to keep it a little longer as a kind of insurance—in case she made demands, or claimed that Laszlo was more to her than he had been. It was—just abnormal enough to make us concerned.' She left the room and was back within three minutes with an envelope. 'Here,' she said, holding it out to Montgomery.

He extracted the card and read it silently before passing it on to William Bird. It was, as Anna had said, 'just abnormal enough'. Fay clearly wanted someone to lean on, to make decisions for her. Laszlo had been mature, her father's generation, Keith perhaps her first ever date, Morgan had been young but physically big and strong, a rock...and Jason: Jason had offered direction, a cause.

'I'm no Madame Heger,' insisted Anna, a glow of colour high on each cheek-bone. 'Laszlo told me everything.'

Montgomery leaned towards Sergeant Bird for enlightenment. 'Charlotte Brontë wrote unwise letters to her Belgian professor, Monsieur Heger,' he was told. 'It's thought that Madame stitched together the torn pieces and read them.'

'You see, I know your cultural icons,' said Anna from across the room. Montgomery noted the 'your' even as he recalled that the Kovacses had assumed British citizenship.

'Thank you for being so frank,' he said. 'I'll let you know the results of all our current investigations as soon as possible. When do you go away?'

'Tuesday,' said Laszlo. 'Professor Byrne has agreed. On Monday I shall brief him on all the department business.'

'Give me the address and telephone number.'

Laszlo dutifully scribbled them down. 'It's a farmhouse near Ross-on-Wye,' he said. 'They promise log fires.'

'You'll need them in this weather.'

As the detectives prepared to leave, Anna appeared hesitant for the first time. 'Inspector,' she said, long fingers fidgeting with her skirt, 'do we take it that Hubert no longer interests you?'

'Not until we've actually charged someone else.'

'Oh. You see... I remembered something after you last came here, but we were sceptical ourselves about Hubert until you actually took him to the station...'

'What did you remember, Mrs Kovacs?'

She paused for a moment, then looked Montgomery straight in the eyes. 'Inspector,' she said, 'he has a gun.'

19

Hubert came to the door of his flat wearing a silk dressing-gown of arabesque design, but Montgomery knew he had not been in bed; a bluish fug of smoke filled the sitting-room, and a smouldering cigarette butt was visible on the edge of the table ashtray.

'I might have guessed,' sneered Hubert when he had identified his visitors. 'You can't leave it even for one evening, can you, Montgomery? I don't know why you bothered to let me go.'

Montgomery forbore to supply the answer—that they would have had to charge him, and were not yet ready. 'May we come in?' he said evenly.

Hubert shrugged his assent, but his eyes were blow-pipes of venom.

'We came to ask if we could see your gun,' said Montgomery.

'What?'

'Your gun, if you please. I believe it's a revolver.'

'You know bloody well it's a revolver—you've got the damned thing. What *is* this?'

The small one... Suddenly Montgomery knew exactly what had happened, and the cold clutch of apprehension paralysed his lungs even as his mind ran on headlong. Hubert had only recently discovered the gun was missing; he thought *they* had taken it during the search. Presumably it was unlicensed, and *that* was the charge he had been waiting for...

So who had found the weapon?

'Cat and mouse,' Hubert was hissing furiously. 'The State lets you get away with it, but Christ! the individual must have some rights! Who is your superior, Montgomery?'

'Detective Superintendent Tillner,' said Montgomery tiredly. He was hardly concentrating on Hubert, but weighing up the magnitude of the disaster.

'He'll be hearing from me. This is pure harassment.'

'Dr Pomeroy, where did you keep your revolver?'

Hubert was almost beside himself. 'What is the *point* of this charade?' he demanded through clenched teeth.

Montgomery stood his ground. 'Dr Pomeroy,' he said, 'I'm afraid we don't have your revolver. We've only just been made aware of its existence. If it's missing from the premises, then someone else must have stolen it.'

Hubert's jaw fell. There was no mistaking the amazement on his face.

'Was it locked away?' asked Sergeant Bird, since progress seemed to be woefully slow.

'You know it wasn't...that is, no...it was under the bed, in a box...' He stared at them as if he was in some kind of dream.

'With the ammunition?' Montgomery could guess the answer.

'Yes.'

'Describe the weapon,' he ordered.

'It was a .357 Magnum: Smith and Wesson. Er, gunmetal blue, with a black rubber grip...double action...'

'Six-inch barrel?'

'No, four-inch.'

'Licensed?'

'No.'

'How did you come by it?' The Kovacses

had said that Hubert was in a gun club, but he might have spun them a tall story.

'A friend—acquired it for me, after we were beaten up in London. Someone else had lifted it from a gun club...' Abruptly he turned his back on them. 'I wonder if you've any idea what it's like,' he whispered, 'being beaten half senseless by a baying pack of hate-crazed yobs... We hadn't done *them* any harm. We were minding our own business... God, I thought I was going to die. Afterwards, I knew that as long as I was in London, I had to have protection. Something to scare them with, to keep them away...' He slumped into a chair; above his bowed head Montgomery and Sergeant Bird exchanged bleak glances.

Carole, too, was wearing a dressing-gown. At two a.m she glided into the downstairs room where Montgomery was waiting by the telephone.

'Why don't you come to bed?' she asked softly. 'They said they'd only ring if there was some news.'

He shook his head. He had unplugged the bedroom extension phone so as not to disturb her. 'Night-clubs are only just getting going at this time,' he said. There would be news, he was sure. It was all beginning to fit together.

'Would you like cocoa?' she asked.

'No, thank you. Carole—what do you think of homosexuals?'

She raised her eyebrows. 'Are you trying to tell me something? Bit late, isn't it, after seventeen years of marriage?'

'Seriously.'

'I think lesbian couples have a lot of sense. Who needs a great, crude man about the place leaving all the drudgery to them? Sorry; you said seriously. Homosexual men? Oh...I suppose I'm sorry for many of them. They seem to be born with a certain propensity, and go through a lot of misery trying to come to terms with it. Let's face it, few people would actually *choose* to be in a misunderstood minority.'

'But are they misunderstood?' wondered Montgomery. 'Isn't some of the hostility because we know all too well what they're about? They're promiscuous not because they're homosexual, but because they're men, and the practices they accept as normal abuse the functional anatomy of the species.' Montgomery knew that he shared the instinctive abhorrence of the truly straight man for the gay one. It was a kind of primeval unease, as if he had come across something subtly alien masquerading as a human being. He had 'diagnosed' Hubert Pomeroy at a glance, while Pomeroy's more effete colleagues had failed to do so.

'I didn't realize you were going to get technical,' said Carole. 'I must say, all the homosexual men I've encountered have been absolute sweeties. They'll gossip like any woman, and they appreciate those things which improve the quality of everyone's lives: things artistic and creative, the importance of caring...'

'You can't have the tinsel without the rest of the package.'

'True—but I know two monogamous homosexual couples whom I'd regard as among the most decent, reliable people I'm ever likely to meet.'

'So you wouldn't mind if, say, Justin came to you one day and said, "Sorry, Mum, but I think I'm gay"?' said Montgomery mischievously.

'Thank you. At two a.m I'm not sure I can answer that.' Carole curled her feet beneath her on the settee. 'If he was certain, then I'd support him. But if he'd been influenced by one of those "It's okay to be gay" campaigns at school, then I'd be very concerned indeed. Every child should be allowed a phase of being unsure, like schoolgirls with a crush on the gym mistress. No, I don't think it should be promoted as a *desirable* state, and I don't think the label of one's sexuality should be tagged on to other issues: one-legged lesbian women against the bomb, or whatever...'

She smiled at him. 'On a lighter note, and as a former English teacher, I must say I'm annoyed at the way our language has been hijacked in the cause. The use of the words "queer" and "gay" has been thoroughly bastardized! You can't apply them these days without unwanted innuendo.'

'Some of our foremost literary figures have been homosexual,' mused Montgomery.

'Yes—poor old Oscar Wilde! Reading Gaol wrecked his health, and just think what masterpieces he might have written had he lived longer.'

'You don't go suing for libel when someone writes the truth about you,' said Montgomery darkly, his legal awareness in evidence despite the lateness of the hour.

The phone rang.

'I'll go to the kitchen,' whispered Carole, handing him the receiver.

'Sir?' Jackson sounded excited, and not a little drunk. 'We found him. His name's Anthony. When we bought him a few jars and promised him discretion, he started talking nineteen to the dozen. Pomeroy's been seeing him for months. Wants to wean him away from his life of sin—he's

315

a rent-boy, by the way. He pretends that Pomeroy's his only lover, and sees him every Saturday night, but in fact he picks up clients in the Lynx every Thursday and in a pub on Tuesday nights. Busy little beaver...'

'What about December the twelfth?' broke in Montgomery.

'I was just coming to that. Pomeroy met him in the Playhouse Bar and they spent the whole evening together in exactly the manner we were told. Pomeroy often stopped over at Anthony's place, but on this occasion he left for the campus at one forty or thereabouts, saying he had things to do the next morning. Looks as if he's in the clear, sir...'

Yes, it did.

William Bird returned from Maple Green, the psychiatric hospital with records of Fay, the following afternoon.

As Montgomery listened to the report, his face growing more and more pinched, further pieces of the jigsaw inexorably slotted into place. He remembered something Hubert Pomeroy had said long ago...something Magda Hepworth had said, and something Eleanor Ransome had told one of his colleagues...

'William,' he breathed as his sergeant finished speaking, 'she's lethal.'

'I shall be buying just a few provisions for our journey, and a new pair of gloves,' said Anna Kovacs to Laszlo as she stood by the front door of the Bramcote home with her shopping bag.

'Take your time,' he said generously. 'Have a coffee and a bun in town. It will take me a while to tidy up my paperwork here.'

He watched her drive away, then wandered to the back of the house to view the garden through the french windows. Thin morning sunlight assuaged the winter drabness of the lawn and borders, but it was another chilly day, and an assortment of sparrows, starlings and coal-tits were fluffing out their feathers in a valiant effort to catch his eye.

Laszlo liked birds. He had never owned a family pet, preferring instead the freedom to travel without ties, but he took great pleasure in preparing nourishing hand-outs to sustain the local bird population when the weather was harsh. Their bright-eyed company was its own reward.

He went to the kitchen and took down a tin from a high shelf. Inside was a slab of nuts and seeds bound together with lard; he broke the slab into manageable pieces and put them on a plate, then opened the newly repaired french doors and carried the plate outside. Despite the cold, he walked steadily to the bird-table half-way down the lawn and carefully spread out the fragments. He wondered what he could do for the green woodpecker he had noticed the previous weekend—an anti-social bird, so vulnerable to starvation whenever the ground was frozen over...

Contemplating whether or not a purchase of live bait would solve the problem, Laszlo returned to the house and locked the french door behind him. He moved through the dining-room, intending to settle down in his study, but suddenly he paused; the door to the sitting-room was ajar, whereas he was sure it had been closed minutes before...

A *frisson* of fear rippled across the back of his neck, but he admonished himself even in the same moment: it was a Saturday, broad daylight, and in three days he was going to be in Ross-on-Wye. The door must have sprung open in the draught from the french windows. (But the air was still...) Surely no one could have...

He found himself backing away from the open door, retreating silently into the kitchen. He stood near the cooker, his heart making great soggy thuds, and from somewhere on the ground floor came a faint creak...

Where to go? The kitchen door to the outside was both locked and bolted—far

318

too much noise, too little time. In any case, the garden would be a trap. He could dash up the hall to the front door, but that would mean passing the other sitting-room door. He imagined it flying open, the intruder glaring from the threshold.

Another noise decided him. Very softly, he eased open the inner kitchen door, praying the hinges wouldn't squeak. He slid past it into the hall and began to tiptoe along the carpet, but as he brushed alongside an umbrella leaning against the wall, it fell and hit the radiator with a sharp *thunk*.

Ahead of him, a handle turned. Magda Hepworth stepped out of the sitting-room, her face grim and implacable, and the hand which held the gun was very steady.

20

'Are you going somewhere, Dr Kovacs?' she asked him frigidly.

'Magda—I...what...?'

'Such a hero. Thinks a borrowed uniform and a gun give him licence to shoot people in the back.'

'Magda—please.'

'Get in here.' She gestured to the

sitting-room, and he was forced to precede her into its comfortable, plant-festooned depths. The slam of the door sounded funereal.

'You are Hungarian, Magda?' His throat felt tight and raw.

'Yes.'

'Your father...?'

'The police officer you murdered in Budapest.'

'Who told you? How did you know?'

'My mother. What happened that day drove her mad. Do you know what they did with his body—they strung it up from a tree, inverted like St Peter! She never recovered. When I was old enough to understand I swore to her I'd find you and make amends. We knew you were in England, as we were; that was sufficient.'

Laszlo felt desperately weak, but managed to remain upright by leaning against a chair-back. 'For four months you've worked with me,' he said in wonder.

'Laszlo is a popular Hungarian name. So is Kovacs. I had to be sure.'

'But you saved my life...'

Magda's eyes kindled with fanatic fury. 'You were *mine*,' she thundered. 'I've lived my whole life for this moment. Was I to let some pathetic little anarchist steal the prize from under my nose? You've got to suffer. You have to know *why* you're going to die, and who is killing you.'

She took a step forward and raised the gun, two-handed, sighting expertly down the barrel. Laszlo couldn't even cry out in protest; he was sinking in a maelstrom of emotions from the past. He, too, had been waiting for this moment, only the nemesis he had envisaged still wore its blue lapels and peaked cap, and stood tall in polished boots... This woman with her jeans and black jumper was in the wrong time, the wrong place.

Magda lowered the gun and regarded him levelly. 'His name was Joszef Szepesi. I don't suppose you knew that, or were even interested. I would have liked to have killed you with *his* gun.'

As she took up her stance again, Laszlo found his voice. 'He was using a child as a shield,' he said. 'Did you speak of heroes?'

She paused for a second, then murmured, 'Lies are futile from one who is on the brink of meeting his Maker.' With pitiless precision she pointed the gun at his chest. 'This is from Julia and Magda Szepesi,' she said, and calmly squeezed the trigger.

There was an empty click. Magda tried again immediately, but the result was the same. Incredulous, she attempted to fire four more times in rapid succession. The final failure shattered her composure into splinters: with a bellow of frustration, she leapt at Laszlo, swinging the revolver aloft like a cosh. At the last moment, he ducked aside.

Suddenly the room was full of people. Three police officers had emerged from their places of concealment; after a brief, bitter struggle Magda was left panting, arms pinioned behind her back by Sergeant Bird.

Montgomery knelt to pick up the gun, holding it carefully by the sides of the trigger guard. He slid it into a flat cardboard box. 'It helps to have a firing pin which can reach the percussion cap,' he said.

Hot blood surged into Magda's face. '*You* did that?' she asked, her voice thick with fury and chagrin. 'You had no right.'

'No? What was *your* right to this gun?'

'I would have used my father's, but it was old and faulty. This one worked: I tested it. You shouldn't have interfered. If you had kept out of this, justice would have been done.'

'Justice? Vengeance, more like. And what of those deaths which have already occurred as a result of your "mission"? Are they just acceptable casualties to you?'

'They were unfortunate. I will tell you

everything—but not here.'

Laszlo tried to suppress his trembling limbs as the officers prepared to lead Magda away, but she could read his state from across the room. 'Coward!' she spat. 'You have always been a coward.'

'Few actions are more cowardly than poisoning, Dr Hepworth,' said Montgomery in an icy voice.

She looked at him oddly for a second, then seemed to slump. 'Excuse me,' she murmured. 'I feel... Please let me go for a moment. I won't run away.' At a nod from Montgomery, Sergeant Bird released her arms and she sagged on to a nearby chair, twisting away from them, her head bowed.

They were almost too late. A movement of her head towards her mouth, a gleam of glass, a crunching sound... Sergeant Bird was just in time to force open her jaws and retrieve the damaged phial with its crystalline contents intact. Robert Allen immediately applied handcuffs.

Montgomery examined the tiny glass object and sniffed it with caution. 'Cyanide?' he asked.

'Yes,' she said defiantly.

'It can take several minutes.'

'I know.'

'Then perhaps you aren't such a coward,' he said. 'But I'm afraid that isn't the way.

We have a lot to talk about.' Stony-faced, he led the small group to the door.

'Magda didn't find the gun by accident,' said Montgomery, as he sat with Jackson and Smythe in their office. 'She broke into Pomeroy's flat with the express purpose of finding it. If we'd known of the existence of the gun earlier on, that would have narrowed our field down considerably; Pomeroy bragged about the weapon while under the influence of sherry at the Dean's dinner last October, so only those present were in the know. As it is, many of them didn't believe him, but he must have said something which convinced Magda it was true.

'She needed a weapon to fulfil her vendetta against Laszlo; her father's relic was unreliable. It was easy enough to get hold of the Calverton master key—cleaning ladies have similar habits in all the campus halls—and I dare say Magda had studied Pomeroy's routines enough to know he went out every Saturday night. So on December the twelfth, sometime around nine, she entered his flat and began to search for the gun.

'Keith Mayhew had been stewing in his room for most of the evening, and must finally have decided to take Chris Shallet's advice. By the way—we're satisfied now that he never was Pomeroy's catamite...

'Keith must have caught Magda in the act. Whether he knocked and she didn't hear, or what, I don't know; that's one bit she isn't telling—but the net result was Magda's exposure in someone else's flat, examining a firearm. She must have soothed his suspicions with a smile: "Come in, Keith. Hubert will be back in a minute; look at this funny revolver he was showing me"—then as soon as the door was closed she attacked him. She forced him on to the sofa and held his face against a cushion; he struggled, and they fell to the floor with a thump which was heard by the student Dez below—but in the end Keith didn't have a chance. He was small and weedy, Magda is built like an Amazon. He died.'

Montgomery glanced across at his officers; their faces were rapt with attention. 'Here was a problem for Magda,' he went on, 'and I have to say she showed diabolical inventiveness in solving it. There had been noises and commotion; someone else might come to the door. In the first instance, therefore, she moved the body to the bedroom, where minutes later Chris Shallet and Morgan Blunt saw it through the window. By the time Magda had tidied up the living-room, she had made her decision: she would simulate Keith's suicide.

'For too long we thought the choice was between Pomeroy's lying about the suicide, having murdered Keith himself, or his telling the truth. We gave no consideration to the third possibility, that someone else might have murdered him and faked a suicide. If we *had* thought of it, we'd have realized that the murderer had to be someone who *knew* how Pomeroy had been tormenting Keith at the Medical School, who knew how desperate Keith had become.

'I've refreshed my memory with our notes and the various statements: they make interesting reading. The first time we met Magda, she claimed she was unable to differentiate Keith from any of the other students. "He must have been one of the quiet ones," she said. But I've heard since that Eleanor Ransome had specifically spoken both to Magda and to Laszlo Kovacs about Keith's problems with Pomeroy: neither was prepared to offer any concrete help. So Magda *did* know.

'Keith was murdered, then, and Hubert Pomeroy obligingly disposed of the body. He was probably in too much agitation to notice that the plastic wasn't sucked tight against Keith's nose and mouth; the fact that he was blue was enough.

'So Magda acquired her gun—and she tells me she practised with it in Sherwood

Forest. She planned to make her move against Laszlo as soon as the fuss about Keith had died down. Unfortunately, Jason Gower stuck his oar in first. His letter-bomb had police buzzing round the Medical School again, and she was stymied. For all her cool competence, this was a time of great strain. She was waiting to kill somebody, and she had the means, but the time was unpropitious for action. I believe *that's* why she became involved with Morgan.'

'The stress-relieving power of sex?' grinned Jackson.

'Exactly. There's something very masculine about Magda. That's just how she would react, even though it was against the isolationist lifestyle she'd set herself.

'But it was her undoing—or more precisely, it was Morgan's. Because somewhere along the line she saw him as a danger. I'm only guessing, but I think I know the reason.We found some odd words scribbled on a notepad in Morgan's room after his death. Robert showed them to a linguist, but they didn't make any sense, and we concluded they were irrelevant. After collaring Magda, however, we tried again, and this time struck gold. The words were *phonetic* equivalents of the Hungarian words *gyilkos, gyáva*—which mean murderer, coward. Magda must have been getting very wound up by then, and talked in her sleep.'

' 'Scuse me, sir,' Smythe interrupted him. 'That's something I have trouble with.'

'What, talking in your sleep?' chuckled Jackson.

'No—this idea of Magda pretending to be Czechoslovakian. Surely Laszlo would have recognized a fellow Hungarian? I mean, if I go on holiday abroad, it's patently obvious who the other British citizens are.'

'That's a poor analogy, Graham,' said Montgomery. 'Laszlo and Magda were both born in Hungary, but the similarity ends there. He spent his first twenty years in Budapest, then fled to England, where all these years later his accent remains strong. Magda's mother fled around the same time, in circumstances which we're still uncovering, but Magda was only two. She spent an unnatural, misanthropic childhood with her mother, who was obsessed with Joszef's death; I suspect words like *"gyilkos"* were daily currency. Later, though, when a social worker found her and sent her to school, she became fluent in English. Her own accent is very slight; I certainly couldn't place it. So we're looking here at two Hungarians in a foreign country, speaking that country's language:

it's perfectly reasonable that Magda's cover story was accepted.

'Morgan was murdered, then, because there was a risk of him exposing her true background. In so far as Magda is able to feel anything for anyone, I sense some genuine regret in her; I think she was so used to behaving decisively that she didn't weigh up the Morgan situation properly, didn't try to find some other way of defusing it. There he was, with a handy nasogastric tube *in situ*. There *she* was, with her own cyanide capsule about her person, made some quiet night in the lab with a test tube and bunsen burner. It was serendipity of the most devilish kind. All she had to do was make a solution of the cyanide, creep up on Morgan, and squirt it through his tube. She'd killed once, remember. No more danger of betrayal. No more distractions from someone who'd perhaps become more demanding than she had expected...

'Magda made haste to carry out the promise she'd made her mother. She broke into Laszlo's Bramcote home and lay in wait for him one evening when Anna should have been out. As we know, that attempt was abortive, but one thing intrigues me. She wore "Endeavour". It was from Morgan's own bottle, which he'd left in her room on the one occasion she'd let him stay there. Was that simply meticulous planning, a contingency red herring to throw us quite literally off the scent if things went wrong? Or was there some more Freudian reason? I suppose we'll never know.

'She planned to repeat the attempt as soon as possible, but before she could do so, Jason Gower leapt to centre stage again.'

'He did her a big favour,' said Jackson, 'blowing himself up like that.'

'I'm afraid he didn't.' Montgomery couldn't help but find the astonishment on their faces gratifying. He shared with them an item of information he had lately received from Chris Shallet, the story of Magda and the 'dummy' car-bomb. 'That was a real bomb,' he said, 'set up by Jason to destroy Magda. Through sheer good luck it didn't explode. Magda must have felt weak as water, yet she managed to convince Chris that the device was a hoax. As ever, she acted very promptly. She knew now that Jason might not only balk her of her prey, but kill her before she had settled her account with Laszlo. Jason had to be removed...

'She had a pass-key which enabled her to enter rooms in D block. She had explosives to use, with which Jason had very kindly provided her. She had a formidable scientific brain...and there was a bonus. Jason had brought back many of his antisocial possessions from E block trunk-room in readiness for his own use. Among these was the Animal Militancy "Methods" manual. With this as a step-by-step guide, Magda had no trouble whatsoever setting up a booby trap in his desk drawer when he had gone off for his chemistry lectures.'

'We did consider a booby trap,' recalled Jackson, 'but only because he'd quarrelled with Fay the night before.'

'Yes,' said Montgomery. 'Chris heard that, as well as the boy in D7. He thought they were arguing about the "hoax" device. But we've spoken with Fay since then: apparently Jason was furious because she'd blabbed to Sergeant Bird about the pamphlets they were working on; he couldn't understand why she'd give police *any* unsolicited information which could be used against him. Fay, of course, was unaware of his more nefarious activities. She could happily mouth the *theory* of scientists being punished for alleged animal cruelty, but she wasn't up to the practical reality.'

'If she's totally innocent, then she's come out of this whole thing rather badly,' said Smythe.

'Yes.' Montgomery wondered why he

was unable to feel more sympathy for Fay. 'Magda always tried to protect Fay from our attentions,' he went on. 'You'd think she'd have been pleased that we were focusing on someone else. But she was terrified our enquiries would lead to Maple Green and reveal her mother—as they did. She tried to interest us in Jason, quite unaware that Jason and Fay were "an item", as they say.'

'William found the old lady?' asked Jackson.

'Yes. He went to Maple Green under the impression that Magda had been Fay's doctor there. When he showed the staff a photograph of Magda, they told him that she'd never attended as a medic, but had been coming for many years as a visitor: her mother, Mrs Szepesi, was a long-stay patient. William got talking with this lady, and out tumbled the story.

'Of course, Fay *did* think Magda must have been a medic when she saw her again in Calverton Hall. Psychiatry staff don't wear intimidating uniforms, and Mrs Szepesi's ward was up the corridor from her own, so she only saw Magda occasionally, leaning over a bed or walking the corridors with that purposive tread of hers.

'If we'd listened properly to Hubert Pomeroy, we wouldn't have made the same mistakes as Fay. During one of his anti-foreigner tirades, he let on that Magda is called "doctor" by virtue of her PhD. Unlike him, she isn't also medically qualified—so she couldn't have been practising psychiatry at Maple Green.'

Montgomery sighed; the events of the previous few days had been more than tiring. 'Proving Magda's murderous intent towards Laszlo would have been nigh impossible with only the ramblings of a deranged woman as evidence,' he said. 'We had to put it to the test, allow the situation to develop. But the risk to Laszlo was enormous; Magda would have emptied that Magnum into him in front of our faces had it still been functional. So we took prophylactic measures: we filed an eighth of an inch off the firing pin while she was out. She wasn't the only one with access to master keys.'

'So much hate,' said Smythe in awe.

'Yes: she was brought up on it. Magda Szepesi was never destined to be normal.'

'But *did* Laszlo shoot her father? He's never seemed the type who could do anything like that. What happened all those years ago?'

'I only have the gist myself,' said Montgomery. 'I'm going to see the Kovacses again tonight; perhaps they'll feel able to tell me.'

21

'I was never the stuff of heroes,' said Laszlo Kovacs.

Anna paused in the act of heaping William Bird's plate high with slices of Hungarian strudel and gave her husband an enigmatic, almost motherly look. From his seat nearby, Montgomery wondered if her thought mirrored the essence of his own: sometimes the reluctant hero can be the most heroic of all.

Laszlo continued, speaking in low tones, looking at the floor. 'I was—what?—twenty when our country rebelled against the Stalinists,' he said. 'Our economy was in ruins thanks to years of senseless over-industrialization. The workers were given poverty-level wages and all they got in exchange were grey, regimented lives where fear of the secret police and their informers ruled every action. *Czengö-frasz*—bell-fever—was very real. You could be sent to gaol or a concentration camp simply for reading a Western book.

'I never considered myself a militant type of person. Though my father had often muttered that he wished Nagy were back again, he was fairly passive about the situation. I think the memory of 1945 was still too raw in all our minds—the Siege of Budapest, when Hungary was crushed between the Nazis and the Red Army. We cowered in our cellar for weeks living on potatoes, beans and a few strands of horse-meat. I was only a boy, but I can still see clearly our beautiful city when it was all over: the shattered buildings, the numb faces of the people. Most of all, I remember the tramlines, grotesquely twisted and torn, like arms reaching up to the skies...'

He shook his head, as if to dispel the image. 'So we had no family instinct for rebellion,' he said. 'My only personal defiance before October '56 had been a handful of visits to the British Legation in Liberty Square to watch films and learn a little English. But I stopped going pretty promptly when one of my friends had his identity card confiscated by the Ávó for doing the same. Without a card, there was no work.

'Risks were for other people,' he said baldly. 'I only started to open my eyes that Tuesday in October when I heard that professors from my own university were part of a great mass of intellectuals and students who were demonstrating in favour of a manifesto for change. The time was right for democracy, they said. I went out into the city with some friends to see what was happening, and found it wasn't just a pipe-dream from one stratum of society: thousands of ordinary workers were joining the throng. Everywhere there was optimism and excitement. As we passed the barracks, soldiers too waved and cheered. I realized with a great surge of emotion that the students truly represented the wishes of the ordinary people of Hungary, and had the energy to act as their mouthpiece.

'I lost my friends in the crowd, but I stayed out on the streets and in the evening witnessed an astonishing sight: in the square off Dózsa György Street, people were trying to pull down the huge bronze fifty-foot statue of Stalin. They failed with ropes, but succeeded when metal-workers attacked the legs with blow-torches. The statue toppled with a reverberant crash, and only the hollow boots remained on their rosy marble plinth.'

Laszlo's face grew grey, the eye-sockets cadaverous. 'The exultation we felt then was abruptly dissipated,' he said. 'News came that unarmed demonstrators who had gone to the radio station had been fired on by Ávós from the rooftops, and thirty or so were dead. To my particular grief a boy I knew had been killed by a tear-gas canister exploding in his face.

Things had gone badly wrong...'

He made a helpless gesture with his hands. 'As you will know, the Russians came with their tanks within hours of these events, invited by their henchmen. We were shocked: only two weeks before there had been similar unrest in Poland, but Khrushchev had declared he would stay out of it and let them find their own way to socialism. We felt he had wanted to avoid duplicating an earlier confrontation with the Poles which had resulted in scores of Polish dead. It was a false sense of security—suddenly here were Soviet tanks, rumbling through Budapest!

'We could either lose all we had gained, or fight them, shame them before the world. My friends said we should fight; I wanted to believe that we could win, but in my heart I couldn't. I imagined us all dead, our city in ruins once more. I said I needed to think...

'Then Anna spoke up. She said whatever I decided, she was going to join the freedom-fighters. We had been going out together for a year; I told her to think of her parents. She was adamant in her view, however. We quarrelled; I could not change her mind, and I left.

'The next day, I searched everywhere for Anna. Eventually someone told me she had joined a corps of freedom-fighters. I found her wearing a baggy uniform, with boots and a rifle. One of her comrades said she had that very morning scrambled on to a T54 tank and smeared the driver's window with jam.'

'Plum jam,' said Anna softly.

'Of course, I joined,' went on Laszlo. 'I had to keep an eye on Anna, if nothing else. The army, who had given us weapons, instructed us in their use. We fought in various parts of the city, including the Corvin Cinema where schoolboys of twelve held out for days. We knew the country was with us: peasants were bringing us food, factories gave us buses and trucks. All over Hungary, insurrections were breaking out.

'Ours were shifting, guerrilla battles. In between skirmishes we would go home and see our families. I found my father surprisingly supportive. He said they were worried sick about all the young people, but very proud... We also went to factories and police stations, to obtain more weapons; the ordinary police were sympathetic.'

'The situation was not without irony,' interjected Anna. 'In school we had been taught the tricks of such warfare in order to repel "the enemies from the West". For many of us, Fadeyev was compulsory reading.'

'We managed to achieve a military stalemate,' continued Laszlo. 'We couldn't win with our small-arms alone, and the Russians, who were short of infantry, couldn't win with their tanks in the narrow streets. But the Ávó, too, were our enemies. Day after day news of their atrocities reached our ears. Hundreds of unarmed civilians were massacred in Parliament Square—yes, Inspector, it has a familiar ring—and in Magyarovar, a peaceful town near the Austrian border, a further eighty-two were mown down by Ávó machine guns. The Ávó became more vicious as they became frightened for their own situation. They knew that the people had years of pent-up hatred for their brutalities, which was now boiling over.

'A week after the trouble started, we were called to a spot where an incident was brewing up. A detachment of Ávó recruits were barricaded in a building, and they had taken hostage a young boy from a group who had tried to commandeer their meat delivery. They wouldn't let him go, and of course firing started.

'We arrived just in time to see Ávó men shooting at random into the crowd. They were terrified—I realize that now—but at the time I knew only horror and fury as innocent people were cut down. The Defence Ministry sent tanks to clear the square, as two of their own officers were trapped inside the same building, but when the crews saw what carnage had occurred, they sided with us and forced the Ávós out on to the street.'

Laszlo's voice became quieter. 'One of the Ávós tried to make a break for it,' he said. 'He pushed his way through the crowd, seized a small child and ran to the park. I was the nearest fighter. People yelled, "Stop him," and "Save the child." I'd injured my foot and I couldn't run properly. I lifted my rifle, intending to shoot him in the leg, but I was overanxious and my aim was poor...I shot him dead.

'I cannot tell you how I felt, shooting the man in the back. It didn't even register at first that I could have killed the child. When I hobbled up to him and turned him over I saw that all the cruelty and brutishness had melted away from his face, and he was really just a young man like myself. I felt sick, yet all around me the people roared approval.'

'You did him a favour,' said Anna tartly, 'as I have been telling you for years. The others were all killed, some most unpleasantly. You couldn't have saved them.'

'Did you know the man's name?' asked Montgomery.

'No—but he was definitely Ávó. They wore Russian-style uniforms with blue lapels and black boots.'

'Is this the reason you left Hungary?'

'Yes,' said Anna as Laszlo merely nodded heavily. 'For over a week we had the Ávó on the run, but when the Russians launched their second, more devastating attack, out came the Ávó from the woodwork again, and their spies were everywhere. We had never intended to leave our country. For me at least, the whole point of rebellion was to stay and fight for change *within* Hungary... But someone tipped us off that Laszlo was on an Ávó hit-list, which meant deportation or execution. We had to leave immediately, before the Austrian border closed.'

She appeared to study her pale fingernails, but they felt that she saw a different picture. 'My sister Lonci came, with her husband, and also some of our friends—but our parents chose to stay behind. They were too old for such change, too settled... We had a truck, but we abandoned it near the border because a patrol was blocking the road. So we carried what we could, and waded for hours through the mud and reeds of a shallow lake, freezing like statues when a star-shell lit the sky. A family travelling behind us drugged their baby so it would not cry out...

'At last we made it. We were the lucky ones: a cousin of Laszlo's vanished and was never heard of again. I thought we might live in West Germany, but Laszlo chose England—and this has been our home ever since.'

Laszlo was staring pensively at the carpet. 'Nothing is ever black and white,' he murmured. 'There is no simple "us" and "them" in conflicts between and within nations. Some of those poor Russian soldiers believed they were in Berlin, fighting Fascists. The Kremlin was divided over how to handle the problem of Hungary... The Hungarian government itself was split. Even the Ávó, overweening bullies as they were, had their share of martyrs. We heard of Ávó men shot by their own officers for refusing to fire at unarmed fellow Hungarians.

'And I, I shot a young recruit. Not an officer steeped in cruelty but a man perhaps guilty only of greed—Ávó pay, you see, was ten times that of an unskilled worker—and of firing his gun in fear. Which is no more than I did.'

'Why did Julia Szepesi flee Hungary as well as the Kovaces?' Smythe asked Montgomery several weeks later. 'From what I've read, the rebellion was crushed quite quickly.'

'True. But before the second Russian assault, the freedom-fighters actually had the upper hand in much of the capital.

342

Ávó men were being lynched all over the place by civilians, and their families must have felt very threatened. When Joszef was killed, Julia was alone with the child in a hostile environment. For all she knew, this determined uprising would succeed, and those who had helped to enforce the old regime would be made to pay. So she fled in a panic.'

'She went West rather than East,' mused Jackson.

'Wouldn't you, given the choice? She was Hungarian, not Russian; Joszef may well have joined the Ávó with motives other than political conviction. And when the pendulum swung the other way in Budapest, she was able to obtain asylum here by claiming she'd *escaped* from the Stalinists...it was too late to go back. But her path was downhill from then onwards. Her experiences unbalanced her; she ended up living in a country where she didn't know the language, and she had no family to help or skills to offer. They lived in squalor, and Magda didn't go to school until she was eight. Magda had to claw her way to respectability the hard way, all the time blaming the person she saw as the architect of their misfortunes. The only information they had was that he was a medical science student called Laszlo Kovacs.

'Magda had a bent for science herself. She studied at night school while struggling to support her mother, and finally attended university as a mature student. She started off studying biochemistry, but persistently searched the journals and switched to physiology when she came across an academic paper written by one Laszlo Kovacs. The rest is clear.'

'Poor Laszlo; he never wanted to get involved in the first place,' said Sergeant Bird.

'No; what happened was quite in keeping with his character. He followed Anna's lead in joining the fighters; he pulled a trigger because people told him to...all against his better judgement. In her way, though, I think Anna has suffered just as much as he has. She always wanted to return to Hungary, but because of him they couldn't.' Montgomery related how vehemently Anna had striven to correct the 'grey' impression Laszlo had given of their native country, telling him how vibrant and colourful life had been before the Stalinist era.

'Travel writers are back to calling Budapest "the Paris of the East",' put in Smythe, who had been devouring brochures.

'I dare say when you've been ruled by other countries for so long, you develop more rabid nationalistic instincts,' said Sergeant Bird. 'Hungary has been under the thumb of the Ottomans, the Habsburgs, the Germans and the Russians since the sixteenth century, while we haven't been conquered at all. We've tended to take our national identity for granted.'

'Until the EC came along,' said Jackson darkly.

'What will happen to Laszlo?' asked Smythe. 'He gives the impression he's almost glad that everything has come to a head.'

'That's right,' said Montgomery. 'The old story has had to be aired because Magda's defence naturally regard it as mitigation.'

'Mitigation? It was the entire *raison d'être.*'

'Quite. So there's been some digging around in Hungary. Few records are available, but people who knew Szepesi have been found. Laszlo thought he'd killed a virtual innocent, whereas it turns out that Szepesi was a murky character even before he joined the Ávó. It figures, really: the ranks of the secret police were stuffed with psychopathic types and individuals with something to hide.

'Laszlo has British citizenship now, but he was a Hungarian citizen on Hungarian territory when the deed was done. That means no one here can pursue the case, even if they wanted to; we have no jurisdiction at all. The Hungarians certainly won't act—so there's nothing to hold Laszlo back now but his own conscience.'

Anna was preparing *tokány,* a ragout with strips of meat, mushrooms, vegetables and paprika, to which she would later add sour cream. Her guests, near neighbours, were due in two hours.

'They will call this goulash,' she predicted to Laszlo with a smile. 'Anything with paprika.'

Laszlo carefully dried the cutlery in his hand and nodded his agreement; their English friends seemed to find great difficulty in accepting that true *gulyás* was, in fact, a soup. 'No matter,' he answered. 'Soon we shall be in the land of the real thing.' He walked across the kitchen and regarded Anna quizzically. 'Will it be a holiday,' he asked, 'or a pilgrimage?'

'Both, I hope. For Noel and Elizabeth everything will be new. They will want to start with the tourist trail: see horses thundering across the Puszta, hear the gypsy violins, take a boat on the Danube or Lake Balaton. But we can show them the hidden heart of Hungary...'

'Anna,' he warned, 'things will have

346

changed. It's been over thirty-five years.'

'I am not afraid. Do you think I shall worry if I see a McDonald's in Váci utca? I might if I saw *two*... No, what I want will still be possible. I wish to stand on Castle Hill and look across the river at the dome of the Parliament Building, then go to Mátyás Church and say a prayer for all our comrades.'

'I, too...' Laszlo appeared anxious. 'Will this heal the wound, or open it up, I wonder?'

Anna divined the source of his new unease. 'You were right before,' she said, 'when you spoke of a clean break. England is our home now. There is a saying I like, and have come to believe in: happiness is not having what you want, but wanting what you have.'

'You think we should continue the Forfeits Club, then?' Bradley Pike looked eagerly towards Steve and Chris, while Eleanor hovered on the sidelines.

'I think Morgan would have been in favour,' said Chris.

'Unless it's time we got some practice at being mature, responsible citizens,' murmured Steve, tongue-in-cheek.

Brad clearly considered that suggestion beneath notice. 'A modified form, perhaps,' he pondered. 'More emphasis on the game, and less on the forfeit. Some new members...'

'I'm glad you mentioned those aspects,' said Chris. 'Eleanor here would like to apply.'

'A *woman?*' Brad was horrified. 'A paid-up fun-quelling, invective-disapproving, alcohol-censuring, recipe-exchanging crochet-hook wielder? Are there no bastions left for us at all?'

'She's not that kind of woman. More to the point, she plays a mean game of poker.'

'Nevertheless...' Brad scowled in Eleanor's direction and received a wink in return.

'You'll still have rugby nights all to yourselves,' she said.

'Hm.'

Deadlock loomed.

'Let's discuss it over a pint,' proposed Steve.

Brad's expression became more cheerful. 'Or five,' he said.

This Large Print Book for the Partially sighted, who cannot read normal print, is published under the auspices of

THE ULVERSCROFT FOUNDATION

THE ULVERSCROFT FOUNDATION

. . . we hope that you have enjoyed this Large Print Book. Please think for a moment about those people who have worse eyesight problems than you . . . and are unable to even read or enjoy Large Print, without great difficulty.

You can help them by sending a donation, large or small to:

**The Ulverscroft Foundation,
1, The Green, Bradgate Road,
Anstey, Leicestershire, LE7 7FU,
England.**
or request a copy of our brochure for more details.

The Foundation will use all your help to assist those people who are handicapped by various sight problems and need special attention.

Thank you very much for your help.